"You must be Zane. Erin Palmer. Nice to meet you."

Zane returned a welcoming grin and gripped the woman's hand. Her handshake was firm, her hand warm, her skin silky soft. Zane became self-conscious of how work-roughened his own palm must be, but she seemed unfazed by his calloused hand.

"Welcome, Ms. Palmer."

One delicate eyebrow lifted, and she tilted her head. "Ms. Palmer? What happened to Erin? I thought after our phone conversation that we were on a first-name basis. I certainly would prefer to be less formal...Zane."

The way she said his name, as an addendum, her husky voice heavy with innuendo, her rosy lips twitching with amusement, caught him off guard. And shot a spike of lust through his blood.

* * *

We hope you enjoyed the McCall Adventure Ranch series!

* * *

If you're on Twitter, tell us what you think of Harlequin Romantic Suspense! #harlequinromsuspense

Dear Readers,

It's finally Zane's turn!

When undercover private investigator Erin Palmer comes to the Double M to investigate the ongoing sabotage at the McCall family's ranch, she shakes up Zane's staid life. Zane is immediately attracted to the mysterious ranch guest, and he is willing to go to any lengths to uncover her secrets. But with the saboteur's attacks escalating, lives hang in the balance, and before Erin and Zane can find their happily-ever-after, they must face down a villain determined to get revenge.

Since this is a December release, I had to have the McCall family and friends celebrating Christmas, right? I love everything about Christmas, and it was a pleasure to include tidbits that showed the McCalls and crew enjoying the season, as well. So, Merry Christmas! Happy Holidays! And I hope you enjoy this final installment of the McCall Adventure Ranch series.

Happy reading,

Beth

RANCHER'S COVERT CHRISTMAS

Beth Cornelison

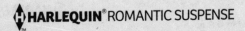
HARLEQUIN® ROMANTIC SUSPENSE

Recycling programs
for this product may
not exist in your area.

ISBN-13: 978-1-335-45667-0

Rancher's Covert Christmas

HARLEQUIN®
www.Harlequin.com

Printed in U.S.A.

Beth Cornelison began working in public relations before pursuing her love of writing romance. She has won numerous honors for her work, including a nomination for the RWA RITA® Award for *The Christmas Stranger*. She enjoys featuring her cats (or friends' pets) in her stories and always has another book in the pipeline! She currently lives in Louisiana with her husband, one son and three spoiled cats. Contact her via her website, bethcornelison.com.

Books by Beth Cornelison

Harlequin Romantic Suspense

The McCall Adventure Ranch

Rancher's Deadly Reunion
Rancher's High-Stakes Rescue
Rancher's Covert Christmas

Cowboy Christmas Rescue
"Rescuing the Witness"

Rock-a-Bye Rescue
"Guarding Eve"

The Mansfield Brothers

The Return of Connor Mansfield
Protecting Her Royal Baby
The Mansfield Rescue

Black Ops Rescues

Soldier's Pregnancy Protocol
The Reunion Mission
Cowboy's Texas Rescue

Visit the Author Profile page at
Harlequin.com for more titles.

Prologue

He needed to be free of his blackmailer once and for all.

A cut brake line should do the job.

One last time, he'd do the man's bidding, but then, no more.

He made his way into the garage where the Double M owners parked the large pickup truck used to tow their cattle trailer. No overhead light. The light might draw attention, he decided, and dropped the hand that hovered near the switch. He fumbled in the dark until he found the snake-necked flashlight on a shelf on a sidewall. Shuffling slowly, his path lit only by the thin moonlight that filtered through the high window, he made his way past the family's personal vehicles. He stopped at the Ford F-350 that would haul the trailer with the largest part of this year's herd to market. Or not.

His goal was to strand the family long enough that

they missed the best sales days. If they didn't make it to market, didn't get top dollar for the cattle, the financial setback would devastate the struggling ranch. And he could finally be finished with the plot to ruin the Double M.

Raising the hood, he stepped up on a stool to lean over the engine. He used the flashlight to locate the main brake line, then centered an empty coffee can beneath the reservoir.

Unfolding his pocketknife, he sliced a thin line in the tube that fed fluid to the brakes. A slow leak of yellow-tinged liquid seeped from the cut. He bent the tube slightly, accelerating the flow into the can. The rapid drip, drip, drip of liquid into the aluminum can synced with the anxious drumming of his heart. He needed to hurry. His absence would be noticed soon, and someone might come looking for him.

He considered allowing a small telltale puddle of the brake fluid to collect on the garage floor. He wanted the damage to be discovered before the trip over the mountains, just not soon enough to repair the damage before the scheduled departure. His goal was to prevent the trip to the cattle market, not to cause an accident.

He heard a noise, a scuff of feet, and he jerked his head up. The overhead light came on, and he blinked in the bright fluorescent glow.

"Oh, hi," the woman at the door said.

He swallowed hard as she approached and, squeezing the pocketknife handle, his gaze locked on hers.

"I didn't realize anyone was in h—" She stopped abruptly when her gaze fell to his handiwork.

The dripping of fluid continued, like gunshots in the still garage. The knife in his hand screamed his guilt.

"What are you doing?" Her tone was sharp, accusing. Her eyes narrowed on him, as understanding and outrage hardened her face. "It's you! You're the one who's been sabotaging the ranch!"

Bile rose in his throat, knowing he'd been found out, knowing what awaited him when she told what she'd seen tonight. His heartbeat stuttered. Unless…

"It's not what it looks like." He rose and moved toward her.

She took a stumbling step back, shaking her head. "I know what I'm looking at. It explains so much. I won't let you get away with this!"

Panic swelled in him. A survival instinct. He lunged toward her, grabbing her arm. "No! You can't say anything!"

"Ow! Let go. You're hurting me!"

He squeezed tighter, shaking her. "You can't say anything!"

"Let go, or I'll scream!"

If he let go, she'd run straight to the main house, tell the family what she'd seen. If she screamed, someone would hear her and come investigate. Neither could happen. He had to make sure she didn't talk. He narrowed his eyes and snarled, "You can't say—"

She drew a deep breath and opened her mouth.

Before she could loose the shriek, he snaked his arm around her, still clenching the small knife. He clapped his hand firmly over her mouth and nose. A muffled grunt of surprise rumbled in her throat, and she struggled to free herself from his grip. Between tightening his grip and her thrashing, the pocketknife managed to cut her, slicing through her sleeve and gashing her arm.

He shifted his grip, only to accidentally jab her belly when she flinched.

Her accelerated pulse meant that she bled faster and droplets began to make the floor slick as they struggled. Finally he dropped the knife with a clatter. With his hand now free, he wrapped his arm across her sternum and dragged her up against his chest. "Be still!"

His fingers dug into her cheek and chin as he smothered her distressed cry.

Damn, damn, damn! What was he supposed to do with her? How could he shut her up?

Her fingers scrabbled feebly at the hand he had over her mouth. But having pinned her arms at her sides with his other arm, she barely reached his palm. Her efforts did little other than anger him. Why did she have to fight? Why couldn't she have just promised her silence and left him alone?

Despite the freezing temperatures, sweat popped out on his brow. His heart thumped hard enough that he would have sworn the whole ranch would hear it. *Do something!* his brain screamed. But the harder she fought, the more rattled he became. The madder, the more desperate.

"Stop it!" He shook her and stumbled when she raised a foot to kick backward at him. His grip tightened as his frustration and fury grew. "I said stop!"

A whimpering mewl escaped from beneath his muffling hand. Her tears dripped from her cheeks to his fingers. Blood continued to leak from her wounds, saturating her clothes and dripping on the floor. Guilt sawed his gut, adding a bitter bite to his agitation. He could feel himself losing the tenuous hold he had on his temper.

When she tried again to break free, twisting her hips,

bucking, he gave her another hard shake. "Stop it!" He gritted his teeth, growling, "Stop, stop, stop!"

She wrenched to the left, and he jerked hard back to the right. And heard a crack. Felt the give in her neck. Her body went limp and heavy in his arms.

He stilled. Stunned. An icy terror crawled through him. Slowly he peeled his fingers away from her mouth.

Her head lolled to the side, and when he relaxed the arm across her chest, her legs buckled. She slid to the ground. Inert. Silent.

His breath rasped in shallow gasps as he dropped to his knees to feel for a pulse.

OhGodohGodohGod! What had he done?

Her sightless eyes stared up at him, and acid pooled at the back of his throat. A numb stupor settled over him.

She was...dead.

He'd...murdered her.

Dazed, he slogged through the horrible truths, his sins, which flashed like slides on a screen. A review of all his transgressions. Lies. Arson. Betrayal.

And murder.

He'd killed an innocent woman.

Again.

Chapter 1

Two weeks earlier

Deception did not sit well with Erin. Her life's work, her history, her passion was truth. But her client had been adamant. No one was to know her true purpose for going to the Double M Ranch in Boyd Valley, Colorado. Or rather, she would be going, assuming she could sell her cover story to—she checked the notebook where she'd scribbled the names and phone numbers of her contacts—Zane McCall. Of the four co-owners of Mc-Call Adventure Ranch, Zane was the chief business manager and, according to her client, the primary hurdle she had to pass.

Erin Palmer took a deep breath, mentally reviewing her practiced script, and tapped in the phone number she'd been given. The line rang several times, and she was about to hang up, expecting the call to go to voice mail any moment, when a low male voice answered. "H'lo?"

"Hi," Erin said, infusing her tone with cheer, "My name is Erin Palmer. I'm looking for Zane McCall."

"You found him. What can I do for you, Erin?"

An unexpected thrill raced through her hearing her name caressed by his sultry baritone voice.

"Well, Zane—" If he could use her first name, she could use his, too. And no, she wasn't flirting. After all, she didn't know anything about the guy other than the melted-dark-chocolate sound of his voice. And flirting would be unprofessional. And—

"Yes?"

Erin wet her lips and refocused her straying thoughts. "I'm a journalist for *Well Traveled* magazine." She cringed internally as the lie rolled smoothly from her tongue. "I'm interested in writing a feature piece about adventure ranches and McCall Adventures specifically." A pregnant pause followed, and Erin's heart tapped out a staccato beat. "Um…Zane? You there?"

"Yeah. I…" She heard the creak of desk chair and his sigh. "Can I ask why?" His sexy baritone voice was now rife with suspicion.

"Why what?"

"Why McCall Adventures?"

She squeezed her eyes shut and pinched her lips together. Answering his question would require laying out an even more elaborate lie. Her gut twisted as she dug for a believable excuse. She couldn't say, "Because that's the cover I'm going with to get me on-site at your ranch."

She decided to stay as close to the truth as possible.

"I heard about the trouble you had with your soft opening, the failure of the zip line and—"

"Wanted to exploit our accident and drag our business through the mud?" The once enchanting voice now had an edge of steel.

Erin swallowed hard. "No! Not at all. Quite the opposite. I respect the way you've turned the business around and recovered from the setback. In fact, I'd like to highlight the precautions you've taken and the remarkable strides you've made toward your relaunch." She held the phone away from her mouth and pulled a face, shocked at her fawning. *Kiss up much, Erin?*

After another significant pause, Zane asked, "*Well Traveled* magazine, you say?"

"That's right."

Another chair squeak filtered through the line, followed by what sounded like the clacking of a computer keyboard. A moment passed before it clicked. He was looking up the magazine, verifying her credentials! Of course he would check out her story. He was smart to do it. So she had to be smarter to pull off her cover.

"I'm not officially on staff at the magazine," she said, quickly pulling the magazine's website up on her own laptop. "I freelance, and I'm hoping to sell my article to *Well Traveled*. I've queried the editor-in-chief about my article idea, and she said she was interested if I could get her a draft by the end of January."

"You mean *he*? The magazine's website says the editor-in-chief is someone named Bill Sherman."

Erin cursed silently as she brought up the staff page. Sure enough, the editor-in-chief was a man. He smiled at her from his bio picture in all his balding, bespectacled glory. Erin felt a prickle of perspiration pop out on her face.

This. This was why she hadn't wanted to lie to Zane and his business partners. She sucked at it. Along with all her other reasons for eschewing the art of deception and vigorously pursuing truth, her complete ineptitude at pretense meant she had a slim chance at pulling it off. Her go-to was always honesty, even if it hurt.

Yes, Officer, I know how fast I was driving. Just write me the ticket.

Yes, DMV worker, that is how much I weigh. I love cheese.

Yes, little sister, those pants make you look fat. Stick with the black pair.

"Oh, sorry. Not Bill. I meant the assistant editor," Erin countered with what she hoped was a casual-sounding laugh. She scrolled down the staff bio page to the next listing. "Claire Norris is who I queried."

She should call her client back and refuse this job. While the case intrigued her, the ground rules gave her too much consternation.

"Well…" Zane said and sighed. "A positive article in a travel magazine would be good publicity." He paused. "Though I hate to remind people of the accident. I'd rather let bygones be bygones regarding that dark chapter of our past."

Erin wanted to tell Zane that dark chapters were never truly history for anyone. They shaped you, changed you, marked your life forever. But such grim prophesying wasn't likely to win her points in her appeal to Zane, so she tucked her personal experience with tragedy away and focused on her sales pitch.

"Yes, the article would definitely be good publicity. Which leads me to my special request."

"A request?" His guarded tone was back.

A shame. She much preferred the casual, flirty baritone. She tried to imagine the face that went with the seductive voice. Typically she didn't research the subjects of her investigations before meeting them. She trusted her instincts about people, and first impressions, uncolored by personal histories, social media or biased articles, were at the heart of how she operated. She researched businesses, places and things, but people required face-to-face meetings. That intangible but all-important vibe she got by looking people in the eye.

Which brought her back to...

"Yes. I'd like to visit the ranch. Conduct interviews. Get a firsthand look at the business, a feel for the locale. Would it be possible for me to come out there for a week or two? I know it's right before Christmas, but I'm on deadline."

"Uh," he grunted. Clearly she'd caught him off guard. "When?"

"I can be there Monday."

Dang it. Her curiosity was tickling her. Thrashing her, really. She had to know the face that went with that voice! She hesitated only a moment before opening her Facebook account and doing a search for Zane McCall.

"So soon?" he asked. "I don't know. We've got a busy couple weeks leading up to Christmas. It's the end of the season, and we'll be sorting the herd in preparation to go to auction."

Several Zane McCalls popped up on her screen, and she scanned the list looking for the one whose information matched Mr. Sexy Voice's. He was third on the list. Boyd Valley, CO. Rancher/Adventurer.

Single. That tidbit excited her more than it should.

"I promise not to get in the way. In fact, I'd love to

see the sorting process. If it is key to the ranch business, then it will be great fodder for the article."

"I thought you said the focus of your story would be the adventure ranch."

She couldn't tell anything about Zane's appearance from the thumbnail profile picture in the list. She chewed her bottom lip, debating, and her finger hovered over her mouse. Curiosity won. She clicked his listing, and his profile page opened.

"Erin?"

She jolted as if she'd been caught snooping in his underwear drawer and slapped her laptop closed. "Oh, uh, right! It is. But I want a complete picture of the ranch and your operations."

Speaking of pictures… She opened the laptop again, and his Facebook page filled the screen. She zoomed in on his profile picture and caught her breath.

OMG. The photo was of a dark-haired cowboy with a strong, square jaw, wide shoulders and piercing blue eyes. He wore a gray Stetson, a tight T-shirt and a pensive look that sent shivers to her core. Oh, yes. The face matched the voice.

"How much input would we have over what appeared in the final article?" he asked.

Drawing her attention back to her conversation took all of her concentration. Even after she closed the web page, she saw the image of Zane McCall, as if he'd been burned onto her retinas.

She exhaled a cleansing breath, fighting to bring her scattered pulse back under control.

"Pardon?"

"How much editorial input would we be allowed?" Zane repeated.

Since there would never really be an article, she supposed that point was moot. But because she was selling herself, for the time being, as a journalist, she figured her answer needed to reflect a journalistic standard. "Well, I would, of course, want to be sure all of my facts were correct, but beyond that, I would have the last say over my writing. A good journalist can't allow outside influences to dictate the content of her work."

"So what assurance do I have that you're not planning to trash us and get readers by writing some sensational, scandal-mongering thing about the recent events at our ranch?"

Erin settled back in her sofa cushions, intrigued by Zane's wariness.

"You don't," she said bluntly.

She knew his family, the ranch, his new business had been through some rough times. That was why she'd been hired. Maybe his skepticism was understandable, but his distrust of her didn't bode well for the mission for which she had been hired.

"All you have is my promise, my word that I have no intention of hurting your family or causing your business any grief." That much was true, and it felt good to be able to be completely honest in that regard. "I want to help your family get the Double M and McCall Adventure Ranch back on track, not derail you."

Zane was silent, and, conjuring the Facebook picture of him again, she could easily imagine him brooding, mulling his options. Square jaw set. Black eyebrows drawn down in meditation over those pale blue eyes. How would she handle working with him every day during her assignment at the ranch? She'd need to get a handle on her giddy attraction to him. Be professional. Not get distracted.

"Your word?" His doubt was obvious in his heavy tone.

"I know you have no reason to trust me, but it is the best I can offer." Sensing she might have underestimated her ability to sell her cover, she searched for additional arguments to sway him.

Before she could launch into a further spiel, he said, "I'm willing to have you come and get a look at the adventure ranch operation. We've made changes, repairs and are planning a relaunch in the spring."

She released her breath. "Great! I can be there—"

"But—" he cut in, his voice firm and commanding. A delicious shiver slid through her. His take-charge, alpha-male authority was sexy. She liked a man who knew what he wanted and had the confidence to get it. "I can only speak for the adventure ranch. I'll have to speak to my father before granting you full access to the ranch. He's the owner here and has the final word regarding the Double M."

"Of course." Erin smiled to herself and relaxed. "I'll wait until you get approval from your father."

She was in.

Erin knew before Zane could say the first word to his father. Because Zane's dad, Michael McCall, was the real reason she was going to the Double M. Zane's father was her client.

He spotted his blackmailer in Buckley's Feed and Seed, and a black pit of loathing gnawed his gut. He didn't want to call attention to himself and to have to face the threats the blackmailer was sure to make again. Though his business at the Feed and Seed wasn't done, he'd much rather make a second trip into town than linger here and deal with another confrontation.

Moving carefully toward the exit, he lost sight of the blackmailer as he edged past a tall display of winter clothes set up to look like a Christmas tree. The exit was in sight. If he could cross the open area just inside the door, near the checkout counter without being seen…

He paused at the end of the aisle with hardware supplies, peering cautiously around the rack of axes and sledgehammers. The coast appeared clear. He took his opportunity and started quickly and quietly toward the front door.

"Leaving so soon?" The voice sent a curl of acid and frustration through him.

He sensed more than saw the source of the voice edging into his path, blocking the exit. He raised his head, nudging back the brim of his hat, to meet the leering expression on his tormenter's face.

"What do you want?" he growled.

"I think you know damn well what I want." The reply was hushed. Clearly the blackmailer didn't want to draw attention any more than he did. Could he use that to his advantage?

"Step aside," he said. "This isn't the time or place."

"Agreed. So meet me in the restroom. Two minutes."

No. Go to hell, you and your threats. I'm done with you. Dear God, how he wanted to say as much to the source of his anxiety and grief for the past several months. But too much hung in the balance. The blackmailer knew it, too, and gloated over the power, the ability to destroy his life, if he didn't do what was asked.

His enemy stepped away and disappeared down an aisle of nuts and screws. Appropriate, he thought with a derisive snort, since he was putting the screws to him. He thought of leaving, of ignoring the demand for a confrontation. But how could he risk incurring the wrath of his foe? One wrong step could trigger all the threatened repercussions to come down on him like a crapstorm. Worse, the blowback could hurt his family. His family was all he had, and he wouldn't risk them to save himself.

Gritting his teeth, he made his way to the back of the store. He killed a minute gathering himself as he feigned interest in the bridles and bits displayed on the back wall. Then he stepped inside the unisex restroom in the rear hall. His tormentor was waiting for him.

"I'm tired of waiting." No preamble or preliminaries. Straight to the point. "The herd doesn't make it to auction. Understood? Enough with the piddling stabs and pokes meant to slow them down. I want you to slash the throat of the operation. A fatal blow. Now. This year's herd."

He'd been afraid that it would come to this. Bile rose, nearly gagging him. "How? Something that big won't look like an accident."

"That's your problem. Just finish them! If the herd makes it to auction, they'll skim by for another year. I'm not waiting another year to get my revenge."

"But I—"

"No excuses. Either the ranch goes down or you do."

He had to brace himself on the dirty sink as a wave of dread stampeded him.

Chapter 2

Zane studied the spreadsheet his sister, Piper, had prepared with the previous month's expenses, and frowned. "Are you sure this is right?"

When she didn't answer, he glanced up and met her raised-eyebrow, exasperated expression. "No, Zane. I just threw some random numbers on the page for kicks."

He rolled his eyes. "I see marriage hasn't made you less sarcastic."

Mention of Piper's recent wedding brought a quick smile to her lips. "Nor has it made me less meticulous with my numbers." She folded her arms over her chest and leaned back in the chair across the desk from him. "Besides, you ask me that every month, dork."

She added a lopsided grin to soften the epithet his siblings had given him when they were kids.

"Yeah, okay." He turned back to the computer screen

and sighed. "Maybe I was just hoping there was better news than this. If we don't start getting reservations and deposits soon, we'll be out of cash before we open in April. I refuse to go back to Gill for another loan."

Just the thought that his high school rival and all-around SOB oversaw the business loan for McCall Adventure Ranch soured his gut. The sooner he and his siblings could get out from under that debt the better. But the numbers Piper had presented him this morning showed a lot of red ink and expenditures.

"None of us want that," Piper said and leaned down to pat the head of the family's Maine Coon, Zeke. The cat rubbed against her shins and mewed at her. "I know, Zeke! Right?" she said to the cat. "See, even Zeke knows what a putz Gill is." Dusting loose fur from her fingers as she rose from her chair, Piper flashed her brother a conspiratorial grin, which he returned. "I gotta go. I'm late."

"You headed out to pick Connor up from school?" Zane asked without taking his eyes off the computer screen.

"Yep. What time do you expect that reporter to get in?"

Zane's chest tightened. Even though his family had been enthusiastic about having the travel writer come visit, he remained skeptical. Sure, good publicity, *free* publicity, would be great for the adventure company. But he'd gotten a weird vibe from the *Well Traveled* reporter that he hadn't been able to shake. He trusted his instincts about people, and the odd conversation they'd had set him on edge.

He flipped his wrist to check the time. "According to her last text, she should be here anytime now. She's driving in from Boulder."

"Hmm. Guess I'll meet her when I get back then." Piper shouldered her purse and rattled her car keys as she headed out.

"Tell my favorite nephew I said hi," Zane called as she left the office.

Zeke, abandoned by Piper, moved on to demand attention from Zane. The cat hopped up on the desk and walked in front of the computer monitor, his fluffy tail swishing in Zane's face. "Uh, excuse me, Fluffbutt."

Zeke nudged Zane's hand with his nose. Pulling an amused face, Zane scratched the cat behind the ear for a few moments then lifted him down to the floor. "Now, vamoose. I have work to finish before our guest arrives." He gave the cat's head a final pat before returning to the spreadsheets Piper had prepared.

He stared at the dismal numbers with a pit in his stomach. No matter how many ways he tried to rework or reimagine the company budget, the bottom line remained the same. The delays in opening, the expense of rebuilding the zip line and increased insurance premiums had hit the fledgling McCall Adventures hard. Really hard.

Zane jammed his fingers through his short-cropped hair and buzzed his lips as he exhaled his frustration. Zeke, who rarely took no for an answer, jumped into his lap and, purring loudly, head-butted Zane's hand. He ruffled the cat's head. "Thanks, pal. But what I need is about a hundred thousand dollars to get the business back in black."

"Zane," his twin brother Josh said, thumping his hand on the office door frame. "Your reporter just pulled in the front drive."

"She's not *my* reporter," he replied, frowning, and not sure why the pronoun bothered him so much.

"You're the one said she could come stay and write her article." Josh hitched his head toward the front of the family house. "Yours or not, get out here and greet her."

"You heard the man," he told Zeke, shooing the cat to the floor as he pushed his chair back from the desk.

"Dad?" he called down the hall toward his father's office, "Ms. Palmer's here if you wanna come meet her."

From the next door down, his father replied, "On a business call. I'll be there in a few minutes."

Zane traipsed through the family home to the mudroom where he snagged his winter coat from the hook by the back door. Shoving his arms in his fleece-lined jacket, he hurried out into the frigid December air, arriving at the main drive in front of his family home just as the sporty, dark blue Toyota 86 pulled up to the house. While the family's two blue heelers wiggled and wagged their tails in excitement, Josh opened the driver's side door and introduced himself as he offered their guest a hand to help her climb out.

Zane stopped in his tracks to stare as a woman with long, curling, dark brown hair and high cheekbones stepped out, flashing Josh an appreciative smile. He wasn't sure what he'd imagined the freelance travel writer would look like, but this stunning beauty wouldn't have been it. When her gaze met his and locked, his pulse jolted as if he'd been hit by the cattle prod.

The bright smile she'd given Josh faltered briefly as she gazed at Zane, then returned to full wattage as she stepped forward, shucking her gloves to extend a bare hand. "You must be Zane. Erin Palmer. Nice to meet you."

Recalled to the moment and his manners, Zane returned a welcoming grin and gripped her hand. Her handshake was firm, her hand warm, her skin silky-soft. Zane became self-conscious of how work-roughened his own palm must be, but she seemed unfazed by his callused hand.

"Welcome, Ms. Palmer."

One delicate eyebrow lifted, and she tilted her head. "Ms. Palmer? What happened to Erin? I thought after our phone conversation that we were on a first-name basis. I certainly would prefer to be less formal…Zane."

The way she said his name, as an addendum, her husky voice heavy with innuendo, her rosy lips twitching with amusement, caught him off guard. And shot a spike of lust through his blood. Zane arched one eyebrow, matching her gesture, and nodded once in agreement. "Erin, then. How was your drive?"

"Blessedly traffic-free, although I did run across a good bit of ice on the road." She had yet to release his hand, and he found himself drawn to her eyes. Eyes the deep green of—

A loud clatter and shout drew her attention across the ranch yard. Erin's hand dropped from his, her gaze seeking the source of the disturbance.

"Hey, can I get a hand here?" Piper's husband, Brady Summers, shouted. He was carrying a tall stepladder and stood next to the twenty-five-foot blue spruce tree that grew next to the stable. A pile of Christmas lights lay on the ground at his feet.

Even as he tucked his hand in his pocket, Zane could still feel the satin warmth of her fingers, like lingering impressions on his memory-foam mattress. He determinedly steered his brain away from thoughts of Erin and his bed. Clearing his throat, he turned to his brother. "Josh? Would you—?" Zane hitched his head toward

Brady and the ladder. "I need to show Erin where she'll be staying, help her with her luggage."

His brother, who already had Erin's suitcases out of the sporty Toyota, said, "I can—" Josh bit off his words as he met his twin brother's gaze and the silent message relayed in Zane's expression. "I can…help Brady with the Christmas tree lights."

Josh flashed his brother a not-so-secret grin and play-punched him in the shoulder as he headed across the ranch driveway toward the massive spruce, the two dogs at his heels.

"All right, then." Zane moved to the bags and lifted one in each hand, while Erin slid an additional duffel over her shoulder. "If you'll follow me…"

Traces of slush and ice left from a light snow earlier in the week crunched under Zane's boots as he escorted Erin across the ranch yard toward the bunkhouse-turned-guest-quarters. "You'll have the run of the guesthouse. Once the adventure biz gets up and running again, this is where the clients will sleep during the on-site portion of the tours."

"Uh-huh," she hummed distractedly, watching Brady position the large ladder with Josh's help. She strayed from the path Zane was leading to get a closer look at the spruce. Setting the suitcases on a dry spot of ground, he followed her over to the tree that the family decorated each year with a copious number of lights and large red glass balls. The glass decorations were already hung on the tree.

"Um…" Erin said as she approached the tree, putting her glove back on. "Can I make a suggestion?"

Brady turned to face their guest, taking a moment to blow warmth into his hands. "Uh, sure."

Zane jogged a few steps to catch up to Erin and made the introduction to his new brother-in-law. After niceties were exchanged, Erin waved a gloved hand toward the spruce. "It's easier to put lights on a tree if you do them before the other decorations."

"Told you!" another male voice said, and Zane angled his head to see their ranch hand coming out of the stable with an extension cord looped over his arm. Zane introduced Erin to the hand, Dave Giblan, and Dave gave her a smile and a nod of greeting, adding, "We went through this last year, too. But Mr. The-Order-Doesn't-Make-A-Difference didn't remember the hassle we had with the lights last time."

"I don't mean to butt in. I've just learned from experience," Erin said and grinned brightly at Dave.

He was *not* jealous of the spark of attraction he saw in her eyes as she replied to the ranch hand, Zane told himself, despite the niggle of irritation in his gut.

Brady grunted and cast Dave a hooded side glance. "Whatever."

As Brady began plucking the glass decorations off the tree, the ranch foreman joined the crowd, as well. Roy Summers, Brady's father and long-time ranch employee, frowned at the group. "Is this like a lightbulb riddle? How many ranchers does it take to decorate a Christmas tree?" He cast a startled glance at Erin. "Oh, hello, young lady. You must be the writer."

More introductions were made, and Roy put a hand on Brady's shoulder. "Come on, son. Someone's got to do the real business of the ranch. Give me a hand tending the abscessed hoof on that calf I brought in earlier."

"Be there in a minute," Brady said, and Roy firmed his mouth in displeasure.

"I'd say a hurting calf takes priority over some baubles on a tree, son." He nudged Brady more insistently. "Let's go."

"Fine," Brady replied grudgingly, and he handed off the glass balls he'd gathered to Dave. "Okay, Santa Claus. I'm out. You have the conn."

Dave responded with a snort and an eye-roll that made Erin chuckle. He repositioned the ladder, which rattled and creaked as he settled it closer to the tree.

"I can't wait to see it all decorated and the lights glowing." She turned to Zane, her face lit with enthusiasm, her cheeks and nose pink from the cold. "I love Christmas. Even more than spring. And my birthday's in spring, so that's saying something, because I *really* love celebrating my birthday."

His chest tightened as he gazed at her. Her eyes reflected a childlike glee that reminded him of Christmases past, rising before the sun with his brother and sister, filled with exuberance and anticipation. As she stood in the winter sun, gazing up at the spruce tree, her breath clouding in the chilled air, Zane finished his earlier interrupted thought. *Spruce green*. Erin's eyes were the same color as a Christmas tree, he decided as a he felt a small hiccup in his pulse.

He gave himself a mental finger-thump to the forehead. *Don't go all hearts and flowers over her in the first five minutes, dork*. Such an impetuous reaction to a woman was more his flirtatious brother's style than his own. Zane preferred time to build an opinion based on his interaction with a person.

Pragmatic. Reasoned. Grounded. He prided himself on being everything an oldest sibling should be, even if his age advantage was only five minutes. So why did Erin evoke such a visceral reaction from him?

He cleared his throat and tipped his head toward the guesthouse. "I'll just put your luggage inside. Then, whenever you're ready, I can—"

A loud *snap* crackled through the winter air like a gunshot. In the next instant, the tall step ladder where Dave perched buckled and collapsed. He toppled to the ground, landing with a thud and a feral cry of pain.

Chapter 3

Erin gasped her shock and concern as the handsome ranch hand crashed to the frozen ground. If his guttural shout left any doubt to his injury, the odd angle of his leg did not.

She clapped a hand over her mouth as a wave of nausea roiled through her at the gruesome sight. Zane abandoned her bags and brushed past her as he rushed to aid his friend.

"Call 9-1-1!" he yelled to no one in particular.

Pulling her glove off with her teeth, Erin fumbled her cell phone from her purse and tapped in her security code with a trembling finger. She squinted at the screen, trying to make out the image against the glare of the winter sun. Her signal reception was weak at best.

Josh hustled past her. "Landline's more reliable. I'm on it."

As Zane's brother ran toward the main house, Erin faced Zane and Dave again, her heart in her throat. Surely she could do *something* to help. Yanking her knit scarf from under the collar of her coat, she balled the scarf as she dropped to her knees across from Zane. "Here," she said, handing him the messily folded neckwear. "Put this under his head."

A pillow may be a small thing under the circumstances, but she had little else to offer at the moment. And standing idly by while the cowboy suffered was not her style. Action was her go-to mode, and her brain was ticking through more options for the crisis, even as Zane tucked the knit scarf under Dave's head.

As if sensing something was amiss, the dogs barked and paced the yard. When the black-and-white dog tried to nose in next to him, Zane pushed the dog back. "No, Ace. Lie down."

The foreman and Brady appeared at the door of the barn across the yard.

"What happened?" Brady called as he trotted toward them.

"Ladder collapsed. Dave broke his leg, maybe more," Zane returned in a clipped, efficient tone, despite his obvious worry. With a wave of his hand, he directed the father and son to, respectively, fetch someone named Helen and to go to the end of the driveway to flag down the ambulance when it arrived.

Zane's take-charge leadership impressed Erin, as well as the way that the other men followed his directives without demurring. Zane's father had indicated as much, as well. Though the McCall siblings and Brady Summers were equal partners in McCall Adventure Ranch, Zane was the gatekeeper, it seemed.

Zane held one of the injured man's hands, letting Dave squeeze his fingers as he writhed and groaned. "Stay still, buddy. I know it hurts. Help's coming."

Seeing Dave's other hand at his side, his fingers clenched in a tight ball, Erin lifted his fist into her lap. Cupping his fist between her palms, she stroked his taut knuckles with her thumb and muttered, "Hang in there, cowboy."

Zane's gaze darted to her, then dropped to her comforting gesture as Dave loosened his balled fingers to grip her hand.

"Thanks," Dave rasped, casting a quick side glance to her before scrunching his eyes closed in pain. His breathing was shallow and rapid, and she didn't need to be a nurse to know hyperventilating was not what Dave needed.

"Hey, Dave," she said, jostling his hand to get his attention. "Will you try something with me?"

Both Zane and Dave peered at her with curious looks.

"You need to calm your breathing, so I thought we could do some yoga breathing together. Will you do it with me?"

The injured cowboy furrowed his brow and stared at her with shock in his eyes. "Yoga?"

Though Zane's expression was equally leery, she could see his concern for his friend outweighed his skepticism. "What do you have in mind?"

She fixed her gaze on Zane and his stunning blue eyes sent a tremor through her. With her host's penetrating gaze on her, she needed the relaxation technique as much as Dave. "Calming breaths. You do it with us."

Dave scoffed quietly between gasps and grunts.

Patting his hand firmly, she directed him to inhale

with her as she counted two beats in her head. "Now exhale slowly for four seconds."

The cowboys both blew their breaths out through their mouths.

"Through your nose, gentlemen. You're not having a baby, you're trying to relax."

Her comment earned her odd looks from both men, but they followed her example as she inhaled again and let her exhale draw out twice as long. "Now inhale for three seconds and exhale for six."

Dave's demeanor calmed, his hyperventilating quieted, and Erin's pulse slowed, too…so long as she didn't look into Zane's piercing eyes. Meeting his celestial-blue gaze was a bit like staring at the sun. Doing so for too long was risky, as if he could sear something deep inside her with his laser-bright stare.

She continued walking them through the one-to-two breathing ratio for a couple of minutes until Josh ran back across the ranch yard and skidded to a stop beside them.

"Ambulance is on the way," Josh said as he spread a heavy blanket that he'd brought out over Dave. Josh was panting from exertion and stress, and his tense energy and ragged breaths distracted her students.

Erin felt the tension reenter Dave's grip as his eyes darted to Josh, and she saw the muscles in the injured man's jaw flex as he gritted his teeth. She snapped her fingers in front of Dave's eyes and, with a nudge of his chin, brought his attention back to her. "Right here, cowboy. Focus on me."

He gave her a pained grin and rasped, "My pleasure. You're a…heap prettier than either of these…chumps."

"Thank you. Now, less talking and more slow breathing, friend." She flashed him a bright smile, and from her peripheral vision, she noticed the frown that Zane divided between them.

Dave followed her directions for a couple more breaths, then with another thin grin that reflected his agony, he added hoarsely, "Any chance I could...repay you for your kindness?" He paused to drag in another breath. "Dinner sometime maybe?"

Now Zane's whole body tensed, his brow forming a deep *V* as he sent the hand a hard look.

"Why, you flirt!" She sent the injured man a wink. Anything that helped distract him from his pain was acceptable in her book. "I just might have to take you up on that."

"What about Helen?" Josh said, and Zane arched a raven eyebrow and cocked his head as if to say, *Yeah, what he asked.*

"Helen?" She gave him a scolding pout.

The ranch hand grimaced, clearly from his excruciating pain rather than the shame of being caught out. He gulped a couple shallow breaths. "It wouldn't be...a date, so what's...wrong with it?"

She gave him a disapproving grunt, then tapped his nose with her finger. "Through your nose. Let's start again. Three-second inhale..."

Her coaching was interrupted again as a woman's distress cry reached them through the chill air. Erin and the men all turned to look toward the back of the main house where the foreman appeared with a young woman wearing a stained apron and no coat. She ran toward them, calling, "Dave! Oh, my God, Dave!"

Erin scooted aside to allow the sobbing woman access to the ranch hand, though she hated the fact that the woman was clearly upsetting Dave again. She glanced at Zane, meaning to send him a silent message with her facial expression.

As if sensing her attention, Zane raised his head, his gaze clashing with hers. She indicated her concern over the woman's effect on the patient with a twitch of her brow and quick side glance. Zane gave her the merest of nods, then put a hand on the woman's shoulder. "Helen, calm down. Help is coming. Right now, we have to keep him comfortable and breathing deeply."

"Dave," Erin said, gaining the hand's attention again. "With me. Inhale…" She demonstrated the technique again while Helen watched. "Can you keep him going?" she asked Helen and the young woman nodded, though her eyes spoke for her distress. Then to Dave, Erin said, "No hyperventilating, cowboy. Concentrate on your breathing."

Dave gave a nod, his jaw clenched and his complexion a worrisome gray.

Having passed the distraction and deep breathing reins to Helen, Erin pushed to her feet and backed away from the huddle of bodies around Dave. She considered taking her luggage inside, but since she'd not yet officially been shown in to her accommodations at the guesthouse, that seemed presumptuous.

Besides, her curiosity was sparking.

The ranch has had a string of incidents, with evidence of sabotage that have hamstrung our operations, crippled us financially.

Her client's words replayed in her head and his word choice stirred a disquiet in her gut as she glanced back at Dave. Though Josh's back currently blocked her view of the ranch hand's broken leg, the grisly image of Dave's twisted shin was burned on her brain.

With a furtive glance toward the ranchers, she sidled over to the collapsed stepladder and studied the rails, the spreader, the bolts. What had happened to the ladder? A simple slip by the hand or something more sinister? She toed a bent piece of aluminum and searched the ground for the screws that should have attached the loose support bar to the legs of the ladder. Casting her gaze around her feet, she searched the ground for the failed bit of hardware. Finding a rusted screw lying in two pieces beneath the branches of the spruce tree, she stooped to gather the bits. Then hesitated.

If this did prove to be sabotage and not just the failure of an ancient screw, she should leave the evidence untainted for the police. She straightened and backed away from the ladder, but slid her phone back out of her pocket.

With another glance behind her to make sure her actions were not being watched, she quickly snapped a few pictures of the fallen ladder and the rusty pieces of the broken screw. Repocketing her phone, she edged back toward the injured cowboy, making mental notes about who was present and their reactions to the incident. She would be having a private meeting with her client tonight, and she already had something to report.

Seeing that she'd left the cluster, Zane stood and approached her.

"Hardly the welcome to the ranch I'd have planned." He shoved his hands in his pockets and drew his mouth into a grim line.

"And not one I'd have expected. I'm sure this isn't the kind of excitement McCall Adventure Ranch had in mind for customers." She placed a hand over her chest.

"My heart is still thumping." And it bumped even harder when Zane stepped closer, his gaze intense.

"Thank you for your help. I'm not sure I'd have known what to do if he'd passed out or…" He waved a hand, his thought unfinished as he cut a glance back toward the injured man. A frown dented his brow and he started unbuttoning his coat. He shrugged out of the fleece-lined jacket and walked over to drape it around Helen's shoulders. Helen turned a pixie-like, tearstained face up to his and gave him a brief smile of thanks. Zane's gentlemanly gesture touched Erin.

"So chivalry isn't dead," she said to him as he returned.

He gave her a brief puzzled look, then shrugged his actions off. "She needed a coat. I gave her mine. No biggie."

But to Erin his thoughtfulness was telling, as was his modesty. She'd learned through her work, through her life-changing moments, that people can say who they are until they are blue in the face. But actions were the real evidence of character. This was why she typically avoided pre-researching people. She didn't want preconceived notions to jade her observations of people in action. Body language. How they reacted to questions and events…

Zane divided a concerned look between her and the fallen hand. Clearly he was torn between his duty as host and his friend's well-being. Rubbing his hands on his jeans, he started toward her suitcases. "Anyway… let me get you settled—"

The distant wail of a siren reached them, yanking his attention toward the highway and the Double M's long gravel driveway.

She put a hand on his arm. "You go meet the ambulance. I can see myself in."

"I—"

"Zane." She squeezed harder on his wrist and could feel the steady thump of his pulse under her fingers. A jolt of something hot and unnerving skittered from his skin through her fingers and throughout her body when his eyes connected with hers. She'd have to get over her unsettling fascination with his breathtaking eyes if she was going to keep her head as she worked with him in the coming days. She paused a beat, regaining her composure, before she slanted a half grin toward him and bent to gather her luggage for herself. "Go on. I've got this."

She turned and headed for the guesthouse door.

"Erin." The sexy timbre of his voice slid over her like a lover's caress. She stopped. Faced him, trying to pretend his voice didn't weaken her knees.

He reached into his pocket, then extended his hand to her. As he walked closer, gravel and ice crunched under his boots. "You'll need this."

A silver key winked in the sunlight at her. "Oh," she muttered as she lifted it from his callused palm. "Thanks." The metal was still warm from being nestled in his pocket near his body heat.

He ducked his head in a nod, and the corner of his mouth tugged in a strained smile. "Let me know if I can do anything to help you get settled."

With an appreciative nod, Erin let herself in the guesthouse and left her bags in the first bedroom down the hall. Moving to the front window, she parted the curtains, allowing her to keep watch for the arrival of the emergency vehicles. Would the police come? Or was the incident being viewed as accidental by the ranch staff?

If *she* made too much of an issue about the broken ladder, she'd call unwanted attention to herself, raise questions. Instead she pulled out her phone and texted her client, Zane's father. He needed to know what had happened and that she advised he have the police look at the scene before it was disturbed. Within seconds of her text, her phone chimed with Michael McCall's reply that he was on his way to the scene.

Erin pocketed her phone and returned to her suitcases to hang up a few clothes, set out her toiletries and plug her laptop in to charge, all the while wishing she were still out in the yard helping, observing. She needed to maintain her cover, but for such a tragic incident to happen within minutes of her arrival...

She just couldn't believe it was coincidence. Her gut told her it was no accident. She thought hard about exactly what had happened prior to the ladder collapse. Who had been present? What had transpired? She'd met Brady Summers, Zane's brother-in-law. And the foreman, also last name Summers. Some relation to Brady? Zane hadn't said, but she'd wager so. Hadn't he called Brady "son" when he'd requested his help with the sick calf?

She replayed that scene in her mind's eye. Brady had put off the foreman at first. That would indicate no preconception about the state of the ladder. And Dave had climbed right on. To his detriment. Josh and Zane had been involved with greeting her. She couldn't fairly make an assessment there. Had she not arrived when she did, would one of them have been climbing the faulty ladder? And was all this speculation just that? Seeing trouble and misconduct where none existed? The ladder was clearly old. Rusted in more places than the screws. Maybe the worn-out equipment was just an accident waiting to happen and Dave had drawn the short straw.

The wail of approaching emergency vehicles and rumble of engines drew her back to the window. An older man with black hair like Zane's had joined the men standing around Dave. Michael McCall? As the vehicles pulled up, the older man walked over to an attractive brown-haired woman of approximately the same age and wrapped her in a comforting hug. Zane's mother?

Erin didn't linger in the guesthouse any longer. While getting in the way during an emergency would be bad form for a visiting travel writer, she really wanted to have a firsthand, up-close view of the proceedings. A sheriff's department SUV was among the arriving vehicles, and she *really* wanted to observe the handling of the incident, since Michael's chief reason for hiring her was his discontent with the way the local law enforcement had essentially shrugged off previous incidents of vandalism on the ranch. Or so Michael felt. Maybe there had truly been little the sheriff could do, too little evidence to make an arrest. Michael didn't buy that reasoning and that scenario seemed sketchy to Erin, as well. How hard had they tried to find the person sabotaging the Double M?

Snagging her coat off the back of the communal area's couch where she'd discarded it minutes ago, Erin headed back outside. She kept to the perimeter of the gathered crowd, edging closer to the site of the broken ladder.

Initial efforts of the first responders were, understandably, getting Dave stabilized and into the ambulance. Zane approached one of the sheriff's deputies and pointed to the fallen ladder, spread his hands, shook his head. *Oh, to be a fly on the...deputy's hat?*

Erin rolled her eyes at her broken idiom and noticed presumably Michael break away from presumably his wife to join Zane's conversation with the deputy. Michael's jaw was taut. When the deputy said something with a lift of his shoulder, Michael's eyes hardened, and he made an angry gesture toward the rubble of the ladder.

Zane placed a hand on presumably his father's shoulder and said something that was answered with a head shake and grim, tight-lipped expression from the older man. The older woman joined them and apparently encouraged Michael to step aside. "Let Zane handle it, honey," Erin overheard the woman say, then garbled words and "...your blood pressure."

She read on his lips the curse word that Michael loosed as Zane and the deputy stepped aside and his wife guided him away. As the older couple stepped to the edge of the crowd, Michael's gaze drifted to Erin and stopped. He tensed, then softened his facial expression and gave her a tiny nod of acknowledgment. His wife noticed, and Erin saw the woman's lips say, *Who's that?*

Michael turned toward his wife to reply, and whatever he said had the woman towing him over to Erin, a warm smile of greeting on her lips. "Are you Erin Palmer, the writer?"

Erin stuck out her hand to the woman. "I am."

"Melissa and Michael McCall. So nice to meet you." Rather than shake her hand, Melissa folded Erin's hand between her gloved palms and squeezed. "I'm so sorry that your welcome has been spoiled by this terrible accident."

"No apologies, please. I'm just so sorry this happened. How is Dave?"

"Shocky," Michael said, offering his hand.

Melissa dropped Erin's fingers so that she could greet the patriarch of the family.

"But the EMT assures us he'll be fine." Erin gave the older man's hand a firm shake as he continued. "Glad to meet you, Ms. Palmer. Zane says you were quite helpful in calming the patient earlier. Some sort of yoga breathing?"

She shrugged. "Mostly common sense. He needed not to hyperventilate, which was where he was headed, so I got him to refocus his thoughts and breathe deeper."

"Don't be modest, dear. That was a good thing you did. We thank you. Dave is like family to us." Melissa patted Erin's sleeve, and the maternal gesture flowed through Erin like warm honey. She immediately liked the woman, whose kind eyes and generous smile spoke of a gentle soul.

"Melissa and Michael McCall…" she said, tipping her head with a grin tugging her lips. "How very alliterative."

Melissa chuckled. "Says the writer. Yes, we have plenty of Ms around here. That's where the Double M got its name."

Erin furrowed her forehead. "I thought the ranch had been in the family for several generations."

Melissa gave a startled laugh. "Someone has been doing her research!" She sent her husband an impressed look before returning her gaze to Erin. When the mostly gray blue heeler nuzzled her hand, Melissa bent to stroke the dog's head and scratch his ears. "The ranch was my family's for close to fifty years before I inherited it when my father died. We renamed it the Double M at that time because I wanted Michael to feel he was included, that he belonged, that the ranch was truly his as much as mine."

Michael jerked his head toward Melissa. "What? You told me you wanted to change the name because Rocking X sounded like a porn palace."

Erin snorted a laugh and quickly covered her mouth to muffle her mirth.

"It did sound like a porn palace or house of ill repute!" Melissa fussed. "My mother thought so, too. It needed to change. And the Double M achieved both dignity and a sense of inclusion for you. Win-win."

Michael touched his wife's cheek. "Well done, love." He gave her a peck on the lips. "Thank you."

The clack of metal stretcher legs folding called their attention to the back of the ambulance. Dave was loaded in the patient bay, and Zane had to retrieve one of the dogs when it tried to jump into the ambulance with the stretcher.

Helen clambered in next to Dave before the back doors were slammed shut.

"Lord, take care of him. Give them both strength and peace," Melissa said under her breath, then raised a worried look to her husband.

"Why don't you follow the ambulance to the hospital?" Michael said quietly to his wife. "I'll join you shortly, but I want to stay here as long as the sheriff is on the premises."

Melissa gave him a long, anxious stare. "Will you behave? Let your sons talk to the deputies? I don't need another emergency because your blood pressure spiked."

The reminder of his medical condition clearly irritated the ranch owner, but he sighed, nodded. "I'll be careful."

"Thank you." Melissa rose on her toes to press a kiss to his cheek before heading across the ranch yard calling, "I'm going to the hospital. Roy? Josh? Anyone want to ride with me?"

Michael shifted his body so that his back was to the rest of the people in the yard. "You saw the accident happen?"

"Sort of," Erin said, matching his lowered volume. "I was talking to Zane at the time, and suddenly the ladder collapsed, and Dave was on the ground."

"And you suspect foul play?" Michael lifted an eyebrow.

Erin shook her head. "Not necessarily. I just thought it wise for the police to photograph the scene, treat it as sabotage for the time being. Just in case. Considering the history of incidents here, it would be prudent."

"I agree. Unfortunately, the deputy I talked to is not so convinced. I tried to argue the point and was sidelined by my family because I had a cardiac event a few years ago and am at risk of another because of my blood pressure." He grumbled something under his breath, then said, "The best thing for my blood pressure would be to see this menace hanging over us solved, and the ranch put back on a profitable trajectory."

"I'd like to go observe," Erin said, casting a glance behind her client and seeing the deputies milling about the ladder debris. "We'll talk later." She offered her hand and said in a louder voice, "It was nice to meet you, Michael. Thank you for hosting me."

He jerked a nod and stepped aside, and Erin eased closer to the area where the deputy was nudging the parts of the broken ladder with his toe.

"Um," she said and cleared her throat, "aren't you going to photograph the scene before you move pieces?"

The deputy raised his head and eyed her. "We only

do that at crime scenes, ma'am. No evidence of a crime here."

"And how do you know there was no crime if you don't examine the broken parts and try to determine what happened?"

The deputy tucked his thumbs in his utility belt, puffed his chest out and narrowed a glare on Erin. "And who are you?"

"Guest of the ranch. Concerned citizen. Witness to the accident. Take your pick." She tipped her head. "I'm available now if you are planning to interview the witnesses."

"Again, no need. No crime to investigate." He took a step toward her. "Unless you know something about what happened that you'd like to share. You have a reason to believe this was more than an accident?"

She flipped up a gloved palm. "Context. Past incidents of vandalism here. And, in my experience, ladders don't typically just fall apart."

The deputy bent to pick up the bits of the rusty screw she'd found earlier. "They do when the hardware holding 'em together rusts out this much. The ladder was old. Worn out. I don't see enough here to warrant an investigation."

She held the deputy's stare. The hard slash of his mouth said clearly he was miffed that she'd questioned his professional judgment, but she didn't back down. She was no stranger to crimes being brushed under a rug, investigations neglected because of political agendas and the influence of money.

She heard the crunch of boots on slush but didn't take her eyes from the deputy.

"Is there a problem here?" Zane said, stepping up

beside her and dividing a glance between her and the deputy.

"I was just offering to tell Deputy—" she shifted her gaze briefly to the man's name tag "—Morton what happened. What I saw. But he indicated he wouldn't be conducting interviews or investigating the cause of the accident, seeing that he has *no reason* to believe anything untoward happened here." She didn't try to hide her sarcasm, and she earned a scowl from the deputy and a puzzled look from Zane.

Morton cast a disgruntled look at Zane before returning his dark glare to her. "Thank you for your concern, ma'am," he said tightly, his expression flinty. "I'll be sure to contact you if we have any questions for you later. Good day." He turned sharply on his heel and stalked away.

Zane watched the officer go for a moment before facing her with a crease in his brow. "What did I miss?"

"I was just expressing my concern to the deputy that they weren't doing a more thorough investigation of what happened here." She motioned to the broken ladder, then rolled her shoulders, releasing some of the tension that had knotted there as she'd confronted the deputy.

"I see." His lips pressed into a thin line, and he glanced toward the departing squad car. "As I said earlier, I appreciate your help with calming Dave. But if I may be blunt, Ms. Palmer..."

His return to her surname told her all she needed to know about his mood, his opinion of her conversation with the deputy.

"The incident is *not* your concern, and I would ask that you not interfere. Our family needs to maintain a good working relationship with the sheriff's department.

We have other issues pending with them, and it would be counterproductive to antagonize Deputy Morton or any of the other officers."

"Even if they aren't doing their job?" she countered, belatedly realizing that she should have stifled her knee-jerk reaction.

"Not your business," he repeated calmly, though she could see the tick of the pulse in his throat and the twitch of muscles in his jaw.

She blew out a cleansing breath and gave him a nod. If she wanted to do her job properly, she had to try to maintain objectivity and not let her hot-button issues color the facts. She'd only just arrived, and she had far too much fact-gathering and observing left to do. Getting on Zane's wrong side would be a mistake.

Chapter 4

Later that day, just before dark, Erin knocked on the front door of the main ranch house, a notepad tucked under her arm. The door was answered by a pretty young woman with dark hair and a tall, willowy figure. Her gray eyes were bracketed with tiny creases that reflected the strain and concern for Dave that hung over the ranch.

"Hi," Erin said, offering her hand to the woman, "I'm Erin Palmer."

Although the brunette shook her hand, her expression remained puzzled. "Piper. Nice to meet you."

Piper. Erin mentally reviewed the names her client had given her about the ranch staff and family members. Piper was Michael McCall's daughter. Zane's sister. Right... She could see the resemblance in the young woman's pretty face.

Piper bit her bottom lip. "I'm sorry. Am I supposed to know you? Did you have an appointment?"

"Uh, Zane didn't tell you about me?"

Zane's sister twisted her mouth in thought. "Not that I recall."

"Well, with all the confusion this morning because of Dave's accident, I guess he—"

"You know about that?" Piper blinked her surprised.

"Yeah. It all happened just minutes after I arrived."

Piper caught her breath and smacked her forehead with the heel of her palm. "The writer! Of course. I'm sorry." She opened the door wider and stood back. "Come in, please. I've been so flustered since I heard Dave got hurt, I totally forgot about your visit."

"How is Dave doing?" Erin asked as she slipped off her coat.

Piper took the winter wrap from her. "Stable. It was a bad break. Both bones in his lower leg. He's just come out of surgery to put in a metal rod to stabilize the leg."

Erin winced. "Wow. I'm so sorry." She cast a quick glance around. "So…is Zane around?"

"Oh…sure. I think he's back in the office. Let me go ask him if he's available to speak with you."

While she waited in the foyer for Piper to return, Erin noticed a small black cat with a white bib and white toes peek around the corner from the next room. "Hello there." She squatted and held out her hand. The cat crept forward to sniff her fingers, but when she tried to pat the feline, it shrank away from her touch. "I won't hurt you." She tried again to pat the shy kitty, but it turned and trotted away.

The thud of boots on the hardwood floor announced

Zane before he appeared in the front hall. "Hi. Piper said you needed to see me."

She stood and greeted him with a smile. "If you have a few minutes, I thought we could start on the article. I'd like to talk to you and anyone else that's available."

Piper reappeared beside her brother. "I'm free now. I just need to check that Connor's doing his homework like he's supposed to be."

"Great! Can we meet in your office?" she asked, glancing at Zane.

He spread his hands, palms up. "Why not? I'll rustle Josh up, and then you'll have three of the four investors in the adventure company."

Erin dipped her chin in agreement. "Perfect."

"Back in five," Piper said, heading out the front door.

When she glanced from the door to Zane with a confused look and a question on the tip of her tongue, he preempted her query saying, "She lives in the foreman's house across the way. She married Brady this summer. Connor is their son."

"Got it." She flipped open her notebook and clicked her pen open to jot down the relationships and connections as she followed Zane down the hall to a small room that was likely once a bedroom but now housed a desk, bookshelves, printer stand and…a sawhorse with a well-worn saddle.

Erin pulled up short when she saw the sawhorse, and her face must have expressed her surprise because, again, Zane foresaw her question and offered, "I'll be working on it later, oiling the leather and fixing a broken buckle. I try to keep something in here that I can work on during downtime with the paperwork. Saves time trekking back and forth to the stable or barn, and I don't feel like I'm ignoring my ranching responsibilities this way."

"Very efficient."

"Well, it's not much. And I do still pull my weight with the herd and tending the horses. This just keeps me busy in stolen minutes throughout the day and at night."

"No rest for the weary?" She sent him a half grin as she settled in a chair in front of the desk.

"No rest for the shorthanded and trying to stay financially afloat," he replied as he tapped his phone screen without looking at her. He laid the phone on the desk next to neat piles of paperwork. "You get settled in all right?"

"I did. Thanks."

"Good." His phone buzzed, and he lifted it again to check the screen. "Josh will be here in a minute. But before my brother and sister join us, I want to apologize if I sounded...*curt* earlier." He dragged a hand down his clean-shaven cheek and sighed. "I was upset about Dave, trying to deal with the uneasiness between the sheriff's department and my father, run point on the situation with the EMS and..." He exhaled through pursed lips, making an exasperated sputtering noise, then shrugged. "Losing another hand was the last thing we needed. And with us in the middle of roundup, about to head to market."

The last thing they needed... Erin's thoughts spun. Losing Dave just as the family was about to realize their profits for the season...

Certainly the hand's injury put a crimp in the family's ability to get the work done on schedule. Could this explain the *why* of the damaged ladder? Assuming it was purposely damaged and not simply an accident as the majority of the ranch seemed to believe. In light of the upcoming auction, would they hire a new hand? Even a temporary worker to help get the cattle to market would be better than nothing.

She furrowed her brow and picked at the seam along the knee of her jeans as she ruminated on that possibility. When she raised her gaze, she found Zane watching her with a peculiar look on his face. Quickly she schooled her face and backtracked mentally to where she'd allowed their conversation to drop.

"Oh, uh, apology accepted," she said with an awkward smile.

His hands rested on the desk, and he tapped his thumb restlessly. "Where did you go just then? You were frowning."

"Just remembering the accident. Dave's leg…" Her stomach recoiled at the memory.

Piper entered the office and took the second chair that sat at an angle facing Zane's desk. "Okay, the kiddo is squared away."

"How old is your son?" Erin asked.

"Eight going on thirty-eight. He doesn't see the need for learning addition and subtraction in order to help run the ranch someday." Piper rolled her eyes.

Zane snorted, and one of his cheeks twitched with humor.

"You rang?" Josh said as he sauntered in and swept his gaze around the room. "Wow. Is this an official parley? Something up?"

Erin smiled at the third sibling of the McCall triplets. "Nothing formal. I just wanted to get to know you all and begin planning my research for my…article." She swallowed and squeezed the arm of her chair. She'd almost said *investigation*. Her near slip was an unpleasant reminder of the ruse she was operating under.

"So I suppose, since I have the owners of McCall Adventures here—" she made a vague gesture to the three siblings with her hand "—this would be a good time to talk about the company, where it stands and…what happened a few months ago to stall the opening?"

Both Piper and Zane cast looks to Josh, whose chipper expression darkened at her mention of the zip line sabotage. Though she had an encapsulated version of the story from the triplets' father, she was interested to see how the siblings viewed the incident.

"Well," Piper started, "first, let me say that my husband, Brady, is actually an equal partner in McCall Adventures."

"Oh, right. Of course," She jotted a note on her notepad. "Should we invite him to join us?"

"He's not really available. He's helping Connor with his homework. Have you met Brady?" Piper asked.

Erin nodded. "I think so. This morning, right before… well…" She let her words tail off when Piper's face fell, clearly distressed by the reminder of the morning's accident.

"I can tell Brady you want to talk with him later, if you want." Piper tucked a wisp of her dark brown hair behind her ear.

"Thanks," Erin said, nodding. "I'd like to talk to everyone on the ranch at some point." She tapped her pad with her pen and shifted her gaze to Josh. "So the zip line?"

Zane cleared his throat. "Is it really necessary to bring that up? We've moved on from the trouble this spring and are ensuring every possible safety precaution is in place as we go forward."

She made a mental note of Zane's reaction to reviewing the zip line sabotage. *Defensive? Protective of the business or of some other secret he wants to hide?*

"That's good," she said. "And I do plan to focus on the future of the business primarily, but…I think it's important for me to have a full picture of what happened, how it impacted the people involved and the business itself—such as the finances of the company—in order to put the journey forward in perspective."

"I'll tell you how it impacted me," Josh volunteered, shifting his weight and poking his thumbs in his pockets. "And I was the one closest to the incident."

Zane pulled a face as he shot his brother a look that said he wasn't happy with Josh's willingness to discuss the recent trouble.

But why? What was it about the past vandalism the family experienced that had Zane's guard up? Was he just wary in the same way Michael was being cautious by asking her not to reveal her true purpose to anyone?

For his part, Josh returned an even look and said, "Chill, man. It's all good." Facing Erin, he flashed a cocky smile. "The woman on the zip line when it fell is not only safe and sound, she is preparing for our wedding in three weeks."

Josh's happiness glowed from his eyes as brightly as his smile.

"Mazel tov! Congrats!" Erin already heard about the upcoming nuptials for Josh and his intended from Michael, but seeing the groom's joy warmed her inside. Her heart also gave a slow drub of envy. Would she ever find someone who filled her with that from-the-soul glow of happiness?

"Yeah, as much as I like Kate, I have to wonder about her sanity, hooking her wagon to this doofus," Piper said with a teasing smile and pure affection for her brother in the wink she gave Josh.

"I still say it's Stockholm syndrome. Josh had to have brainwashed her while they were alone those two days," Zane added, lacing his fingers behind his head and leaning back in his deck chair.

"Hardy har har," Josh returned wryly as he moved to the saddle Zane had set up on the sawhorse. While his siblings chuckled under their breaths, he swung his leg over the saddle and sat astride it, arms crossed over his chest, his expression as content and smug as a cat with a canary *and* a bowl of milk.

"I just oiled that," Zane said.

"You did?" Josh asked, frowning as he stood and checked his clothes for stains.

Zane snorted dryly. "Made you look."

Josh gave his brother's shoulder a shove before he resettled on the saddle.

"Boys," Piper said, rolling her eyes, "you're wasting the nice lady's time."

Erin wanted to say that the interplay between family members and the ranch employees was exactly what she wanted to observe. She needed to get a sense of hidden tensions, jealousies or competition that could shape her investigation.

She honed in on an element of Zane's jab at Josh. "You were alone with your fiancée for two days after the accident at the zip line?"

Josh nodded. "That's right. Two crazy, drama-filled, brush-with-death days." He curled up a corner of his mouth again, and his eyes—the same shade of startling blue as Zane's—twinkled. "It was great," he said without irony.

Erin was busy comparing how bright and full of life Josh's countenance looked compared to Zane's harsher, more serious expression, and she almost missed the seemingly contradictory postscript.

"Great?"

"Well, maybe not at the time. But in hindsight, I wouldn't change any of it. Except the parts where Kate was in danger." He inhaled deeply, his nostrils flaring and his brow creasing. "That part still gives me nightmares."

"Understandable." She paused, taking mental note of how each of the McCall triplets reacted to the mention of the danger Josh and Kate had experienced.

Piper watched her brother with a knitted brow and a tighter grip on the arm of her chair. *Concern.*

Zane gave his brother a look of disgust...or was it anger? She focused on him. "Zane, Josh's experience seems to irritate you. Why?"

He jerked his gaze to her, clearly startled by her question. "What?"

"He's still ticked off because I didn't do what he wanted," Josh said.

With a peevish side glance to his brother, Zane sat forward in his chair, propping his arms on the desk as he narrowed his eyes on Erin. "My brother has no one to blame for what happened after the zip line fell but himself."

Josh groaned and shook his head.

"He took unnecessary risks, like he often does," Zane continued, ignoring Josh's noises of disagreement, "and put Kate in danger."

"With a guarantee of the same end result, I'd do exactly the same again, too."

Josh and Zane exchanged hard stares, as if challenging the other to be the first to blink.

Erin was following the tense standoff when she felt a hand on her arm. She turned to Piper, whose mouth was twisted in a lopsided moue. "That smell you smell," she said, waving her hand as if stirring a scent in the air, "is testosterone and the reek of McCall stubbornness." With a quick glance at her brothers, she added, "They actually do love each other. They're best friends. Two peas in a pod." She cleared her throat. "Right, guys?"

After a beat, Josh cut a side glance to Erin and cracked a grin. "It's true. Zane and I are like this." He held up crossed fingers. "But lately my twin has been in a perpetual bad mood."

Zane made a rumbling noise in his throat and firmed his mouth as he broke his stare at his brother. "If you hadn't noticed, our family's legacy is about to go down the toilet. We're under attack from some unknown vandal, and our planned adventure business nearly got someone killed. We'll be lucky if we can find the cash to make repairs and reopen in the spring. I'd say I've got good reason to be in a bad mood."

"Fa-la-la-la-la. La-la. La-la!" Josh sang, mocking his brother.

"It's not a joke!" Zane groused. Then, as if remembering Erin was watching them, he jerked his gaze to hers and schooled his expression.

Interesting...

Erin took mental notes, not wanting the siblings to know their interaction was of key interest to her. She wanted them to be as natural as possible, not stifling reactions to put on a good face.

"This pessimistic version of you is getting old, Zane."

Piper tipped her head as she considered her brother. "We may have troubles, but we have plenty to be thankful for, too. Lots to be happy about. My reunion with Brady and Connor. Josh's wedding plans. Roy's sobriety. A roof over our heads. Christmas…"

"Yeah, yeah," Zane said, shrugging a shoulder. "I just get the feeling sometimes that I'm the only one with my eye on the ball. We do have a business to run and financial issues to deal with. Not to mention this other unknown threat looming over us." He sat taller in his chair and squared his shoulders as he centered his cerulean gaze on Erin. "But that's not what you came to write about, nor is what we need to be talking about now. Am I right?"

Erin chewed the end of her pen. "Well, maybe not specifically. But getting the lay of the land, so to speak, will help fill in details for a richer story, one with heart and depth."

"'Heart and depth,'" Josh repeated, nodding approvingly. "There you go. I like that."

At almost the same moment, pings and buzzes sounded in the office. The instant tension was palpable, and the siblings exchanged meaningful looks as they all pulled out their cell phones.

"Crap," Zane and Josh said at the same time.

Erin's gaze darted from one face to another.

"Hoo-boy," their sister added.

While Piper's and Josh's faces reflected frustration and mild concern, Zane's expression seemed almost… relieved. *Curious.*

Erin couldn't wait to get back to the guesthouse and begin making notes on her observations. "What's wrong?"

Josh swung his leg back over the saddle on the saw-horse. "Gotta go."

Piper pushed to her feet. "Roy found a place where the fence is out and some of the herd got loose. Short-handed as we are, it's all hands on deck to get the strays rounded up and fix the fencing." She shoved her phone in her back pocket and extended a hand to Erin. "Nice to meet you. I'm sure we'll talk again soon."

Josh replaced his hat and nodded to her as he hurried out. "Sorry to have to bolt. Catch you later?"

"Sure." Erin turned to Piper. "You're going out to round up cows, too?"

Piper grinned. "I did in the old days, but now I'm headed back to the house to stay with Connor while my husband goes out in the pasture."

Zane tapped a few keys on his computer, closing programs, and turned off his monitor. When he faced her, he turned up his palms and shrugged. "This is life on a ranch. We're all on call 24/7."

Erin stood and flipped her notepad closed. "Understood. No worries. We'll continue this some other time." She studied Zane as he stacked and straightened files on his desk, put away his pen and calculator in a drawer and pushed his chair under the desk. So orderly and neat. Her brother, Sean, an engineering student at the time of his death, had been the same way. She could still hear Sean saying, "A place for everything, and everything in its place."

"Question?" she said as Zane took his gray cowboy hat from a hook made from bull horns by the office door.

"Okay." He motioned with his hand for her to precede him out the door.

"When the call—or should I say the text?—came in

just now about the trouble with the fence, I felt the mood shift in the room. Everyone tensed."

He nodded, his expression flat. "For all of us to get a text at the same time is a bad sign. It means there's trouble." After a slight hesitation, he amended, "Usually."

"I get that," she said as they walked down the hall together. His broad shoulders filled the space between the walls where family pictures and shadow boxes with ribbons and medals had been hung. She wanted to spend more time in this hall with the old photos and awards, but Zane ushered her forward. "My question is this— when you read the text, instead of worry or frustration, like I saw on your siblings' faces, you looked…relieved."

Zane snapped his gaze toward her. "I did?"

"That's how it seemed to me."

A muscle in his jaw flexed as he stared at her. His brow furrowed, and his lips set in a taut line. While he was every bit as handsome as his twin, his more serious countenance and the lines of stress etched around his eyes made him appear older than his siblings.

"I suppose I was," he said finally as he continued down the corridor. He sidetracked briefly to the foyer to retrieve Erin's coat and hold it for her as she slipped her arms in the sleeves.

"Thanks," she said, smiling and adding another mental tick mark in the "gentleman" column for Zane.

She followed him through the kitchen and into the mudroom where he paused to toe off his athletic shoes and jam his feet into a pair of well-worn boots, saying, "Considering everything that's been happening around here lately, I guess I was glad the news wasn't anything worse. Loose cows and a broken fence we can handle. It happens now and then. Nothing new." He exhaled a sigh as they stepped out into the winter chill, and his breath clouded. "The news just as easily could have been another disaster because of our saboteur, or a problem with my dad's health, or bad news from the hospital about Dave, or—"

She grabbed his arm, stopping his progress across the ranch yard. "First, have you ever heard the expression 'borrowing trouble'?"

He nodded. "I know. It's a bad habit…especially lately." He dragged a hand down his face and gave her weak smile of chagrin.

A pang of sympathy prodded her chest, and she had to remind herself that her job required her to stay as un-affected emotionally as she could. She didn't have a heart of stone, but to judge people fairly and accurately, she couldn't let her personal feelings sway her perspective. "Second, where's your coat?"

He hitched a thumb at one of the outbuildings. "I have a work coat in the stable."

"Well." She took a step backward and motioned to-ward the area where she saw Josh mounting his horse and riding out. "Don't let me keep you."

Touching the brim of his hat, he turned and took a couple steps before returning. "Erin?"

"Mmm-hmm?"

He screwed his mouth into a frown of consternation. "I don't want the incident this morning or the tension you saw in my office earlier to affect your research."

She arched an eyebrow. "Easy there, cowboy. That sounds a bit like you're about to try to censor my work."

His brow dented, and he shoved his hands into his pockets. "That's not what I meant. Although…ideally,

I'd like your article not to be a laundry list of all the troubles we've had of late. That'd hardly be a sales pitch."

"I told you before, and I'll say it again, the integrity of my work requires no interference from the subject of my writing. My intent is not to sabotage your—" He flinched at her word choice. "Sorry. I'm not out to hurt your business. Trust me to do my job, okay?"

He hunched his shoulders against the cold as a chilly breeze buffeted them. A shiver sluiced through Erin, as well, but for a different reason. Every time she had to defend her work as a supposed journalist, she cringed internally. She could feel herself sinking deeper into a quagmire of deceit that dragged at her soul. Asking him to trust her, even as she led him to believe falsehoods about her, rankled.

He made a noncommittal sound in his throat. "What I meant was…I *want* you to have every opportunity to talk with the family, interview us, hear about our history, learn the business, get a close-up, inside view of the daily operations…despite the fact that we'll be operating shorthanded. *That*, more than the troubling incidents that have put us on our heels, is what defines my family and this ranch."

She raised her chin. "Oh," she said awkwardly. She flashed him a lopsided smile. "Looks like I owe you an apology. I shouldn't have presumed…" She bit her bottom lip, letting her sentence trail off. Was she already letting herself be swayed by Zane's serious disposition? Was she overcompensating because she found him so attractive and such an enigma at the same time?

The taut lines in his expression eased. "How about a mutual agreement to extend some trust, the benefit of the doubt?"

She released a deep breath, her grin warming. "Agreed."

"In that spirit then…" He shivered visibly and jammed his hands deeper into his pockets. With the wind stirring, he had to be freezing. "How would you like to come with me and help round up escaped cattle?"

Erin gave a startled laugh. "Me?"

"It doesn't get any realer than broken fences and rounding up a straying herd."

She only hesitated a second before throwing her hands up with a snort of amusement. "Why not?"

"Good. This way." He hitched his head toward the outbuilding where she'd seen Josh earlier. "You want a horse or an ATV?"

Falling in step beside him, she wrinkled her nose at his question. "An ATV? That's not very Americana. Cowboys are supposed to ride horses."

"It's the new Americana. More efficient in many cases, and you don't have to muck an ATV's stall or pay for vet bills and feed. Every ranch I know is using some form of motorized vehicle these days."

They reached the outbuilding, and as they stepped inside, the scent of manure and straw grew stronger. As her eyes adjusted to the dimmer light inside, she scanned the long aisle of stalls where a few horses hung their heads over their gates, snuffling and flicking their ears.

While Zane pulled on a coat he'd retrieved from a hook just inside the main door, she walked over to one of the horses and raised a hand to pat its nose. "Hi, beautiful. How are you?"

"So what do you think?" He eyed her as he buttoned the coat, which she saw was stained with Lord-only-knew-what, along with a liberal amount of dust and dried mud. No wonder he kept it in the stable.

"I'll save the ATV for another day and try a horse… if that's okay?"

He nodded and pursed his lips in thought. "I'd recommend Lucy for you. That's who Kate rides."

"Kate?" She flipped through her mental Rolodex, working to recall if she'd met Kate yet.

"Josh's fiancée. She's still learning to ride, and Lucy is one of our gentlest." Zane had taken a saddle and reins from a rack and entered the first stall on the left. He stroked the neck of the large black horse in the stall, and the animal responded with a snuffle, nudging Zane with its nose. "Hey, Sarge. Time to work."

Zane's phone beeped, and he paused long enough to check it. Muttering a curse, he glanced back at Erin. "That was Roy. I need to hurry. The herd got spooked, and they need me ASAP. I really don't have time to saddle Lucy for you. Rain check?"

Erin's heart sank, but she tried to hide her disappointment. "Sure."

As she turned to leave, he called, "Unless you wanted to ride double with me."

Walking back to the gate of the stall, she licked her lips and weighed the option. "Are you sure?"

"I wouldn't have offered if I weren't. But I need an answer now. Those loose cows are getting near a dangerous area in the hills, even as we speak." Zane slid the bit into the black horse's mouth and adjusted the reins while he talked.

"Okay. Am I dressed all right?" She held her hands out and dropped her gaze to her jeans, winter coat and low-heeled suede boots.

"Cows don't care about fashion," he said, not even looking as he tossed a blanket over the horse's back.

"Uh-huh," she replied dryly. "But what about functionality? Do I need to change anything? I can run back to my room, if so."

He sent her a quick side glance as he grabbed the saddle off the floor and draped it over the horse's back. "It'll do. But if you want to preserve the condition of those rather expensive-looking shoes, I'd swap out for a pair of work boots around the corner by the front alley door. While you're there, grab some gloves."

She followed his directions, and by the time she'd swapped her boots out and found a small pair of work gloves in a plastic bin, he was leading his horse—Sarge, he'd called the large black equine—out to the alley. The top of the horse's head rose taller than Zane's by several inches, and the beast's well-muscled flanks were sleek and shiny, his ears perked and alert. Just the same, she asked, "Sarge can manage both of us?"

"For a while. I won't ask him to work with both of us in the saddle." He motioned her closer. "You'll sit in front of me until we get up to the part of the fence where the cows got loose. Then you'll have to get down while Sarge and I round up strays. But you can observe. Maybe give Roy a hand with repairing the fence?" He slapped the saddle and nodded toward Sarge. "Need a leg up?"

"Onto this giant? Definitely." She moved closer and poked her foot in the stirrup, a challenge in itself thanks to her tight, slim-legged jeans. As she hoisted herself up, she felt Zane's large hands on her hips, his fingers digging into her with a firm grip. The heat from his palms sent shockwaves through her, and her breath snagged in her lungs. Erin worked to calm her scattered pulse as she settled into the saddle, sliding as far forward as she could to make room for him. But Zane had a rugged, magnetic presence that was hard to ignore. Especially when his touch made her blood sizzle like Fourth of July sparklers. He swung up to sit behind her, and his broad chest and muscled legs surrounded her. The press of his body against hers was like a vacuum, sucking all the oxygen from her lungs. Dizzying desire flashed through her as his arms circled her to take hold of the reins. "Ready?"

She squeezed the saddle horn, searching for balance as her head swam. She hummed her assent, because she doubted she had the breath left to speak without her voice cracking.

Zane clicked his tongue to the horse. As they rode out, he paused long enough to call to the two dogs that milled around the gate to the pasture.

"Ace! Checkers! What are you two lazybones still doing here? We have work to do." He gave a whistle and the dogs sprang to action, running into the pasture in front of them.

Erin tried to focus on the blue heelers bounding over the frozen ground ahead of them rather than the hard male body pressed against her back. Easier said than done, especially when Zane settled his hand on her belly, anchoring her as he kicked his horse's gait up to a canter. She clutched the saddle horn with one hand and his arm with her other.

"You okay?" he asked, his mouth beside her ear and his warm breath sending a tingle through her.

"I'm good," she said, though her voice sounded choked. She hoped he credited her winded reply to the jostling of the horse.

They rode for several minutes in silence, crossing the rolling hills of frozen pastureland. She drank in the lovely setting, imagining what it might be like to live in this rural setting, working the land and managing a herd for a living. Peaceful, in many respects, she thought, then remembered the stress and concern Michael had expressed to her because of the sabotage. Being at the mercy of the weather was a constant issue for the ranch. Drought, blizzards, storms could all take a toll on the herd.

"Do you ever wish you did something else for a living? That you lived in town and had a nine-to-five job?" she asked.

"No," he said without hesitation.

"Never? Not even when the herd gets loose right at dinnertime and you have to round up straying cows in the freezing cold?"

She felt the rumble from his chest as he grunted. "Inconvenient, yes. But ranching is my life. My heritage."

"That doesn't mean you can't want something else for yourself. You really don't ever think about getting a different job?"

"No." His tone was so certain, so final. She had to admire that he was so sure of his life path. She wondered sometimes if she'd chosen to be a private investigator for the right reasons. If Sean hadn't been killed, what would she have done with her life?

When the cattle and other ranchers on horseback came into sight, she pushed the philosophical questions aside and took in the scene before her. She recognized Josh in his black hat riding in a wide arc around the straying cows. Brady was further out in the pasture, while another man sat with his back to them, astride an ATV near the fence line, talking to the foreman, Roy Summers. Zane rode up to these two and addressed them. "Erin came to observe. Dad, want to give her a hand down?"

When the man on the ATV glanced over his shoulder, she saw it was Michael McCall, his face marked by lines of strain and worry.

Roy stepped forward first and reached up to help her down from the saddle. She caught the faint whiff of alcohol as the foreman set her on the ground. "Thank you, Roy."

"Ma'am," he replied, dipping his chin briefly.

"You can ride with me," Michael said, patting the ATV seat behind him, "or you can stay up here with Roy."

With another whistle to the dogs, Zane set off to help his brother and Brady head off the wandering cattle. She watched him ride away, a strange twinge in her chest. His command of his horse, his poise in the saddle, his whole confident demeanor struck her as infinitely sexy. He embodied the classic cowboy of American folklore, the rugged masculinity made famous by Madison Avenue advertisements. Her heart kicked, and her breath snagged as he galloped away.

"Ms. Palmer?"

She jerked her gaze back to Michael. "Oh, right. I'll watch from here. I don't want to be in the way."

He touched the brim of his hat in acknowledgment and said something to Roy she didn't catch as he revved the ATV engine and drove off in the same direction Zane had gone.

"Can I do anything to help you?" she asked Roy. "I brought gloves." She pulled out the leather work gloves to show him.

"Sure. You can hold the posts while I work on the barbed wire."

A stiff cold wind blew up across the pasture, and she

dug in her coat pocket again for the bright purple knit hat her sister had given her last Christmas. After tugging the hat on, she moved to kneel beside Roy, who worked to wind new wire on the downed posts. The longer she held the posts, the more she doubted the value of her contribution. Roy was clearly humoring the ranch guest. But the simplicity of her task allowed her to follow the action in the pasture. The flow of the men on horseback, the dogs and the ATV, gathering the far-flung cows and guiding them back toward the open section of fence, was mesmerizing. More and more, though, she found herself less observing the process as a whole and more tracking one man in particular. *Zane.*

She furrowed her brow when she realized what she was doing. What was her fascination with him? Josh and Brady were every bit as handsome, if happily attached. The other men had been more cheerful, though she couldn't find fault in Zane's behavior toward her. She'd witnessed his courtesy and thoughtfulness. Was it the veil of mystery and wariness that surrounded Zane that intrigued her?

She gave her head a brisk shake. She didn't need to form any leanings one way or another about any of the McCalls or the ranch staff without further observation and interviews. She'd been on-site less than twenty-four hours, for Pete's sake! Yet her first impressions had always been a valuable guide in the past. So…what did it mean that she had such a visceral reaction to Zane?

"Now when they come around that hill with the herd, they'll drive 'em right up here. Once they're all inside the fence, you take that post over there—" Roy pointed to the last place the fence was standing "—and I'll start driving in the new posts."

"Got it." She sniffed the air discreetly, more certain now that she smelled liquor on the man's breath. Michael had told her, when giving her an overview of the state of the ranch, that Roy had recently done a stint in a rehab center. She didn't want to stick her nose where it didn't belong, but she wondered if she should let Michael know she suspected Roy had been drinking.

"Now when the cows come through, you'll need to stay way back. You don't wanna get trampled."

Her pulse jumped, and she gave him a nervous laugh. "Uh, no. Certainly not!"

Roy glanced up from his manipulation of the barbed wire with a pair of long-nosed pliers. "The boys will do their best to steer 'em straight in, but you can never predict when a cow will veer off track."

"Thanks for the heads-up."

A whoop sounded behind her, and she turned to see Josh headed toward them, the first of the herd charging up the hill.

"Stand clear!" Roy gave her a gentle push, backing her away from the gap in the fence.

She scuttled away, her heart racing with the thrill of seeing the beasts beating a path toward her. The ground shook, and the low bleats and moos escalated the din of thundering hooves and the roar of the ATV engine as Michael guided the left flank.

Erin scanned the terrain, searching for Zane. He and Brady were bringing up the rear with the dogs racing along beside the cattle, tongues lolling. As he neared, Zane cast a glance her way. She smiled and gave him a thumbs-up.

But instead of returning a grin, his face darkened, and he shouted, "Erin, look out!"

She jerked her head around in time to see one of the cows at the edge of the herd veering away from the others. The cow was running straight at her.

Chapter 5

Adrenaline spiked in Erin's blood. She stepped back, only to come up against the barbed wire of the fence. Without a moment to second-guess, she whipped off her purple hat and waved it and her arms at the approaching cow as she yelled.

The cow tossed its head and turned sharply left, seconds before it would have trampled her. Relief left her limp, her knees shaking, and she would have collapsed if not for the strong arms that wrapped around her and pulled her into a hug.

"Geez, Erin, are you all right?"

She tipped her head back and met the intense blue of Zane's concerned eyes.

"I am. Thanks." Her breath shuddered from her, and she clenched her back teeth, steeling her nerves. His steadying grip both calmed her and started a different kind of excitement in her core. "My fault. Roy warned me to be alert, and I let myself get distracted." *By you.*

"Hey, Zane, enough flirting! We need you!" Josh called.

Zane pulled back from her, sending his brother a disgruntled look. "I'm not—" He cut off his protest with a grunt and shook his head. Catching her eye again, he asked, "You're sure you're okay?"

She nodded, and Zane backed toward Sarge, his gaze still studying her.

"That's all of 'em," Roy shouted. "You're up, little lady!"

Erin gave a little gasp as she startled from the hold of Zane's attention. She hurried across the gap with the new fencing, closing the herd inside. Zane and Roy rushed to set the new posts and tighten the barbed wire.

When the pasture was secure once more, Roy approached her, wearing a crooked grin. "Close call there, Ms. Palmer. You've got the makings of a ranch hand in you. That was some quality wrangling you did to redirect that cow."

She chuckled. "I don't know how quality it was. Mostly it was desperation and survival instinct."

"Just the same, I'm glad you're okay." He winked at her as he ambled away.

Michael pulled up beside her on his ATV. "Hop on, Erin. I'll give you a lift back to the house."

"Um…" She cut a side glance to Zane, who was deep in conversation with his brother and showing no indication of heading back to the ranch yet. A thread of disappointment twanged inside her. She'd rather ride back on Sarge, snuggled up to Zane again.

But feeding her ill-advised fascination with Zane

wasn't smart. Objectivity and focus were what she needed. Her near-miss with the runaway cow was proof of that concept. Giving herself a mental thump on the forehead, she accepted the senior McCall's offer and climbed on the back of the ATV.

She held on to Michael as they bumped over the ruts and hills back to the ranch yard. He let her off at the door of the guesthouse, quieting the engine so they could speak.

"Has anyone invited you to dinner yet?" he asked.

"Can't say they have. But you don't have to—"

"Don't be silly. You're our guest. Besides, one of your best opportunities to catch the whole family at once is at supper. We make a point of gathering around the table to eat as a family." He paused, frowning. "Although tonight will likely be an exception, seeing as Melissa is sitting with Helen and Dave at the hospital."

"Any update on Dave?" she asked.

"I'm about to call Melissa and check on him. Our meal tonight won't be anything fancy, but you're more than welcome." He checked his watch. "Say in half an hour?"

"All right. Thank you." She headed inside to clean up, remembering that she'd left her shoes at the stable where she'd changed into work boots. She considered briefly fetching them now, but decided she could pick them up on her way to dinner.

Zane detoured by the guesthouse on his way in from the stable. Erin answered his knock after a short wait. She stood behind the door and only poked her head around to peer out at him. "Oh, hi."

Her hair was wet and her skin looked freshly scrubbed. The light, floral scent that wafted out to him added credence to the theory she'd just climbed out of the shower.

Lust in its purest form kicked him hard, and he gritted his teeth, choking down the groan of approval that swelled in his throat. His body remembered far too well the feel of her round tush against his groin as they'd ridden out into the pasture. With her silky hair blowing in his face, he'd had her feminine scent filling his nose and fantasies filling his head of sinking his fingers in her coiling tresses while he kissed her wide, raspberry mouth.

Zane firmed his lips, frustrated by how easily she sidetracked his thoughts. Drooling over the visiting journalist was all kinds of bad form and highly impractical. He wasn't the sort to indulge in one-night stands, and she wasn't staying long enough to form a relationship with any real depth or merit. Better to rein in his impulses regarding her now than to pursue what was surely a nonstarter.

She raised her eyebrows and quirked her mouth in a lopsided grin. "Yes?"

He was staring like a dope, he realized, and shook himself out of his stupor. "I brought you your boots. You left them in the stable."

"Oh!" Her face lit like a child's on Christmas morning. "Thank you. Saved me a stop on the way to dinner."

She reached around the door for the boots, and he caught a peek of the towel she'd wrapped around her. A beat later, her words registered. "Dinner?"

"Mmm-hmm. Your dad invited me to eat with you. I'll be over in a few minutes. Just need to dry my hair and throw on some clothes."

Another flash of heat pulsed through him with the reminder of her dishabille. He fisted his hands and cleared his throat. "Guess I better hurry and get cleaned up myself then."

He touched the brim of his gray Stetson and nodded as he stepped back from the door, then turned to march toward the house. Was it his imagination, or did she linger a moment watching him go, despite the winter air that had to be chilling her wet skin?

He showered in record time, wanting to be finished and out front when she arrived. Sure, someone else from the family could greet her and play host, but he was the one who'd given her the okay to visit the ranch and conduct her research. He felt a personal responsibility to see to their guest's needs and to be her escort as needed. His damnable attraction to her had nothing to do with it. *Yeah, keep telling yourself that, pal.*

When a knock sounded at the back door a few minutes later, he and Josh both moved to answer it. "I got it," they said at the same time.

He took a quick step or two to get ahead of his brother, shooting him a stand-down warning glance.

Josh returned an amused, knowing grin. Sometimes Zane hated that his brother could read him so well.

When he opened the door, the frigid December air that blew in stole his breath. Or, more likely, the vision of Erin in a cream-colored sweater that clung to her feminine curves and navy slacks with her dark brown hair curling around her wind-chapped cheeks did the job. Nothing about her clothes was revealing or scandalous, but she managed to look sexy as hell regardless.

She gave his freshly pressed jeans and pale blue button-down shirt an assessing gaze, too. "Well, well.

You do clean up nicely, cowboy. No one would know you were wearing an inch of mud half an hour ago."

"Likewise, ma'am." He ushered her to the living room via the back hall, bypassing the kitchen where the rest of the family was pulling together the meal. He couldn't say why, but he wasn't ready to share her with the others just yet.

When they entered the living room, he lifted Kate's black-and-white cat, Sadie, off his father's recliner. "Scoot cat. You don't get the best seat in the house."

"Oh, don't bother the sweet thing! I can sit over here." She motioned to the couch but stepped closer to Zane and the cat. "Hello, kitty. We meet again." When Erin reached out to pat the feline, Sadie gave her a wide-eyed look, jumped from Zane's arms and scampered away. "Was it something I said?" she said, chuckling.

"Sadie is skittish and still getting used to all the people in and out of the main house. Kate only moved in here with her a couple months ago."

"So I shouldn't take it personally?" Her cheek dimpled as she grinned, and he felt a funny catch in his chest.

"No." He stood in front of the recliner, waiting for Erin to sit first. But her attention had been caught by something across the room, and she headed toward the far wall.

"Oh, wow." She stopped in front of an old aerial map of the ranch that his grandfather had framed and hung in that spot nearly sixty years earlier. "That's the Double M?" She pointed to the superimposed white line that demarcated the property lines and denoted the different pastures and hay fields.

"That's the Double M circa 1960 or so. Our property lines have changed somewhat over the years."

He crossed the room to stand next to her. Growing up, the old map had filled him with wonder and pride, knowing how the Double M had grown under the guiding force that was his grandfather. The ranch had expanded further when his dad had taken over. Only in recent years had the future of the ranch come into question. Now, as he stared at the familiar old map, his chest tightened. Would his generation be the last to call the Double M home? He'd give anything to preserve the family's heritage, but recently he'd felt as if the deck was stacked against him. No matter how hard he and his father tried to streamline finances, find new income streams and reduce debt, the ranch seemed to be slipping through their fingers.

"So what's changed?" Erin asked, and he had to mentally backpedal to put her question in context.

"On the map?"

She nodded.

He rubbed his hands on the seat of his jeans, drying the clamminess that had accompanied his latest worry spell. Pointing to the top of the map, he said, "Well, we lost a bit of land here when the state put in the new highway. Granddad got a nice check out of it that he used to upgrade equipment, though, so that was no biggie." He tapped the bottom right corner. "This area down here is ours now. We bought it from another rancher when he went bankrupt about ten or fifteen years ago. And this area here—" he pointed to the left side of the map "—was bought when the owner died and Mr. Miller's kids decided they wanted out of the ranching biz."

She nodded and pointed to a spot in the middle of one of the pastures. "What's that black spot?"

"Lightning started a prairie fire a few weeks before this aerial shot was taken. That's the burned area."

"And this?" She pointed to another spot. "Is that water?"

"A pond. Yeah."

She glanced at him. "The one that got poisoned last year?"

He frowned. "How do you know about that?"

She hesitated. "I… Your father told me."

He did? His pulse jumped in surprise. He hadn't realized she'd had much chance to talk to his father yet, although his dad had driven her back to the ranch this afternoon. So maybe…

He folded his arms over his chest and turned back to the map with a scowl. "Yeah. That's the one."

"So where did the herd drink after that?"

He tapped the map. "We moved them to this pasture. This pond is smaller, but it sufficed. It'll be years before we can safely use that pond again."

"How did you—?"

"Dinner's ready!" Josh bellowed from the kitchen, cutting her off.

Rather than get any deeper into the discussion of the trouble the vandal had caused, Zane quickly ushered Erin into the adjoining dining room, steering her with a light touch at the small of her back. Zane pulled out the chair at the end of the table where his mother usually sat, and Erin slid into the seat. He took his place, immediately to her right, just as his dad, Kate and Josh arrived from the kitchen with platters of pancakes and bacon.

"As I said, the ladies who usually do the food prep around here are at the hospital with Dave, so we went with one of the only things we know how to prepare.

Breakfast," his dad said, setting the plate heaped with bacon on the table.

She smiled gamely and put her napkin in her lap. "Breakfast for dinner was a favorite at my house growing up. And who can argue with bacon anytime of day?"

"Erin, have you met my fiancée, Kate?" Josh asked.

The willowy blonde who'd stolen Josh's heart smiled warmly and offered her hand to Erin. "Nice to meet you. So you're a writer?"

Zane thought he detected a slight hesitation before Erin nodded and said, "That's right. Congratulations on your engagement. I hear the wedding is in just a few weeks."

Josh helped Kate with her chair and gave Erin a goofy, slap-happy grin. "Seventeen days."

His brother and Kate exchanged a sappy look. Zane was happy for his twin, but at times he felt a twinge of something he hated to think was jealousy. Marriage and family was something he'd always thought he'd have before Josh did. Not that it was a competition. Even though so many other things in their history had seemed a battle for them. Who had lost their tooth first? Who had gotten better grades? Who had made the football team? Who had dated the prettiest girls? Who had stayed on the bronco longer?

Or maybe that had been all his own perception, his own need to succeed. Often Josh didn't seem to care about anything other than having fun and doing his own thing.

Once Josh and his father had seated themselves and the food had been blessed, Zane passed the bacon to Erin before helping himself.

"Aren't Piper and Brady going to join us?" she asked.

"No," his dad said. "They live in the foreman's house across the way with Roy and their son, Connor. They fix their own meals, except for special occasions."

She nodded. "Ah, got it. So Connor is Piper and Brady's son, and Roy is Brady's father..." She wagged a finger in the air as she mentally processed the information, squaring the relationships in her head.

Zane handed his brother the plate of bacon and asked, "So you got your first taste of ranch life today. What did you think?"

Her eyes widened, along with her grin. "Amazing. Exciting. *Muddy.*"

The men chuckled, and his father said, "Oh, yeah. It's dirty work for sure."

Erin took a bite of her bacon, and her eyes closed as a satisfied moan rolled from her throat. "Ooh, that's good."

Her hum of pleasure stopped Zane in the middle of forking two pancakes onto his plate. The sultry noise reverberated through him, and a sweet heat like maple syrup puddled low in his belly.

"How long did it take to train the dogs to help herd the cows like that?" Erin divided her gaze between Zane and his father.

"They were already trained when we got them," Zane said. "Training dogs takes time, and there's enough work to do around here without adding that job."

"Oh, right. I can imagine." She took a bite of pancake, then once she'd swallowed, added, "They were amazing to watch. It's incredible how they responded to your whistles and commands and knew just what to do."

"They definitely earn their keep," his dad said with a laugh.

Zeke chose that moment to jump onto the table and sauntered across to sniff the plate of bacon.

Erin gave a startled laugh, and Josh shot out of his chair to grab the feline before he could steal any meat. As Josh lifted Zeke from the table, the cat's long fluffy tail swished and knocked over the red taper that his mother had stuck in the middle of an evergreen-and-holly Christmas centerpiece.

Zane groaned as he righted the candle. "Clearly not all of our animals are as well trained."

"My apologies," his father said, "My wife spoils that cat. Gives him free rein."

"No problem," Erin replied, her amusement glowing from her eyes as well as her grin.

Damn, she was beautiful. Even without makeup as she was now, her skin was flawless. Her fringe of dark lashes framed her bright evergreen eyes, and her smile shone brighter than the spotlight that drew customers to the Christmas tree lot at the edge of town. Having had her mahogany curls teasing his cheeks as they rode out into the pasture today, he knew firsthand her hair was every bit as soft as it looked. His mind's eye conjured an image of himself threading his fingers through her unruly mane while their bodies tangled and she moaned with the same sexy pleasure she'd expressed for the bacon. When she cast a glance his direction, he realized he was staring, and he jerked his attention to his plate.

Damn! He didn't need a distraction like her around when the family was struggling to stay afloat and an unknown vandal was attacking them. He wouldn't be surprised to learn that the downed fence today was the handiwork of their saboteur.

"So what happened to the fence? How did it get torn

up, so that the herd got out? Do you think it was the same person who has been wreaking all the other havoc around here?" Erin asked, as if she'd read his mind.

He glanced toward his father, knowing the topic of the vandalism could stir him up and raise his already high blood pressure. Josh, too, sent a concerned glance to the end of the table where Michael sat.

His dad drew a slow, measured breath and set his fork on his plate before raising his eyes to meet Erin's. "While it certainly could have been further sabotage, the fact is that fences are in constant need of repair. The weather, the wildlife and the herd can all do their share to damage the fences. We ride the fence line daily as part of our maintenance schedule."

"And what do you think was responsible for the section out today?" she pressed.

"Who's to say?" Josh wiped his mouth, then took a sip of his water. "Could be a combination of things. I didn't see evidence of tampering. Although, Roy was the one working the fence. Guess we should ask him what he saw."

"Tell me more about the other incidents of sabotage," Erin said, crunching another strip of bacon. "Who discovered the damage? What evidence did the culprit leave behind?"

Zane tensed and sent his father another covert glance. "Maybe that's a conversation for another time. Not a topic that's good for digestion."

His father shook his head. "No, don't put her off, Zane. She needs the full picture to do her job."

Zane turned toward Erin, and his gaze clashed with hers. "But her job is to write about the adventure business and highlight the positive, tell people an inspirational story of siblings with a passion for the outdoors."

"That doesn't mean she can't ask about the trouble we've had lately." Josh stabbed a bite of pancake, and syrup dripped from his fork as he added, "I mean, that's one of the main reasons we decided to start McCall Adventures—the extra income to get the ranch out of the red."

Zane tensed and sent his brother a stern look. "Things not to discuss in mixed company—politics, religion... and personal finances."

Josh snorted. "Well, shoot! That's all the fun stuff!"

Kate sent her fiancé a lopsided smile and poked him with her elbow. Turning a polite smile to Erin, she said, "Why don't you tell us about yourself, Erin? Where is home for you?"

Zane gave Kate a nod of thanks for rescuing the conversation. He couldn't say why talking about the family's recent troubles bothered him so deeply. Erin might need certain insights about the family to promote the best aspects of the adventure tours, but he still had an unexplained wariness about her. Her questioning of the sheriff deputy's handling of Dave's accident might have been on point, but it had felt like an intrusion to Zane. Or maybe an indictment of how he'd been overseeing the incident for the family.

"I live in Boulder at the moment," Erin said. "I love the area, but I'm not married to it. If I got the chance to move to the west coast, say Portland or Seattle, I think that would be cool."

"And wet..." Zane and Josh said at the same time.

Erin divided a look between them, grinning. "Did I just witness a woo-woo kind of twin thing?"

"Yes," Kate said.

"It's not woo-woo," Zane countered.

"It's kinda woo-woo," their dad said with a lopsided grin. "They've done stuff like that their whole life. Sympathy pains, reading reach other's minds, saying the same thing at the same time…"

Erin shifted an intrigued gaze toward Zane. "Now this is interesting. Tell me more!"

He shrugged. "Typical twin stuff. No big deal."

Josh aimed his fork at his brother. "Now see, I *knew* he was going to say that!"

Zane gave Josh a wry look. "Yeah? What am I thinking now?"

Josh pressed his fingers to his temples, pretending to be tuning in to Zane's thoughts, then gave a mock-offended gasp. "Zane, such language! There are ladies present!"

Erin and Kate chuckled, and Michael rolled his eyes. Zane lifted a corner of his mouth in amusement as he shook his head at his brother. "Doofus."

"Dork," Josh returned.

"Now seriously," Erin said, putting her hand on Zane's wrist, "I want to hear the twin and triplet tales. I find the link between twins fascinating. As your triplet, does Piper share any of the woo-woo stuff with you or is it just you two?"

Warmth curled in Zane's belly, and he dropped a surreptitious glance to Erin's hand on his. Could she feel the none-too-subtle drubbing of his pulse?

"We have the usual sibling bond with her," Josh said, "but it's not quite the same as the connection Zane and I have being identical twins. Some of that is because we're brothers. I understand him better than Piper. Women are...weird."

Kate chuckled. "Excuse me?"

Josh leaned over and kissed Kate's cheek. "Your weirdness is part of the reason I love you."

His fiancée shook her head. "Nope. Still feel insulted." She glanced to Erin. "You?"

Erin grinned. "Well, I rather like being a little weird. Keeps life interesting."

Josh raised his glass to her. "Exactly."

Zane snorted. "In that case, Josh is very interesting."

Erin set her fork down and leaned back in her chair, waving a finger to the family in general. "I love this. The family banter and teasing. I'm learning a lot that will help me with my research, give it depth and a framework."

She gave his father a long look, and Zane's father returned a subtle nod. A funny niggle told Zane the silent exchange between them was significant, but he couldn't guess why. Through the years, he'd sent his sibling enough covert glances and silent messages around the dinner table to know when something was up. That he couldn't decipher the message passed between his father and Erin unsettled him.

For the rest of the meal, conversation turned to the progress in preparing for Kate and Josh's Christmas wedding. Dress alterations, flower selection, the music for the reception. Not having much to add to that discussion, Zane was better able to sit back and observe Erin. Her eyes grew animated as she shared ideas with Kate, showing the same enthusiasm Piper and her mother had for such details. Meanwhile Josh, who wouldn't know an amaryllis if it hit him in the head, had only occasional contributions to the discussion of poinsettias and evergreen sprigs, sweetheart necklines and keyhole backs. Zane studied his twin across the table with a mix of amusement, joy…and uneasiness.

Zane thumped his thumb on the arm of his chair as he followed the conversation and tried to analyze why Josh's wedding bothered him. He liked Kate a lot. She really was a great fit for his brother and a welcome addition to the family. She wasn't the issue.

He loved the idea of a holiday wedding, so it wasn't the timing of the nuptials. And Piper's wedding hadn't phased him in the slightest. Piper's marriage to Brady seemed like fate finally working itself out.

"Will you live here at the ranch once you're married?" Erin asked.

And Zane's gut clenched. Josh had been like his right hand, his other half, his best friend for twenty-eight years. With Josh's marriage, he felt a bit like he was losing his brother, their special connection, a piece of his history.

"Eventually we'll get a house in town," Josh answered. "Or maybe we'll build a house somewhere on the property?" His twin divided a look between their father and his intended.

Michael nodded. "Sure. That could be arranged."

Troubled by the negative track of his thoughts, Zane turned to Erin, offering a new topic of discussion. "I understand Connor is playing one of the wise men in his school's Christmas play on Friday evening. If you're interested in getting a feel for the town and meeting more people from Boyd Valley, you'd be welcome to join the family for the school's production."

Erin shifted her bright smile and Christmas-green

eyes to him, and, just like that, his mood lifted. "I'd love to! That sounds like fun."

"Fun?" Josh pulled a face. "Kids singing out of tune and stumbling through awkward lines sounds tedious to me."

Kate elbowed him. "Josh! It'll be great."

Josh arched an eyebrow and snorted. "See? Women are weird."

"I didn't mean to put you on the spot about the school play on Friday," Zane said as he walked Erin back to the guesthouse after dinner. "You don't have to go if you don't want to. Truly."

"No! I want to go!" She grabbed the sleeve of his coat and met his querying side glance. She knew she was shamelessly flirting with him, but having indulged in a glass—well, two—of wine with the family after the dinner dishes were washed and put away, she was at the mercy of her host's good looks, his low-key charm and the mellow warmth the wine created in her. She could pull back and regroup with a more professional distance in the morning. Right?

"All right, then." He gave her a small, crooked grin, one that hinted at what his chiseled face would look like if he were to smile as brightly as Josh had throughout dinner. She made it her goal to bring that kind of relaxed and glowing smile to Zane's face before she left. She had the distinct feeling he hadn't smiled nearly enough in recent months.

Erin inhaled the crisp winter air redolent with the scents of hay, mud and animals. Ranch smells. When she'd arrived, the earthy scents had offended her urban sensibilities. But now, only one eventful day into her stay, and she was already growing accustomed to the feculent odors.

"Thank you for dinner and the warm welcome your family has given me." She stopped on the stoop of the guesthouse and faced him. "I have to say…even though I'm here to work, I'm really looking forward to the next few days. A beautiful setting, nice people…" *A possible vandal lurking among them that she'd been hired to root out.* When the reason for her presence at the ranch flashed in her mind, she furrowed her brow and sighed.

Zane mirrored her frown. "What?"

"I—" She cast about for a reasonable explanation for her mood shift. "I was just thinking about Dave. Have you heard from your mom or Helen recently?"

He nodded. "He's been moved to a room for observation. Mom was going to get some dinner for Helen then head home. She should be here in a little while."

She nodded and turned to open the guesthouse door. "Well, thanks again for…" She hesitated when she met a deeper frown denting his brow. "Zane?"

"It may seem overkill, seeing as we're kinda isolated out here, but…I'd feel better if you'd keep your door locked while you're here."

She blinked. "Oh, I, uh…"

"We don't know who is sabotaging the ranch or why," he rushed to explain. "What they might do next, but… why make it easier for them? Better safe than sorry."

She dipped her head briefly in agreement. "All right."

His warning stirred a mixture of cold apprehension over hidden dangers on the ranch and a warm swirl of gratitude for his protectiveness.

"Good night," he said, touching the brim of his hat. Zane walked backward a few steps, his gaze clinging to hers before he turned to head back toward the family home. She watched him go, studying the wide set of his shoulders, the brisk, almost military, long-legged stride. He had a commanding presence, a surety about him evident even in his confident walk. He knew how to own a room...or a ranch yard.

Despite her own counsel against biasing attachments, she hadn't been immune to his charisma, his unspoken power. His bright, piercing gaze that she felt like static in her bones. He was pure alpha wolf, and her instincts about him told her there was plenty left to discover beneath his serene, solemn and imposing exterior.

And she saw the way the others on the ranch tended to defer to him.

Well, maybe not his siblings. She smiled remembering the lighthearted teasing from Piper and Josh. The rapport of the triplets, his ready thoughtfulness and concern for others spoke volumes to her about what she'd find when she finally got a chance to peek behind the curtain of Zane's brooding and wariness.

As she closed the door behind her and scanned the empty guesthouse, she remembered the deception she'd agreed to and sent up a silent prayer that her attempt to help the family didn't come back to bite her.

Chapter 6

Erin conscripted Zane to take her into town a couple days later. Though Michael would have been the logical choice to take her, being her client, he'd already headed out to the pasture with Roy and Brady by the time she'd gotten herself out of bed, caffeinated and moving. She was undeniably happy about having Zane as her chauffeur, though—which was trouble. She'd only been at the ranch two days, and she was already breaking her own rules about biasing preconceptions about the people she was investigating. And while she thought it was a long shot that Zane was the culprit behind the sabotage to the ranch, giving that leaning too much credence could blind her to the truth.

Having spent yesterday meeting everyone on the ranch at least in passing and observing as they completed their daily routine, today she wanted to get a feel for the community. She thought she could poke a few rocks regarding the McCalls' sabotage and see what crawled out.

As she'd driven to the Double M earlier in the week, Erin's focus had been on the road and her phone's GPS application, making sure she didn't miss a turn. With Zane behind the wheel of his pickup truck, she could savor the landscape of snow-dusted hills and evergreens.

"It's beautiful here. What a joy to be surrounded by the mountains on one side and rolling farmland on the other. The best of both worlds."

"I've never lived anywhere else and can't see any reason to leave." He shifted his gaze to the landscape out the driver's window as if seeing it with fresh eyes. "This place is a part of my soul. I know it sounds trite, but it's true. When you've grown up working on the land, depending on the land, nurturing the natural resources, it becomes more than just the place you live."

The passion in his voice was subtle but spoke for the heartfelt emotion behind his statement. A warmth stirred deep in her chest. His love for his home reinforced her gut-level instinct that Zane couldn't be responsible for the vandalism. The vandal had burned crops and poisoned a pond, both crimes against the very land that sustained his family. The land that he held so close to his heart. If she *were* a writer, that sentiment from Zane would be part of her article.

And you want him to believe you are a writer so...

She dug a notepad from her purse and clicked open her pen. "I love the way you put that. Can I quote you for the article?"

He jerked a startled glance her way, and a smile flickered at the edges of his mouth. "I, uh, sure."

When she raised her head from scribbling her notes,

his whole demeanor had changed. He seemed pleased with the direction of the conversation, proud to be introducing her to the industry, the landscape, the way of life he loved.

"We aren't far from the turn-off to go to my grandfather's land if you want to see it." He cut a quick querying glance to her.

"And the significance of your grandfather's land? Is it part of your ranch?"

"No. It's not suited to ranching. Too rugged. It's where we will run the adventure part of the adventure tours when we're up and running. I figure it's important for you to see it for your article. You'll want to take pictures. It's really scenic."

"Well, sure. Let's go."

Zane flipped his turn signal and pulled onto a side road while she took the opportunity to study his profile. Now *that* was a scenic view. The contrast of his black hair and eyebrows to his bright blue eyes gave her chills. The good kind. And his full lips, square jaw and straight nose were Hollywood-worthy. But other little details she'd never noticed about a man before caught her attention when it came to Zane. The veins in the back of his large, callused hands struck her as ruggedly sexy. The clean, neatly trimmed fingernails, despite the dirty work he did in the pens and pastures impressed her, and the peek of his collarbone in the open *V* of his work shirt tantalized her. His collarbone, for crying out loud! She was getting palpitations over the man's clavicle!

She shook herself from her distracting thoughts and noticed the serious furrow on Zane's brow. "Why the grim look, cowboy?"

"Just thinking about what we were discussing earlier."

He tapped the steering wheel with his thumb. "Ranching is a hard life," he said. "No doubt about it. But in our family, it's a tradition that has been passed on for generations."

She clicked her pen again and continued taking notes. She had to bite her tongue not to ask questions, but she didn't want to put words in his mouth or to taint his commentary. For a change, he was talking, more relaxed, more open. Her best move was to stay quiet, other than an occasional "Mmm-hmm" to tell him she was listening, and let him have his say.

"So there's a certain unspoken pressure to make the ranch a success beyond simple economics. I don't want to be the generation that failed our forefathers, let all their blood, sweat and tears come to nothing."

Erin frowned at the notion that Zane was laboring under such a burdensome concept. His admission bolstered her impression that he took on more than his share of responsibility and leadership. No wonder he seemed so serious and unhappy much of the time. The man was trying to carry the whole ranch and his family legacy on his shoulders.

"It's sobering to see neighboring ranches fail. Other families with the same history behind them, the same love of the land and sweat equity on their side, have had to sell land and shutter their doors. We are just one bad season away from being the Carvers or the Andersons."

Erin jotted the names Carver and Anderson on her pad. She wanted to ask Michael about those families and the circumstances surrounding the failure of those ranches. Could the saboteur be working his way from ranch to ranch, causing all of the local families to go out of business?

"That's so sad. What are they—?" She snapped her mouth closed. No questions. Let him talk…

He cut a side glance to her before turning back to the highway and tightening his grip on the steering wheel. "What happened to the Carvers and Andersons?" he guessed correctly.

"Yeah. Are they still in the area?"

He nodded. "Yeah. Hugh Carver works for another ranch now as a hand, and his son went into banking. He's our loan officer." He made a face saturated with disgust.

"Why the funny face?"

He grunted. "Gill is…" He twisted his mouth and wagged a few fingers, apparently searching for the right word. "Well, he's an ass. No sugarcoating it. Always has been. He's been trouble for my siblings and me since high school. Junior high even. But he happens to work for the bank with the best loan terms, and even a small difference in interest rates makes a big difference long-term for our finances."

She hummed her understanding and jotted *Gill Carver—banker and historic ass* in her notes.

"The Andersons took jobs in various places. Mrs. Anderson is one of the librarians in the next town down the highway. Mr. Anderson works at the Feed and Seed. Their daughter married and moved out of town, and Henry became something of a miscreant. Drugs, petty theft, trespassing…"

She sat taller in her seat, and he shook his head without looking at her. "I know what you're thinking, and no. He's been serving time for car theft and drug possession for the last five years."

"He hasn't been paroled? You've checked?"

"We mentioned him to the sheriff, and they confirmed with the state that he's still behind bars."

"Oh." She sagged again in her seat, scowling. "That would have been too easy, huh?"

He barked a humorless laugh. "Yeah." Then frowning at her he added, "And again, not your concern."

"Hey, I like your family and hate seeing what's happening to you all. So sue me if I take a personal interest in who is behind the vandalism." When he met her gaze, she gave him a raised-eyebrow, challenging stare.

Zane huffed and turned back to the road, muttering, "Stubborn."

She chuckled. "Yes, I am."

He gave her an exasperated half smile, and once again, she longed to see a full smile on him. His twin was understandably floating on air these days, and his face, so like Zane's, positively glowed when he grinned. How breathtaking would Zane be if he allowed a real, soul-deep, joy-borne smile to grace his lips? She ached inside knowing Zane had so little to smile about. Had he become so mired in his family's troubles that he couldn't enjoy the simple things? Couldn't share his brother's happiness? Couldn't cut loose for a few minutes and just enjoy a belly laugh over something silly? Even when she'd been witness to his teasing with his siblings, he'd only managed a weak facsimile of a grin.

She glanced out the window at the beauty of the rugged terrain. "So tell me about this property we're going to."

His face brightened a bit, clearly warming to the subject. "It's been in my mother's family for generations, going all the way back to the 1850's gold rush. My great-great-great-grandfather came to Colorado during the first wave of the gold rush and staked a sizable claim. As other miners around him gave up the search, he bought them out. In the years that followed, he and his sons refused to sell their land, and so this huge piece of unblemished wilderness is still in the family. Because of the early deaths of her great-uncles and my mother being an only child, the land was eventually deeded in entirety to her."

Erin blinked. "How many acres do you own?"

He told her, and she goggled at him. "Holy moly, Zane! You realize, don't you, that if you sold that land to a developer, your financial worries would be over, right? You and your whole family could retire in style."

He sent her a hooded glance. "First, what you're suggesting is blasphemy. If Otis Ferguson and his sons could hold the land when the railroad came calling, the McCalls are not going to sell to developers."

"But—"

"Second," he said and frowned. "I already considered that option, to my mother's dismay, and learned that her father anticipated growing pressure to sell the land and did some fancy legal and real estate maneuvering to make selling virtually impossible."

"How so?"

"He made Swiss cheese of the property, deeding very small pockets of the land to environmental charities and trusts in his will, with strict stipulations attached. We can't sell the land without permission from the various charities and private investors, and he made it worth their while to hold on to their small bits of property instead of selling. He knew the environmental causes would not want the land turned into subdivisions and shopping malls."

"A wily old coot, your grandfather. Eh?"

Zane slanted a half grin at her. "Wily, yes. But we really don't want to sell the land. It's so beautiful, and if we can get the adventure tours running—"

"*When* you get the adventure tours running," she corrected. "You *will* do it. I have all the faith in the world you will."

Another half grin. "*When*, then. The adventure tours will mean the land is helping us turn a profit. So for now, we hold on to the property and another link to our family history."

They drove for several more minutes, taking narrow, winding roads up steep hills until they reached a plateau where he parked. She shouldered open the truck door and as she struggled down from the high seat, he rounded the front, headed toward her.

"I was coming to help," he said, seeming disappointed he hadn't been allowed to give her a hand down.

"Oh, thanks. Just…used to managing alone." She flashed a grin and tucked her scarf into her coat against the chill.

"So…no boyfriend then?" he asked, trying to act casual and failing miserably.

She laughed. "No boyfriend. Not in a while."

He nodded, again clearly trying to be blasé but a satisfied grin twitched at the corner of his mouth.

"And you? Dating anyone?" she asked as he showed her to the edge of a cliff where a beautiful river flowed through ice-sheeted stones.

"Nah." He hunched his shoulders against the stiff, cold breeze and jammed his hat down more securely on his head. "When would I have the time to date? The ranch keeps me busy sunup to sundown."

"Hmm." She ruminated on that as she gazed out across the river ravine at the lovely winter landscape. "My philosophy is we make time for the things that are important to us."

He cut a side glance to her and arched an eyebrow. "By that standard, I could assume that means dating isn't important to you."

"I date!" she protested and pivoted toward him, giving him props for the way he'd turned her comment back on her. "Just...not so often anymore. I've gotten..." She twisted her mouth as she searched for the right word. "Picky. I don't want to date just anyone."

He inhaled deeply and faced the river, nodding slightly. "Good. You shouldn't settle."

"Is that your excuse? Not settling?"

He didn't even look at her. "I don't intend to settle, either, but following your axiom, I'd say it was because my priority is the ranch. My family and our way of life is the most important thing in the world to me."

"I believe that." And she also believed that when Zane McCall did find a woman to love, he'd cherish her the same way he valued and prioritized the ranch. Zane didn't do things by half measure. The woman that stole his heart would be lucky indeed.

She couldn't deny the frisson of jealousy that tickled her for that unknown someone in Zane's future. Shoving the jab of envy aside, she refocused on the gorge.

"Is this where you had the zip line?" she asked.

"No. This is the pickup spot." He leaned forward and motioned to the sheer rock down to the river in the ravine. "Folks will raft to the bank below us and scale the rock using a belay system. The anchors are set and ready to go."

She slipped her phone out of her coat pocket and took several pictures. Not only did photos add credence to her cover story, the landscape, with ice twinkling in the tree branches and the river tumbling through the rocks, was magnificent.

"Next stop is the landing area for the zip line, though, and the first night's camp spot. Ready to go?"

She swept one last encompassing gaze over the scenic view and bobbed her chin. "Ready."

The campsite and zip line terminus were equally impressive. Erin forced herself to set aside her goggling at the forested valley over which the zip line stretched to focus on the landing deck and new equipment. "So what happened this spring? How did the zip line fall?" She walked around the wide steel pole and studied the extensive bolts and clamps securing the thick cable. "This setup looks like it's ready to withstand a hurricane."

"That's the idea. Our last setup was good, but not good enough to deter our saboteur. We're not taking any chances this time."

"What did the saboteur do? Cut the line?" She kept her attention focused on the cable attachment above them, hoping he'd not brush off the question as he did so often when the sabotage was brought up.

"He cut the tree the line was anchored to. Weakened the wood just below the cable so that the tree toppled when the stress of weight was added to the zip line. The first passengers over that made that happen were Josh and Kate."

She did look at him then, hearing the tension in his tone. She rubbed his arm, and even through his thick coat, she felt the firm muscles and the quiver of stress as he recalled the tragic event. "But they survived, and look at them now. About to be wed. It all worked out fine."

He gave her a withering glance. "You know how to put polish on a cow pie, don't you?"

She snorted a laugh. "Wow. Is that a compliment or…?" She turned up her gloved hands in query. "Not sure what to make of that."

He chuckled softly. "It was intended as such. I have a hard time being optimistic at times. Thank you for re-minding me to count my blessings."

Her stomach growled, none-to-subtly in the stillness of the winter woods. She clapped a hand to her belly and laughed. "Excuse me!"

"Hey, I can take a hint. Let's head to town for some lunch." He put a hand at the small of her back, escort-ing her through the trees and underbrush to the dirt road where they'd left his truck.

Once back on the highway to Boyd Valley, Zane asked, "After lunch, do you have someplace specific you want me to take you or am I dropping you off in the middle of Main Street and letting you wander?"

"Well, I want to get a feel for the community, so I'll probably do a bit of wandering. But let's start at a hub. Where do people gather in Boyd Valley?"

"They don't. Not this time of day. Boyd Valley isn't like a college town or big metropolis where people sit around coffee shops and chat. Families are working, kids are in school, business is being conducted."

She didn't hear any condescension in his tone, just a statement of facts. "All right."

"Fact is, the diner where I thought we'd have lunch, called Zoe's, is as close to a hub as you'll find this time of day."

"Zoe's, huh?" She wrote the restaurant name in her notepad. "What about evenings? Does Zoe's get the dinner crowd or is there a bar in town where folks go after hours?"

"Well, sure." He rubbed his clean-cut chin and cast her a quick side glance. "I understand the hard-core drinkers head outside the city limits to a honky-tonk called Broncs. But I don't imagine they're open at this hour."

"Okay. We can save Broncs for one evening soon…if you're game to go honky-tonking with me?"

"You want to go to Broncs? Seriously?" He scoffed. "You don't strike me as the honky-tonk type."

"Is that a no? You won't take me?" He didn't strike her as the honky-tonk type, either. Josh, maybe. But Zane seemed too business-like and serious to ever cut loose at a bar or nightclub.

He faced her with a wrinkle in his brow. "I didn't say no, just that your request surprised me." He tapped the steering wheel with his thumb. "In fact, I'd be remiss if I let you go in that place alone. The clientele is not known for gentlemanly behavior. Especially once the booze starts flowing."

"Then it's a date?" she asked.

He blinked and faced her with a frown. "A date?"

She grunted. "Not a *date* date. But…I have your word you'll go with me, maybe tomorrow night?"

He turned up his palm and snorted wryly. "Sure. Why not?"

She mock punched him in the shoulder. "Who knows? Maybe we'll even have fun."

He gave her another half grin. "Who knows?"

As they entered the town limits of Boyd Valley, she

shifted her attention to the small houses and businesses that lined the main drag. A tiny post office, a beauty parlor called Snips, a liquor store. Across the street, she spotted a bank, a small grocery store and Buckley's Feed and Seed. All the lampposts that lined the sidewalk had been decked with lighted holiday decorations of some sort. Bells, elves, snowflakes, reindeer and candles were the most prominent. Storefront windows had been sprayed with faux snow or filled with displays featuring fuzzy red stockings, cheery Santas and announcements of holiday discounts.

She gave the Feed and Seed closer scrutiny as they passed. "Is that the store where Mr. Anderson works now?"

"Yep. Wanna stop?"

She checked her watch. "Depends. What time do people eat lunch around here? I don't want to miss the crowd at Zoe's."

"*Crowd* might be a bit of an overstatement, but if you want to catch people at lunch, we best go there first. This town rises early, eats early, goes to bed early."

"Rancher's hours?"

"That's right."

"Can I buy you lunch while we're there?"

He shook his head. "No need. You're our guest. I should pay."

"And you are doing me a favor. So I insist on buying."

He shook his head again and repeated, "Stubborn."

He parked in front of the small diner, and before she could unbuckle her seat belt and gather her purse, he'd circled the front fender and was opening her door for her.

"Thank you, sir," she said, feeling a tingle when he gripped her hand to help her down from the high truck seat. She followed him inside the restaurant where what seemed like miles of silver and gold garland had been hung on the walls and draped along the polished wood bar. The stale scent of fried food hung in the air, mingling with the savory aroma of today's lunch offerings. A Christmas tree loaded with twinkling lights occupied one corner, and a mechanical, life-size Santa with his stuffed sack over his shoulder guarded the door, greeting everyone who passed with a somewhat creepy-sounding, "Ho, ho, ho!"

Zane gave creepy Santa the stink-eye as he walked by it, then motioned for Erin to come with him up to the bar. He introduced her to the woman behind the cash register at the end of the polished wood bar, who turned out to be the owner, Zoe Taylor. Erin estimated her age in the late fifties or early sixties based on the threads of gray in the long, thick braid of her dark hair and the tiny laugh lines bracketing her mouth and brown eyes.

"Nice to meet you, Erin. Will you two be eating with us today?"

Erin had only finished her breakfast a couple of hours earlier, but she nodded. "We'd love to."

Zoe wiped two plastic-encased menus and handed them to Erin and Zane. "What brings you to this corner of the world?"

"Research." Erin took the menu and glanced at the list of entrées. She avoided eye contact with Zoe as she told her practiced fib. "I'm staying with the McCalls while I work on an article."

"You're a reporter?"

"Well, more like a features writer," Erin said.

"She writes for a travel journal. *Well Traveled* magazine," Zane offered.

Zoe laughed. "Uh, are you sure about that, Zane? Maybe you should check her credentials."

Erin's pulse thumped. Had she done something that gave her away? Could the restaurant owner see through her lie? She cleared her throat. "I'm sorry?"

Zoe waved a hand at her. "Just teasing, hon. There was another *supposed* writer and photojournalist in here about a year ago. Turned out he was no reporter but was actually stalking Zane's sister, Piper." She faced Zane. "You remember?"

Zane's countenance could have been carved in granite. "Kinda hard to forget. That cretin wasn't a joke to our family."

Zoe schooled her face. "Sorry, hon. Didn't mean to make light of it. I just…"

When the older woman's voice trailed off awkwardly, Erin prodded Zane. "Piper was stalked by some creep?"

"Yes." His terse answer signaled his unwillingness to discuss the matter further. "I'll have the club sandwich and vegetable soup."

Erin ordered a cup of the potato soup and followed Zane to a table near the front door. She wanted to talk further with Zoe, knowing the woman's business likely made her privy to much of the town gossip. Perhaps she could steal away from the ranch under some pretense or another and drive up here on her own later in the afternoon or tomorrow. One way or another, Erin needed to learn more about Piper's stalker and his whereabouts.

As she pulled her chair up to the table, she glanced around the mostly empty restaurant. "Do you know any of the other people here?"

Zane looked over his shoulder at the other diners. "I

grew up in this town. I know all of them. Who do you want to meet?"

"Who has the most interesting tales about your misspent youth?" She curled up a corner of her mouth and wiggled her eyebrows.

"What makes you think I misspent my youth?"

"Didn't you?"

His expression softened, and he shrugged one shoulder. "I hung out with Josh and Brady, so…yeah. I had my moments."

She gave a greedy-sounding chuckle and rubbed her hands together. "Now we're talking! Spill. Or point me toward the person who can reveal all."

Zane rolled his eyes and shifted on his chair to scan the other tables again. "Well, the man in the gray sweater was my high school math teacher. And the man he's talking to coached the baseball team I was on in elementary school."

"Excellent." Erin scooted her chair back. "Target sighted. Engage interview."

"You're going over? Now?"

"That *was* the purpose of my trip today." She left her purse on her chair but pulled out a pen and notepad.

"But—"

She approached the two older gentlemen with a smile, leaving Zane to follow her. Or not. His choice.

Zane sighed and shoved out of his seat to trail Erin to Mr. Finklebine and Mr. Garrison's table.

"Good morning, sirs." She flashed her brilliant grin, and the men looked up, clearly intrigued by the stranger in their midst. And why not? She was beautiful, and her smile captivated. What man wouldn't give her his attention?

She launched into her introduction, shaking each man's hand, and laid out her spiel concerning the article she was writing. "I'd love to get your perspective on the McCall family, the Double M, the ranch's history and contributions to the town…or any scandalous tales about Zane, here, that you want to share." She lightly jabbed his ribs with her elbow and winked at him.

The men laughed, obviously charmed by her.

"Not sure how much scandal you'll find about Zane," Mr. Finklebine said, waving his fork. "Zane was always one of my best students and a model citizen, as I recall. Piper was a good student, as well. Now Josh got up to some no good now and then, but all in all, the McCall kids are good folks. Raised right."

Zane nodded politely to his former math teacher. "Thank you, sir. That's kind of you."

Mr. Garrison snorted and wiped his mouth on his napkin. "It may be kind, but it's a lie."

Erin faced his Little League coach with an arched eyebrow. "A lie? How so?"

Zane narrowed a puzzled look on the stoop-shouldered man.

"He got into plenty of mischief, just like any boy. My own sons included. My boys told me about the beer and cigarettes that were filched outta various homes and passed around behind our garage. You were in that crowd," he said, aiming a finger at Zane. "Don't deny it."

Zane opened and shut his mouth like a trout out of water.

Erin gave him a mock shocked expression. "Scandalous!"

Raising both palms, he sighed. "Guilty."

"And you were one of the boys suspended for a few games after you put Bengay in Freddy Brown's catcher's mitt."

Erin curled her lips in over her teeth, apparently fighting laughter.

"I…was." The heat of embarrassment climbed his neck and tingled in his cheeks. Zane jabbed his fingers in his pockets. "But that's not helpful to Ms. Palmer for her article."

"Not so fast, Bucko. Everything is grist for the mill," Erin said with a sly grin dimpling her cheek. "You never know where you may find inspiration."

He grunted. "In that case, I'll bow out. My ego can't handle the ignominy." He nodded to the two older men and took a step toward his and Erin's table. "Gentlemen, be merciful."

Erin waited until Zane had stepped away before she pulled another chair up to the men's table to join them. Despite the tug of regret that he'd been put on the spot that way, she was pleased to have the opportunity to speak to the men without Zane listening. "What I'd really like to talk about is the McCall family and the Double M Ranch in general."

"Good people. The ranch has been a stalwart in this community for decades," said Mr. Finklebine, a gray-haired and potbellied man with wire-rimmed glasses and bushy silver eyebrows.

His leaner redheaded companion nodded. "Agreed."

Erin smiled at the men, deciding how to word her inquiries so they weren't leading. She kept her volume low so that Zane wouldn't overhear. "To the best of your knowledge, is that an opinion shared by the rest of the town?"

Mr. Garrison leaned back in his seat and rubbed his pointed chin, his lips pursed as he thought. "Can't recall hearing much of anything spoken against them."

Mr. Finklebine lifted his coffee mug. "Like I said. They're good people."

"If anything," Mr. Garrison added, "folks feel bad about the trouble they've had of late."

Erin's pulse picked up. Now they were getting somewhere. "Trouble?"

"Some fool idiot dumped poison in one of their ponds and killed a bunch of their cattle last summer," Mr. Garrison explained, his tone gruff.

"Nah, it was summer before last. Eighteen months ago," Mr. Finklebine corrected. "I remember because I heard about it while I was in the hospital for my knee surgery." He faced Erin. "That was just the beginning of their trouble." He narrowed his pale eyes at her. "I'm surprised Zane didn't tell you about all this."

"I know some of it. But to write my article, I need to hear all the versions of the story. What has been said around town. What the sheriff's report says…" A trip to visit the sheriff without Zane was in her plan for later today or tomorrow. "What the family says. I'm interested in your take on what's happened at the Double M recently."

"Damn shame," Mr. Finklebine said then slurped his coffee. "That's my take."

A bubble of frustration swelled in her. She needed more specific answers, but she hated to steer the conversation too much for fear of tainting their answers.

"Here's the thing," Mr. Garrison said, pushing his

plate away and folding his arms over his chest. "There's not a person I've talked to who can imagine a good reason for the Double M to have been targeted. Rumors have been circulated that it's an inside job. It's no secret that Roy Summers went to rehab a few months back. Some folks say he committed the vandalism while in a drunken stupor. But even drunk, Roy Summers is one of the most loyal men I know. He and his boy, Brady, are like family to the McCalls."

Mr. Finklebine snorted. "They *are* family now that Piper and Brady got hitched."

Mr. Garrison swept one hand toward his friend. "There you go. They are family."

"I heard the sheriff was looking into the possibility that Michael—that'd be Zane's father—" Mr. Finklebine added, looking over the top of his glasses as he leaned toward Erin "—might be behind it all for the insurance money."

Her chest tightened, knowing how badly Michael had taken those suspicions and the lengths he was going to in order to clear his name and save his business, his family. Erin worked to hide her feelings about that theory. She cleared her throat. "How do you feel about that possibility?"

Finklebine scoffed. "If Michael McCall's committing insurance fraud, I'll eat my hat."

"I don't believe it, either. Not for a second," Mr. Garrison echoed.

"So then...do you two have any theories?" she asked, noticing from the corner of her eye that Zoe had brought out her and Zane's food.

"Well..." Mr. Garrison knitted his brow, a deeply thoughtful expression molding his face. "I've wondered if some big corporate outfit could be trying to buy out the Double M and Michael won't sell."

"I hear the mafia is into every kind of business these days." Mr. Finklebine wagged his finger at her. "It could be some crooked big-money corporation or the mafia."

Erin kept a straight face. Barely. She'd seen crazy hypotheses borne out before, but the notion that the mafia had decided to drive the Double M out of business was a bit far-fetched to her. She tapped her lips with a finger and nodded.

Over Mr. Garrison's shoulder, she could see Zane trying to catch her attention with a small wave. "Gentlemen, my meal has arrived, but it was lovely speaking to you both." She slid them each one of her faux writer business cards with her cell number. "If you think of anything that might be useful to me concerning the McCalls or their ranch, please reach out to me. I'll be in the area for a few more days and would love to treat you to a cup of coffee in exchange for your ideas."

Both men pocketed the cards, and Mr. Garrison stood when she did. "Pleasure meeting you, ma'am. Good luck with your article."

"We've got trouble." He paced the floor, his gut in knots as he reported in to his blackmailer.

"What are you talking about?"

"There's a woman at the ranch. A reporter of some kind. She's asking lots of questions, nosing around."

He heard a terse expletive then a strained silence.

"What kind of questions is she asking? What news outlet is she from?"

"Some travel magazine, I think. Supposedly she's doing a thing about the adventure company, but her questions have included the incidents I set up. She's pokin' her nose in all aspects of the business and family history."

His blackmailer grunted. "Then you *do* have a problem. Your job is to see that nothing she learns comes back to me. Because if I go down, I'm taking you with me. And murder is a whole lot bigger deal than anything that can get pinned on me."

He plowed his fingers through hair damp with flop sweat. "It wasn't murder!" Then realizing how loud he'd become, he choked down his panic and grated through clenched teeth, "It was an accident."

"It was a death caused by your negligence. And you left the scene. Between the two charges, you'll do serious time, my friend."

His gut roiled. His blackmailer was no friend. A friend didn't put your nuts in a vise and force you to hurt people you valued and respected. Family.

Not for the first time, he considered going to the cops himself, confessing what he'd done, taking the lumps. Before this went any further. Before anyone got hurt. Before anyone *else* got hurt, rather.

But the thought of life inside a prison cell made him sick to his stomach. Claustrophobic. He needed the outdoors, the fresh air and wide-open spaces of ranch life. He'd die on the inside. Maybe that was what he deserved, but he wasn't ready to concede that fate. Yet. Maybe he could fix this. Maybe he could meet his blackmailer's demands and still find a way to fix the damage he'd caused.

Maybe. Maybe. Maybe. When had he become such a pushover?

He squeezed his eyes shut, self-loathing a living thing clawing his heart.

"What do I do?" he asked. He really didn't want to hear how his blackmailer expected him to handle the reporter. He'd been talking to himself, asking a rhetorical question.

But his blackmailer took the query at face value and said flatly, "Deal with her."

His pulse stuttered. "What do you mean?" he asked, stunned. But he had a horrible sense that he knew exactly what the demand implied.

He heard a sound outside—voices—and knew he had to get off the phone. Quick.

His blackmailer huffed impatiently. "Do I have to spell it out? We can't let some snooping bitch ruin everything now. Get rid of her, whatever it takes."

Chapter 7

"So did you learn anything interesting?" Zane shoved his napkin in his lap and arched one eyebrow as Erin stirred her soup.

"Well, your family has an excellent reputation in town." She paused to sip from her spoon. "And Mr. Finklebine has a theory that the sabotage at the Double M is the work of the mafia."

Zane choked on the soup he'd just swallowed. Grabbing his napkin, he covered his mouth as he half coughed, half laughed. "Pardon?"

She tugged her lips into a wry grin. "You heard me right." She leaned toward him, across the table, whispering, "The mafia."

"Wow. That's…" He screwed his face in a frown of amused disbelief.

"Mmm-hmm." She sipped her drink then added,

"You'll be happy to know I didn't get any more tales about tainted baseball gloves or beer behind the barn."

Zane took a bite of his sandwich and chewed slowly. Then crooking a finger for her to come close again, he leaned across the table. "What Mr. Garrison doesn't know is that I'm the one who convinced his sons *not* to put the Bengay in Freddy's jock strap. It coulda been worse."

Erin covered her mouth as she laughed, and Zane's heart lifted at the melodious sound. The mirth in her eyes rivaled the lights on Zoe's gaudy Christmas tree. He felt a lightness in his soul as he shared lunch with Erin that he hadn't known in a long time. Too long.

She blew on a spoonful of soup and sipped it. "Tell me about Piper's stalker. Where is he now?"

And just like that the light disappeared behind a cloud. Zane set his sandwich on the plate and chewed slowly, deciding how much and what to tell Erin. "He's in prison back in Massachusetts, where he'd committed a murder."

Erin's eyes widened. "Whoa. Murder? Did he hurt Piper? How was he caught?"

"Long story. He scared her, scared us all pretty good, but she wasn't harmed physically. He nearly killed Roy, Brady and Connor though."

"Seriously?" Erin blinked and leaned toward him. "What happened?"

Zoe arrived at their table to refill their drinks and bring their check, sparing him from going into the grisly details of that nightmarish chapter of his family's recent past. Or so he thought. As soon as Zoe stepped away from the table, Erin's questions continued.

"Is there any chance this stalker is responsible for the sabotage events at the ranch?"

Feeling the first pulses of a headache coming on, he squeezed the bridge of his nose with his thumb and index finger. "No. The police have looked into that."

She nodded. "And the police eliminated him because...?"

Zane groaned his frustration.

"I know. Stubborn. Right?" She grinned unrepentantly. "Humor me."

"All right! But then we change the subject, because none of this helps your research for your article." Zane poked at his sandwich but didn't pick it up. The reminder of how he'd nearly lost his sister and some of his closest friends just over a year ago had squelched his appetite. "He lived in Boston and worked with Piper. He has solid alibis for all of the incidents except the burning of our alfalfa field. He copped to everything he did in stalking Piper as part of a plea deal, but he vehemently denied any part of burning the field. In fact, he may have seen the saboteur, and he gave a vague description of someone he saw in that field while he was spying on Piper and the ranch."

Erin perked up. "He *saw* the vandal?"

"Allegedly. But his description was so general as to be useless. A man in blue jeans and a cowboy hat. That describes half the population of Boyd Valley." Zane rubbed his sternum, behind which his acid reflux had returned. He'd kept mum about the irritating health issues he'd started having lately. The family had enough to worry about without telling them he'd started having bad heartburn, headaches and sleeplessness. He was pretty sure they were simply a result of his constant aggravation over the ranch finances and concern for his father's high blood pressure. "Can we go back to discussing my misspent youth now?"

"Hmm, good point," she said, arching an eyebrow and tapping a fingernail on her glass of diet cola. "Have you considered that Freddy Brown could be your vandal, seeking retribution for the Bengay incident?"

"Seriously?"

She flipped up a palm. "It makes as much sense as anything else. And more sense than the mafia."

Zane stirred his soup idly, thinking about her suggestion. "It's not Freddy. His family moved away when we were all in sixth grade."

The tinkling of the bells over the front door signaled a new arrival to the restaurant, and when he saw who entered, his heartburn blazed hotter.

Gill Carver. His loan officer. Aka local pain-in-the-ass, burr-under-his-saddle and all-around source of ill-will. He couldn't help the moan of displeasure that rumbled in his throat.

Erin frowned. "What?"

"Don't look, but trouble just walked in."

She started to turn, despite his warning, and he grabbed her hand and squeezed. "Don't…"

But Gill had spotted him and moseyed up to their table, his gaze falling to Zane's grip on Erin's wrist. "Ma'am, is this fella bothering you?"

She raised her eyes to Gill. "Excuse me?"

Gill turned to Zane. "You have to hog-tie or man-handle your dates to get them to stay through the whole meal these days, Zane?"

Instead of releasing Erin's arm, he turned his hand

so he could lace his fingers with hers and gently stroke the underside of her wrist with his thumb. "What's the matter, Gill? Don't recognize affection and petting when you see it?"

"Gill?" Erin asked. "You're Gill Carver?"

Zane shot Erin a startled look. The woman had an excellent memory.

Gill's expression was equally surprised. "I am." He extended his hand for her to shake. "And you are...?"

"Erin Palmer." She untangled her hand from Zane's to shake Gill's.

Zane immediately missed the contact.

"I'm using the excuse of writing an article about the McCall Adventure Ranch to renew an old romance with Zane." She winked at Zane. "Right, babe?"

God bless her for following his lead. Zane felt a funny catch in his chest when she used the term of endearment and a matching tone of voice.

"An article on the adventure ranch?" Gill faked a jaw-cracking yawn. "Ma'am, you can find a lot of things way more interesting than his failure of a business."

"It hasn't failed," Zane said through clenched teeth, though he struggled to keep his tone civil. The last thing he wanted was to escalate a confrontation with Gill in front of Erin. In the past, he'd prided himself on being the most levelheaded of his siblings in dealing with the menace that was Gill Carver. Some days it was harder than others. "We're restructuring and will open in a few months."

"So you've said, but that remains to be seen." Gill flashed a smug grin.

"You have reason to believe they won't reopen?" Erin

furrowed her brow and tipped her head in query. "Why is that?"

Gill lifted a shoulder. "Just a theory. Word on the street is the Double M and everyone on it are circling the drain."

In his lap, Zane fisted his hand. *Must. Not. Punch. Gill.*

"Interesting," Erin said, putting her hand on her chin as if deep in thought. "From what I've heard since I arrived, the McCalls have a first-class operation and are widely respected in town. Everything I've been told indicates they expect to pull through these rough times and come out stronger than before."

A muscle in Gill's cheek twitched, and his eyes grew cold. "You've been drinking the punch they're serving out at the Double M, huh? I thought journalists were supposed to be unbiased."

Zane caught her almost imperceptible flinch. He was prepared to come to Erin's defense, put Gill in his place, but Erin got there first. "And I'd have thought a loan officer would want his clients' business to succeed. I mean, if nothing else, I'd think there would be ethical issues at stake if not legal."

Gill stiffened. "Are you threatening me?"

Erin scoffed. "Just asking a question. That's what journalists do." She looked puzzled for a moment then added, "Why? Do you feel threatened?"

Zane mustered all his composure to keep from laughing or cheering…or kissing Erin on the lips. He needn't have worried about her. Clearly she could take care of herself.

Gill squared his shoulders and divided a glare between Zane and Erin. Zane held his loan officer's gaze, silently daring him to push him further, to give him cause to break a few teeth. Instead, Gill took a step back and jerked a nod, his expression cold. "A pleasure, as always, to see you, McCall," he said in a tone that contradicted him. "Enjoy your meal."

Zane remained silent as Gill marched away and took a table on the opposite side of the dining room.

"So…that's Gill," Erin said, studying Zane over the rim of her glass as she sipped diet cola.

"Yup." Zane took a deep, restorative breath, trying to shake loose the tension coiled in his chest.

"You're right. He's an ass."

He raised his cup of coffee to her in a toast. "You were magnificent, by the way. Bravo."

She scowled and shook her head. "No. I let him get to me. I was unprofessional. I'm supposed to remain neutral. Objective. But I let him get under my skin."

"Gill's good at getting under people's skin. He's like a chigger that way. Don't kick yourself."

"What he *is* is a bully. He wanted to get a rise out of us, and I gave him what he was angling for. I know better."

"I've been trying to be the voice of reason with my siblings and Brady for the last fifteen or more years in regard to Gill. But some days he pushes all the right buttons and…" He exhaled through pursed lips, making his lips buzz. "When he started in on you, I was this close—" he held his thumb and forefinger a millimeter apart "—to serving him a knuckle sandwich."

A startled, somewhat awed, expression crossed her face. "Really? You were going to fight him to defend me?"

"Hell, yeah. No one insults a lady in my presence and

gets away with it. But when I saw you had everything in hand, I ceded to your less violent and probably more effective means of putting him in his place." He ducked his chin toward her. "Good job."

Her gaze shifted across the room, presumably to Gill, though Zane had his back to Gill's table and wasn't going to turn to look.

"He's so openly hostile to you," she said quietly, her tone and expression contemplative.

"Yeah—why?"

"His attitude toward your family makes him such a natural, obvious suspect in the sabotage." She met his gaze, her brow dented in concern. "Too obvious, really. Why would he draw attention to himself like that if he had something to hide?"

Zane tensed. "Because he's an ass, and he can't help himself?" He paused, sighing. "Erin, like I've said, that's not your concern. I don't want your article to be about our problems. I don't want you to waste your energy digging into matters best left to the sheriff." He covered her hand with his again to emphasize his point, but the contact sent electricity through him. He took a moment to recover from the shock that rippled through him when he touched her silky skin, then whispered hoarsely, "Please. Drop it. For me?"

Her gaze clung to his, her evergreen eyes softening with his request. As he'd done when Gill appeared, now she flipped her hand and laced their fingers. "Have you considered that I want to help you figure this mess out? Maybe I can bring an outside perspective that will clarify things that have escaped your notice. Why not let me help where I can?"

"I appreciate your concern. I do." He tightened his

grip on her hand. "But you're a travel writer, not a cop. And the last thing our family needs is for you to poke a hornets' nest or put yourself in harm's way by asking questions and forming hypotheses that aren't part of your article."

A shadow passed over her face, and he could tell by the way she caught her breath and bit her bottom lip that she was deciding how to respond.

"Why do you think I'd be in harm's way?"

He sighed and firmed his mouth. Why wouldn't she let it go? "Maybe you wouldn't. But I'd rather not find out the hard way. The last act of sabotage was the damage to our zip line, and my brother or Kate could have been killed. They both nearly were. The vandal seems to be escalating from damage to property to acts that put our family and employees in danger. I don't want anything to happen to you."

"I can understand that, but—"

"No!" he said firmly, his aggravation sharpening his tone. On this point, he wouldn't vacillate. "Erin, listen to me. You drop your nosing into the vandalism, or I will have to ask you to leave the ranch and ditch the article."

Her head jerked back as if he'd slapped her. She disengaged her hand from his and leaned back in her chair. She scowled at him with disappointment in her eyes. "Wow. Ultimatums? Really, Zane?"

He kept his tone low and unwavering, but without animosity. "I didn't want it to come to this, but you won't quit. The sabotage, our financial troubles, our rocky relationship with our ass-hat banker are all off the table. You either write about the opening of McCall Adventures in the spring, keeping the article focused on the positive aspects of the community and ranch and the opportunity we'll offer for thrill seekers, or don't write it at all."

She stared at him with a heartbreaking disappointment in her eyes that hurt more than it should have. He'd only known her a couple of days, and already her opinion of him mattered too much. He wanted to see her smile at him, wanted her moxie on his side, wanted an openness between them that allowed a deeper level of sharing and understanding.

Erin was bright, witty, challenging. She fascinated him. Her beautiful face and womanly curves captivated him. Her sense of humor and joy for life gave him a hope he wanted to build on. He'd actually thought she might be the reason he began clawing his way out of the dark hole of stress and despair that had swallowed him in recent months.

But his family came first. Now and always. And he had an itchy feeling between his shoulder blades that Erin's inquiries into his family's troubles, her challenging the sheriff deputy's procedures, her unwillingness to stand down despite his repeated requests, could lead to greater problems for the Double M. Maybe even danger for his family. For her. He couldn't let that happen, even if Erin hated him for his stance.

She took her napkin from her lap and placed it neatly beside her half-eaten bowl of soup. "Well." She inhaled through her nose and blew it out through pursed lips. She was calm but clearly disheartened. "Your position is duly noted."

He hated the chasm he felt between them now. She wasn't railing against his rigid bluntness and the line he'd drawn, but the distance he sensed between them, the discouragement that shaded her expression stuck under his ribs like a knife.

"I'm finished with my lunch and still have a few people I'd like to speak to in town." She pushed her chair back. "About the Adventure Ranch and what it can mean to the tourism industry for the town. You needn't wait for me. I'll call the ranch when I'm ready to return. Maybe Brady or Piper could get me when they pick Connor up from school?"

"Erin, I don't—"

She raised a hand. "I promise to be good. I don't need a babysitter, and I don't want to take up your time."

Sure, he'd put a few things on hold to come into town with her, but nothing he couldn't handle later. He was used to being on the computer late into the night, after the hands-on part of his ranch work was finished for the day. But being dismissed by her stung. He enjoyed her company, and before this tiff, he'd been having a good time with her, something in short supply recently.

Maybe he had gone too far with his ultimatum. Maybe—

She rose from her chair, swiping the bill from the table. "My treat. You drove me into town, so I'll buy lunch."

"Erin, no." He tried to get the bill from her, but she snatched her hand away and held it out of his reach… unless he wanted to create a scene. "Erin," he repeated, his shoulders slumping, "don't leave. At least let me take you around town to interview—"

"Really, it's fine." She gave him a polite smile that lacked her usual ebullience. "I'll see you back at the ranch."

She breezed up to the bar where she handed Zoe the bill and some cash, saying, "Keep the change."

As Erin walked out of the diner, her motion set off the creepy Santa display, which emitted a droning "Ho, ho, ho!"

But Santa wasn't the only one laughing. He heard a snigger behind him and turned to find Gill watching him.

Gill clapped slowly and shook his head. "Lost another one, huh, Zane? Tough break."

Zane choked down the bitterness that rose in his throat and stalked out to the parking lot, looking for something to punch.

Chapter 8

Erin tamped down the frustration and annoyance that scrabbled in her chest, strangling her breath. She'd been having a nice time with Zane, thoroughly enjoying his company until…

She huffed and strode faster down the sidewalk. The first business she reached was Buckley's Feed and Seed, and she ducked inside out of the brisk winter wind. Mr. Anderson, one of the men who'd lost his ranch, worked here now, according to Zane. Perhaps she could get a few words with the former rancher, feel out his attitude toward the Double M and, more specifically, the members of the McCall family.

A man in a flannel shirt and vest glanced up as she approached the sales counter. "Hello there, young lady. How can I help you?"

She introduced herself and gave her false narrative

about the article again, the gnawing inside her greater every time she repeated the fib. She pulled out her notepad and pen. "May I ask you a few questions, um… I'm sorry. I didn't get your name."

"Walt Anderson," he said, offering his hand to shake. "Ask away."

Bingo!

"Pleasure to meet you." She gripped his hand, relieved that she hadn't had to ask for Mr. Anderson, which would have raised questions. "Well, I want to get a good picture of the community and what it is like to live here. Have you always worked here at the Feed and Seed?"

He shook his head as he slid a stool closer to the counter and took a seat. "No, ma'am. I started here about twelve years ago."

She waited a beat, hoping he'd give her the opening she wanted without making her drag the information out of him. No luck. "What did you do before that?"

"I had a cattle ranch."

Again he let the statement lie without further comment. She pretended to write this in her notes. "Why did you make the change?"

He scratched his balding head and sighed. "Hit some bad times. A couple years of drought and disease got most of my herd. I couldn't afford to stay in business any longer. I sold my ranch before the debt swallowed me like it did some other ranchers in the area."

She gave him a genuinely sympathetic frown. "I'm so sorry. I understand ranching is a difficult life."

"Difficult, yeah. But I loved it." He flashed a rueful smile. "Not a day goes by that I don't miss it. But life, fate, God, call it what you will, had other plans for me." He spread his hands. "So here I am."

She chewed her bottom lip, deciding how to get the information she needed. "Forgive me if it's insensitive to ask, but…can you tell me more about your ranch and why you had to sell? For instance, what happened to your ranch when you sold it?"

Twisting his lips in a thoughtful moue, he grunted and folded his arms over his chest. "Well, the land was divided up and sold at auction. Other ranchers with adjoining property bought some of it and a developer bought a lot or two. A lot of my equipment was so old as to be no good to anyone else, so some of it went to the scrap yard, some of it was sold for parts. The rest was included in the auction."

"And your herd?"

"What was left after that last devastating summer went to market in late fall, as usual. I had one stud bull that brought a good price." He rubbed the side of his nose. "Saved one of the beasts to fill our freezer for the winter."

Her gut turned. She wasn't ignorant about where her cheeseburger came from, but she didn't like to think too much about that aspect of ranching. She made a few notes then met his gaze. "And how have you dealt with the loss of your ranch since then?"

He gave her a small smile. "Like I said, I miss it. But what's done is done. No point in crying over what you can't change. You pick yourself up, dust yourself off and carry on. I still had a family to feed and bills to pay. I came to work here—" he motioned to the aisles of the Feed and Seed "—and counted myself lucky to have a job."

She nodded. "A good attitude goes a long way."

"Indeed it does, ma'am."

"And is it difficult seeing your neighbors come into the store? The ranchers who bought your land and equipment?"

He appeared to ruminate on the question. "At first it was hard, but I knew it was just business. Could just as easily have been me buying their land." He tipped his head and narrowed his eyes on her. "Don't know if you're aware or not, but the ranch you're writing about, the Double M, is in a bit of a financial bind at the moment. That adventure tours business the kids started was supposed to help save them from bankruptcy."

She held her breath. "Oh?"

"Afraid so. Hate it for Michael and Melissa. I really figured if anyone would survive the hard times, it would be them. Michael's one of the best ranchers and businessmen I know."

"Ms. Palmer?"

Hearing the voice behind her, Erin turned. Roy Summers stood behind her with a metal doohickey of some description in his hand. "Oh, hello, Roy. What brings you to town?"

He held up the object in his hand. "The de-icer for the stock tank went out. Gettin' a replacement." He lifted an eyebrow. "I'm surprised to see you here. This is hardly the most interesting place for a young lady like yourself."

"Hold on, Roy," Mr. Anderson said, grinning wryly. "Are you calling me boring?"

Roy shrugged and gave the store clerk a deadpan expression. "Just calling 'em like I see 'em."

Erin hid her grin and cleared her throat. "We were actually having an interesting conversation. I'm trying to get a feel for the town, the people and the history of the area for my article." She cocked her head. "And I'm glad I ran into you. Do you think you can give me a ride back to the ranch?"

"How'd you get into town?" Roy set the de-icer on the counter.

"Zane drove me, but—" She didn't get a chance to finish her statement before Zane entered the store and spotted her.

"There you are." He strode to the counter, his long legs eating up the distance quickly.

She felt an instant shift in the atmosphere around her as he neared, like the zing of ozone in the air after a storm, and her breath hitched. Zane's mere presence seared her consciousness so that all else around her faded away. He had a commanding presence, a confidence in the way he carried himself that attracted attention and respect.

Or maybe that was just the woman in her responding to his raw masculinity. Either way, she needed a moment to regain her equilibrium before she met his gaze and straightened her spine.

"I was just asking Roy for a ride back to the Double M. I thought maybe I'd use the time in his truck to interview him."

"Interview me?" Roy folded his arms over his chest and frowned at her. "Now you *are* getting into boring material. What could I possibly have to say that'd be any help to you?"

"Aw, come on, Roy. I bet you have some good stories about life on the Double M." She winked at him, then tipped her head, asking, "You've been with the family how long?"

Roy shifted his feet and hesitated. "I started as a hand about the time the senior Mr. McCall died and his daddy—" he jerked his head toward Zane "—took over running things. I moved up to foreman about five years later, when the previous foreman retired."

"See, I'm learning things already," she said with an encouraging grin for the reluctant foreman.

Zane sighed and took her elbow. "Can I have a word with you?" He hitched his head toward the nearest aisle. "Alone?"

"I—" He propelled her away from the counter with a hand at her back before she could state her objection.

She could hear Mr. Anderson and Roy talking as Roy's purchase was rung up and charged to the ranch account.

When they were out of sight of the other men, Zane faced her with deep creases in his brow. "Look, I'm sorry I upset you. I didn't mean to sound so..."

When he paused, looking for the right word, she offered, "Authoritarian? Dictatorial?"

He clearly didn't like her characterization, and with his mouth twisted in a disgruntled frown, he pushed both hands into his back pockets. The pose pulled the lapels of his coat back and the material of his long-sleeved T-shirt taut across his chest. She had to divert her eyes to keep her mind on track.

"Erin—" he said at the same time she said, "Look, Zane—"

He nodded to her. "You first."

She moistened her lips and drew a breath as she began calmly, "My intent is not to trash your family or your business in my article. I thought I'd made that clear. In fact, I want to help your family." That much was true, which made it a little easier for her to continue her charade, hoping at least that much honesty would buy her some grace down the road. "I'm asking you to trust me. Why is that so hard for you?"

His dark eyebrows winged up then, but she pressed on. "I want to know as much as I can about both the good and the bad surrounding the ranch, so I can do my best work and present an honest picture of the grit and determination your family has shown. I'm learning so much about the family loyalty and community respect that make the Double M special." She reached for his shoulders and felt a tiny tremor when she gave his biceps a squeeze. "I understand your desire to protect your family, but give me a chance. Trust me to do my job. Please?"

Except that her real job was far from what he expected, and she hated the necessary deception, even as she was begging for his trust.

Zane looked away, his feet shifting as if the idea of offering his faith in her was giving him pause. "Erin, it's just that—"

"Excuse me, Ms. Palmer?" Roy said from the end of the aisle. "Do you still need a lift?"

"Oh, yes. Thank you." She stepped back from Zane, but before she could walk away, his hand shot out to catch her wrist, stirring a twitter in her belly.

"Erin, I'll drive you back to the ranch."

"I know you can, but I want to go with Roy."

He seemed hurt by her assertion, so she added, "Roy's been so busy in the pastures and working with the animals, I haven't had a good chance to get to know him. I figure the drive to the ranch is a good time to bend his ear and get his perspective on things." She glanced at the foreman. "Assuming that's all right with you?"

Roy shrugged one shoulder. "S'pose so."

"Great! Thank you, Roy." She turned back to Zane. "So…see you back at the ranch."

Perhaps it was wishful thinking on her part, but she thought Zane looked disappointed with her decision. In truth, she would have preferred to spend the time with Zane. But she had a job to do, and the sooner she got to the bottom of the vandalism incidents at the Double M the better. Instinct told her Roy knew something that would help her. He was such an integral part of the work that happened at the ranch, and he had a long history not only at the ranch but within the community.

She followed him out to a large truck, one even bigger than Zane's, with a higher step to the front seat. She goggled at the behemoth a moment before Roy opened the passenger-side door for her, and she hoisted herself up onto the bench seat. The cab of the ranch vehicle was dirtier than Zane's, which had been surprisingly neat and odor-free. This truck had mud and, judging by the smell, manure on the floor, dust on the dash and clutter—including foam cups, old receipts and a rusty wrench—scattered across the bench seat. In addition to the manure smell, she detected the scent of stale coffee, oil and—she sniffed discreetly as Roy rounded the vehicle to climb into the driver's seat—the subtle odor of alcohol. Roy had a lidded travel mug in the drink holder, and if she'd had more time, she'd have opened the top to take a whiff and confirm her suspicion that Roy's coffee was Irish.

The seat beneath her vibrated as Roy cranked the powerful engine and pulled out onto the main road through town. She took her notepad out, and the foreman shot a nervous glance toward her.

Erin chuckled. "I promise I don't bite, Roy."

His cheek lifted with a shy smile. "I know. I just…

don't guess I've ever been interviewed before for nothin'. I'm not sure what I'm s'posed to say."

"Just relax and answer the questions as best you can. This isn't an interrogation," she teased. "I simply want to talk about the ranch and the McCalls and the adventure tours business that the younger generation has started."

He seemed to relax a fraction, but he took a big swig of his drink before nodding to her. "All right."

"I understand your son, Brady, is a partner in McCall Adventures, too. Is that right?"

Roy nodded. "He is."

She waited a moment for him to expand on his son's partnership, but Roy said no more.

Ooоо-kay. This was going to be one of *those* interviews. Short answers. No exposition.

"How do you feel about Brady going into business with the McCalls?"

He lifted a shoulder. "Fine."

"You're not worried about McCall Adventures failing and him losing his money?"

Roy shot her a concerned look, then squeezed the steering wheel harder. "I don't…" He hesitated then frowned. "I hope not. Brady doesn't have much, and what he's got, he worked hard for."

She kept silent, watching his expression. Something was on his mind. She could see the play of emotions on his face. Finally she prompted, "But?"

He jerked a glance toward her. "But what?"

"I just thought you had more to say on the subject. If you do, please share it."

He scratched his chin and sighed. "Nah. I was only thinking how Brady would do anything for those McCall kids. Especially Piper."

"Understandable, since they're married," she said, grinning.

He nodded. "Yeah. But even before they got married, he'd have given his left nut for—" He stopped abruptly, and with his face flushing, he amended, "Pardon, ma'am. I mean, he'd have done anything to make her happy. He's been in love with her most of his life. And the boys… they've been his best friends. They were raised together, living on the ranch like we were."

"And you?"

He wrinkled his forehead. "What about me?"

Hoo-boy. "Do you consider yourself close to the family?"

A shrug. "Sure. I've worked for 'em a long time."

She gritted her back teeth. Apparently she was going to have to bend some rules of interviewing to get any valuable information from him. "So, um…what can you tell me about the trouble the family has been having? What do you know about the sabotage to the ranch?"

He jerked his gaze to her, frowning. "Pardon?"

"You do know about the sabotage? The burned field? The poison in th—"

"Sure. I know about it." He squeezed the steering wheel then reached for his coffee and took another sip. "What is it you want to know?"

"Just your thoughts about who could be behind it and why? How it has affected your job. Anything really. Just tell me your thoughts on the subject."

He grunted and stared silently out the windshield at the road for so long she was about to decide he was refusing to answer when he finally mumbled. "It's a hell of a thing, the damage to the ranch. It's hurt us, no doubt.

But…the McCalls, they're smart. They're strong. They'll bounce back. At least, I pray they will."

"And if they don't?" She watched his face closely. His jaw muscle was flexing and tightening as if he was grinding his back teeth.

"Well… I'll be out of a job. Brady, too." He sighed. "It'll mean the end to one of the oldest ranching businesses in the state."

"Hmm," she hummed sympathetically, hoping to encourage commentary.

His expression grew more serious, and he shook his head. "Won't happen. Michael knows his business, and I'll do anything I can to help turn things around, 'spite the run of bad luck."

"Ever think about leaving the Double M for another, more secure position with another ranch?"

He shot her a look that suggested she'd spoken blasphemy. "Never. The Double M is my home. The McCalls…" His voice cracked, and he blinked rapidly as if fighting back tears. Roy sniffed hard and took another drink from his cup. "Sorry. I… I was sayin' the McCalls are like family."

He wiped his nose with his sleeve, and his expression hardened. "This sabotage has got to end eventually. Somehow. And then Michael and the boys will build the ranch back to its glory days." He nodded. "They will."

"Just the boys? Not Piper or Melissa?"

He scoffed a laugh. "Well, sure. Them, too. Just… it's the boys that get their hands dirty, most of the time. Piper even left for a time. Went off to school and to work up in Boston for a while."

Erin scratched her head with the tip of her pen and bit the inside of her cheek. She still wasn't getting where she wanted with the foreman, and they were nearly back to the ranch. "Roy, as an observer of all that's happened in recent months, the vandalism and so forth…"

He tensed and cut a quick glance to her.

"And…well, as a longtime resident of the town and with your knowledge of ranching and the other ranchers and all…"

"Who is the vandal?" he asked for her.

"You have ideas?" she prompted.

His jaw tightened again. "The police and Michael have asked me the same questions over and over."

"And what do you tell them when they ask?"

"I have nothing. Only my promise to work hard to help Michael put things right when it's all over."

"Just between you and me, do you have any suspicions? Or hunches?"

Roy turned off the highway onto the drive to the ranch. "Sorry, Ms. Palmer. I can't help you with that."

She exhaled a big breath of frustration. No wonder Michael was at his wit's end. How could *no one* have any notion who was behind the trouble at the Double M? Well, any reasonable idea anyway, she amended, remembering the older gentlemen's mafia theory.

Someone was hiding something. Her gut told her as much, but she hadn't yet discerned who that someone was. Frustration and impatience chafed down her spine as she jammed her notepad back in her bag.

As they pulled up to the end of the long drive, Roy's attention caught on something that had him squinting, then mumbling, "Well, looky there."

Erin shifted her gaze out the dusty windshield and spotted the car parked near the front door of the family home. A dark-haired man with crutches stood near the passenger door while Michael, Melissa and a pretty blonde fussed over him. "Is that Dave?"

"Mmm-hmm."

"Well, good! It's nice to see him up and about."

Roy hummed again in agreement as he pulled the truck alongside the family's car. He touched the brim of his hat and gave a nod when Dave lifted a hand in greeting.

Erin unfastened her seat belt and thanked Roy for the ride.

He dipped his chin. "My pleasure, ma'am. Sorry I wasn't more help."

After gathering her belongings, she climbed from the front seat with a big smile for the returning hand. "Dave, welcome home!"

As soon as she closed the truck door, Roy pulled away, headed toward an outbuilding where a few other vehicles and farming machines were parked. She frowned as she watched Roy drive away. The foreman seemed…*underwhelmed* by the hand's return from the hospital. Erin twisted her mouth. Maybe she was reading too much into Roy's subdued reaction.

"Is something wrong, Erin?" Melissa asked.

She turned a polite smile to her hostess. "No. I just thought Roy would be happier to see Dave."

Zane's mother glanced in the direction Roy had driven. "Oh, I'm sure he's thrilled, but Roy's not one to show much emotion one way or the other. He's the king of laid-back and low-key."

Michael waved a hand toward the other woman with Dave. "Did you meet Helen? She's our cook and also Dave's girlfriend."

Erin greeted Helen. "We met…sort of. I'd just arrived when Dave fell."

"Of course. You showed him the calm breathing technique." Helen shook Erin's hand. "Nice to meet you… again."

Dave nodded to her. "Thanks for your help. Not the kind of first impression I wanted to make."

Erin waved off his comment. "I'm just glad to see you back home and on your feet…sort of." She motioned to his cast and pouted.

"Oh, well…" He released his grip on one crutch long enough to swipe at his cold and runny nose. "This isn't my home, but Mrs. McCall insisted I spend a week or two in Piper's old room while I recover."

"That way I can still work and keep an eye on him," Helen said, scooting closer to him and looping her arm through Dave's.

"We can all take care of him. Better than him being laid up at home alone," Melissa said.

Dave looked embarrassed by the fuss. "I won't be laid up. I can get around with the crutches."

Melissa propped a hand on her hip. "Pfft! You've earned a little downtime, Dave. Allow us to take care of you."

He shrugged. "Well, I have been wanting to catch up on the latest seasons of *Longmire* and *Game of Thrones*."

"And now you can," Helen said and kissed his cheek.

"But I'm missing round-up and getting the herd ready for auction." Dave gave Michael an apologetic frown then glanced toward the spruce tree, which still sat half decorated, and regret slid over his face.

Michael lifted a hand in a what-are-you-going-to-do

gesture. "Can't be helped. We'll manage. Don't worry yourself over it."

But the furrows in Michael's brow said clearly the senior McCall *was* concerned about being shorthanded. He turned to Erin and cocked his head in query. "What were you and Roy up to?"

"Oh, he just gave me a lift home from town. I had lunch with Zane and took the opportunity to chat with some townsfolk about the ranch for my…article."

Michael raised an eyebrow. "Why didn't Zane bring you home?"

"I, um…wanted to take the opportunity to chat with Roy. And speaking of which…" She flipped up a hand in inquiry. "If you're free now, may I *interview* you… say, in your office?"

His eyebrows dipped, knitting his brow with concern. "Is something wrong?"

Now she knew where Zane got his wariness. She glanced at the others who were listening to their exchange and flashed a smile. "Not at all. Just doing due diligence for my article." She swung a finger to point to the rest of the small crowd. "And you all are next. Interviews in the next couple of days, one and all."

"This way, then," Michael said, and he escorted her through the house, pausing long enough to lift Zeke out of the Christmas tree where the cat was chewing on ornaments. The smaller black and white kitty watched from the floor with wide green eyes.

When Erin chuckled at Zeke's naughty behavior, Michael shook his head, grumbling, "That cat is exhausting. Always into something. And now he has help from Sadie."

She patted the feline's fuzzy cheek then hurried to

catch up as Michael entered his office and closed the door behind them.

"So? Any luck so far finding the person responsible for sabotaging my ranch?" He circled his desk and sank wearily into his worn chair.

"No conclusions yet, but I'm learning a lot." She reported on all she'd uncovered in her conversations that morning, briefed him on her plans to follow up on a few ideas, and reminded him she'd only begun her investigation. "I know it is hard to wait, but I want to be thorough, talk with everyone, explore some unconventional outlets."

Michael rocked back in his desk chair. "How unconventional?"

"Broncs."

She explained her plan to chat up patrons at the bar, and he shrugged. "Worth a shot. Nothing else has turned up anything useful."

He laced his fingers over his chest and tapped his thumbs together restlessly in a gesture that reminded her of Zane's fidgeting when worried.

"Michael," she said, meeting his eyes, "I promise you, I will do everything in my power to find the person who has been hurting your ranch. It is a slow process, and I don't want to raise unnecessary suspicions. But I swear to you, somehow I will get the person responsible and find you justice."

Chapter 9

Pretty bold words, considering you have no real leads yet, Erin thought to herself as she reviewed her conversation with Michael that evening. After a grand dinner, featuring roast beef, potatoes, apple pie and a warm welcome home for Dave, Erin needed a walk to ease her full stomach and clear her muddled mind. She strolled across the yard toward the large, half-decorated spruce tree and tipped her head back to take in the breathtaking sight.

From the stable, she heard a soft bark and turned to see one of the blue heelers—Checkers maybe?—standing at the small door to a doghouse just inside the stable door. Beside Checkers was a Labrador she'd not seen before. The Lab stood and wagged its tail. The orangish glow of a heat lamp illuminated the canines and assured her the family wasn't letting the dogs get cold. "Hi, pups," she said, receiving another tail wag in response, and kept walking.

The night was clear, and the sky over the ranch full of stars. Even the near-full moon's glow couldn't hide the glorious array of heavenly bodies. Living in town where the city lights made it hard to see so many stars, Erin took the opportunity now and stood for a moment just staring in awe at the twinkling lights.

"Erin?"

She started at the male voice and turned slowly, peering through the darkness of the ranch yard for the person who'd spoken. She recognized Zane's gray Stetson on the figure standing by the corral fence. She crossed the yard toward him, lifting a hand in greeting. "I was just admiring the stars. You can see so many out here!"

He tipped his head back, squinting at the night sky. "Yeah. I suppose I take that for granted. Having grown up here, I've always seen this many."

She arrived at the fence, where he leaned on the top rail, and gave him a playfully scolding frown. "Shame on you, taking any of this natural beauty and breathtaking landscape for granted."

He tugged the rim of his hat. "Touché."

After a beat of awkward silence, she said, "Zane," at the same time he said, "Erin."

They chuckled, and he waved a hand toward her. "Ladies first."

"I wanted to apologize for being—"

"No," he said, putting a gloved hand on her arm. "I'm the one who should be sorry. And I am. I was rude and… What was your word? Dictatorial? I let my worry over the ranch and the things that have been happening override common sense."

"Common sense?"

"Or maybe just common trust."

She felt something bump her leg and glanced down to see the yellow Lab she'd spotted earlier, the dog's eyes bright and eager.

Zane bent to scratch the Lab behind the ears. "Hi, Kip. What are you doing out here?" Then to Erin, "You've promised you're not out to write a sensationalist, yellow journalism piece about us, and I want to take you at your word."

She clutched her coat closed at the neck when a chill breeze buffeted her. "Do I hear a 'but'?"

"Trust is hard to come by for me lately. Someone I know, possibly someone I care about, is quietly working against my family, trying to hurt us." He shook his head and turned his gaze out across the corral, where a couple of the horses, wearing stable blankets, shuffled through the darkness and nibbled grass through the far fence.

"Someone, but not me. I don't want to hurt your family. Quite the opposite. You have a charming, warm, loving family that has been so kind to me since I arrived. I like you all very much." She stepped closer to him and stroked a hand along his square jawline. "Some more than others."

He arched an eyebrow, and even in the pale moonlight, she could see the flare of heat in his eyes. "We like you, too." He covered her hand with his own gloved hand, the hint of a grin playing at the corners of his mouth. "Some more than others."

"So then…can we start over? Be friends? Put today's tensions behind us and make a fresh start?" She canted closer, curling her fingers into his coat and savoring the added heat of his body blocking the gentle stir of brumal air.

He wrapped an arm around her, anchoring her close with one arm while his free hand tucked coils of hair that escaped her knit cap behind her ears. She gave him a quick hug, then turned in his arms to face the corral and take another gander at the brilliant stars. A cloud or two had drifted in, cluttering the view with shadowy wisps.

The yellow Lab pawed at her leg and whined, seeking attention. She rubbed the dog's head and cooed sweet nothings to the canine.

"Excuse me for a minute," Zane said, his voice heavy with regret. "Kip here is not supposed to be out. I need to take her home before she gets herself into trouble."

"Oh, sure," she replied, shivering a bit as he stepped away from her and a cool stir of air swept away the heat of his body. "Where does she belong?"

"She's Connor's dog, but she stays in the fence of their yard. She's not trained to work with the cows like Ace and Checkers, and she causes problems when she gets in the mix."

"I see."

Zane took the Labrador by the collar. "Back in a minute. C'mon, Kip."

She watched him lead the dog across the yard toward the foreman's house, where Piper and Brady lived with Connor and Roy. And Kip. She smiled to herself as she scanned the quiet ranch yard. The McCalls truly had a little community here with the ranch hands, the foreman's family and all the family pets and work animals. Her gaze settled on the half-decorated spruce that had been neglected since Dave's fall from the ladder. A pang twisted in her chest. She ruminated on a plan until she saw Zane approach again, Kip safely delivered to her warm house.

"Isn't that your truck over there?" she asked as he

joined her again at the corral fence. She aimed her thumb at the pickup near the front of the family home.

He lifted his chin a notch, and his expression reflected wary curiosity. "Yeah. Why?"

Without answering his query, she held out her hand. "Do you have the keys on you?"

His countenance grew more suspicious. "Again, why?"

"Because I'd like to borrow them for a moment." She could see his hesitation, could almost hear his internal debate on whether to trust her. "Fresh start, remember? You don't have to look at me like that."

With an amused snort, he dug the keys from his pocket and, with one eyebrow arched as if in warning not to let him down, he dropped them on her upturned palm.

She chuckled. "You'll be a great father one day. You already have the don't-disappoint-me evil eye perfected."

He blinked his surprise. "What evil eye?"

"I'll be responsible, Dad," she teased. With that, she winked at him and sashayed to the truck while he stood in the pool of moonlight and watched.

Erin climbed into the truck, inhaling again the scents that lingered there. Hay, mud, sweat—but overriding them all was the distinct scent that she could only call *Zane*. A spicy tang, a clean crispness that held notes of pine and leather...and was it citrus? Whether the aroma came from his deodorant, an aftershave or some other grooming product, she couldn't say. But the fresh odor filled her nose and sent a tingle of awareness scampering down her spine. She'd only been at the Double M a few days, yet she already knew she could pick Zane from a lineup based only on his seductive scent.

She cranked the truck engine, then to tease Zane, she

raced the motor. Predictably, he jerked his chin higher and took a step closer, a look of panic filling his chiseled features. Chuckling to herself, she shifted into gear and drove slowly across the yard until she'd pulled alongside the tall blue spruce. The strings of Christmas lights had been abandoned at the base of the tree, as if disturbing them was bad luck. All of the decorations for the tree were just where they'd been at the moment Dave had fallen and broken his leg.

When she climbed down from the front seat, Zane was waiting for her, a sarcastic grin twisting his mouth. "You're not funny."

Her grin spread wider. "Oh, but your reaction *was*." She patted his chest, and even through his thick winter coat, she could feel the solid muscle that lay beneath the suede and fleece. "You need to unwind a little, cowboy. Life is more enjoyable if you're not tied in knots all the time."

Her assessment met with wide eyes and a stunned sort of choking noise. Brushing past him, she bent to scoop the strings of lights, draping them over her arm, then piling them on the bed of his truck.

Roused by the new activity, Ace and Checkers trotted back out and hopped onto the bed of the truck, wiggling with excitement and thumping their tails.

Zane put his hand on Erin's shoulder as she stooped for a second armful. "You don't need to do that. Some else will get those."

"Will they? It's been how many days? And I'm kinda afraid that whoever does move them will just put them back in a box." She carried the lights to the back of his Tundra, then hoisted herself onto the bed, laughing when Checkers licked her face. "And I'm of the opinion that the Double M could use a bit of Christmas cheer." She plucked one strand from the bed as she stood. Erin saw immediately that the truck bed didn't get her as high as she'd need to be to reach the top branches. "That is one tall tree," she said, tipping her head as she considered the spruce.

The truck jostled as Zane joined her. "What are you doing?"

Although his tone made it clear he knew perfectly well what she was up to, she sent him a side glance and a smug grin. "Decorating the tree. Want to tune that satellite radio I saw in the cab to some Christmas tunes to set the mood?"

"Seriously?" He tried to take the lights from her hand, and she tugged them back.

"Either help or get out of the way. But this tree is getting its halls decked with yuletide…something or other."

He snorted. "For someone who loves Christmas, you're kinda twisting those carols a bit."

She thunked him in the stomach with the back of her hand. "Are you going to play the radio or what?"

He rolled his eyes and jumped down from the truck bed, the dogs following him. While he scrolled through satellite stations, searching for seasonal music, she draped the strand of lights on the closest part of the tree, weaving them through the branches and around the glass balls that had never been removed. She quickly needed more elevation to reach the higher boughs. Moving a few strands to the top of the cab, she used the walls of the bed as footholds to climb. Balancing carefully, she crawled to the roof of the cab and rose to her feet. Keeping her center of gravity shifted to her heels, she stretched to place lights on the evergreen.

"What the hell?" Zane shouted, startling her. "Erin, are you crazy?" He quickly climbed on the truck bed again and hurried toward her. "Are you trying to break your leg, too? Or your neck?"

"Of course not. But I want to reach—"

"Get down!" His tone reflected panic more than anger.

She glared at him. "Do you have another ladder we can use?"

"I— Not that I know of. But that doesn't matter." He edged closer and put a hand on her ankle. "What you're doing is risky."

"So…you come up here. You can hold me."

From the door he'd left open to the cab, the jingling refrains of "Santa Claus Is Coming to Town" played into the cold night. With a frustrated-sounding sigh, he hoisted himself onto the roof of the cab.

As Zane got to his feet, Erin had to brace her legs in a wide stance and shift her weight to keep her balance as the truck rocked.

He eased over to her and, with a scowl, put a hand at her waist. "You really are stubborn, you know that?"

"My father called it *persistence*. I know what I want and don't settle." She flashed a teasing grin as she faced the tree and raised a string of lights toward a top branch. She hummed along with the radio and looped the electric wires around the limbs.

Through her coat, she could feel Zane's grip tighten, and she heard his boots thump as he rearranged his feet. Finally, with a tug, he pulled her away from the tree. "Hang on."

She glanced over her shoulder and gasped her surprise when she found him shucking his boots and yanking off his socks. "What are you doing?"

"Sacrificing my feet to your little project." He quirked an eyebrow as if to say, *I hope you're satisfied.* "I have no traction in my boots. I'll have a better grip with my bare feet."

She glanced down at said feet. Long and sturdy-looking, no crooked toes or bunions for her cowboy! She shook the pronoun from her head. Not hers. Just...Zane. "You don't—" Erin shivered, imagining how cold the truck roof and night air must be for him. "But that's—"

"Let's just get done with this, okay?" He wiggled a finger, motioning her to turn around. This time, he planted his feet, squared his hips and wrapped an arm around her waist, reaching under her coat to grip her sweater.

Confident in his hold, she leaned forward, stretched up and flung the remaining light strands onto the highest branches. Standing on her tiptoes, his solid strength mooring her, she poked and fiddled until the arrangement pleased her. As she settled back on her heels and pivoted toward him, she said, "You realize that's just one side of the tree. We need to move the truck to get the other sides."

He replied with a grumble from his throat. "All right. But you *will* step down onto the bed before this truck goes anywhere."

His eyes glittered with determination, and her pulse kept time with the rat-a-tat-tat of the Little Drummer Boy's drum from the radio as she held his gaze. She could too easily imagine herself climbing onto a different sort of bed with him. Zane would be a caring but commanding lover, she decided, and a trill of anticipation stirred under her skin when she considered testing her theory.

"FAST FIVE" READER SURVEY

Your participation entitles you to:
✱ 4 Thank-You Gifts Worth Over $20!

Complete the survey in minutes.

CAVANAUGH'S SECRET DELIVERY
TOP SECRET DELIVERIES
Marie Ferrarella
USA TODAY BESTSELLING AUTHOR

BRAVING THE HEAT
Regan Black
USA TODAY BESTSELLING AUTHOR

Get 2 FREE Books

Your Thank-You Gifts include **2 FREE BOOKS** and **2 MYSTERY GIFTS**. There's no obligation to purchase anything!

See inside for details.

Please help make our
"Fast Five" Reader Survey
a success!

Dear Reader,

Since you are a lover of our books, your opinions are important to us... and so is your time.

That's why we made sure your **"FAST FIVE" READER SURVEY** can be completed in just a few minutes. Your answers to the five questions will help us remain at the forefront of women's fiction.

And, as a thank-you for participating, we'd like to send you **4 FREE THANK-YOU GIFTS!**

Enjoy your gifts with our appreciation,

Pam Powers

To get your
4 FREE THANK-YOU GIFTS:

✳ Quickly complete the "Fast Five" Reader Survey
and return the insert.

"FAST FIVE" READER SURVEY

1	Do you sometimes read a book a second or third time?	○ Yes ○ No
2	Do you often choose reading over other forms of entertainment such as television?	○ Yes ○ No
3	When you were a child, did someone regularly read aloud to you?	○ Yes ○ No
4	Do you sometimes take a book with you when you travel outside the home?	○ Yes ○ No
5	In addition to books, do you regularly read newspapers and magazines?	○ Yes ○ No

YES! I have completed the above Reader Survey. Please send me my 4 FREE GIFTS (gifts worth over $20 retail). I understand that I am under no obligation to buy anything, as explained on the back of this card.

240/340 HDL GM37

FIRST NAME	LAST NAME

ADDRESS

APT.#	CITY

STATE/PROV.	ZIP/POSTAL CODE

"Right," she said in answer to his directive. Her voice sounded winded and raspy to her own ears.

Zane cocked his head, narrowing his gaze on her briefly and drawing a deep breath that made his nostrils flare, before he stepped back. Offering his hand, he helped her step down, then after shooing the dogs off the front seat, he climbed back into the cab to pull the truck up against the opposite side of the spruce.

They repeated the process—him holding her waist while she leaned against his strong arms to reach the top boughs—until all the lights had been evenly strung on the tree. Satisfied with her work, she rocked back on her heels and stepped away from the edge of the cab's roof…and onto his toe.

He hissed in pain, and she quickly sidestepped, only to have her shoe slip on the slick metal of the roof. When she stumbled, he grabbed her arm and quickly hauled her up against his chest. She clutched his shoulders, and Zane's arms slipped around her in an instant, anchoring her.

Adrenaline had stolen her breath, but as she lifted her face to Zane's, she sucked in a lungful of chilled air. "Oops."

"Mmm-hmm." His black eyebrows went up again in another silent *What'd I tell you?* "You okay?"

She bobbed her head but didn't let go of him. The moon had come out from behind a wispy cloud and cast a pale silver light across his face. His gaze—that damnably hypnotic gaze of his—reflected the lunar light like stars set against his dark features. Mesmerized, she stared up at him, and again her breath stuck in her lungs. The tip of her tongue slipped out to moisten her chapped lips, and his pupils grew like those of a predator spotting its prey.

His splayed hand skimmed up from the small of her back to the nape of her neck. He nudged her forward, and her pulse spiked.

As he dipped his head, his piercing gaze remained locked on hers. He gave her the merest of kisses, a brush of his lips against hers, while his gaze delved deeply into hers. A ripple of desire rolled through her, shaking her to her core.

How could such a small kiss have such a huge impact on her? Her heart drumming against her ribs and the whoosh of blood past her ears played harmony to Nat King Cole crooning from the radio about chestnuts on an open fire.

Let me tell you about open fires, Nat. Because, oh, yes. Flames licked her veins and heated her core.

Zane's scrutiny was still fixed on her, his mouth hovering just over hers while he silently searched her face, questioning her. Erin answered his unvoiced query by plowing her fingers into his hair and dragging him to her. She slanted her lips over his in a deep kiss that left nothing to chance or uncertainty.

A growl of approval rumbled from his throat. His arms wrapped around her, one hand on the back of her head, another on her buttocks. He held her tight, pressed close to his body...which was fortunate, because the sensation of his warm lips devouring hers made her head spin and her legs buckle. Shimmering sparks sizzled from her core to her limbs until her whole body was alive, jangling, yearning. She locked her knees, stretched up on her toes to reposition her mouth, to open wider to his exploration and delve more deeply into the mysteries that were Zane.

Her head spun, drunk on the crisp scent of evergreen,

winter air and manly musk. The romantic melody of "The Christmas Song" and Nat King Cole's velvet voice wrapped them in a sensual cocoon, and the moonlight painted them in silver intimacy.

She lost track of how long they stood on top of his truck, kissing, touching, straining to press closer to each other, but one Christmas song blended into another, then another. Only when the jarring squeak of a chipmunk on the radio shouting "Okay!" blasted through the still night did Zane raise his head and suck in a ragged breath.

"Wow," she whispered, fighting to regain her mental balance. As she canted back from him, she bumped his foot with hers. Squashed it, really. "Ooh, sorry!"

He shook his head. "You didn't hurt me. At this point, my feet are basically numb."

She jerked her gaze to his bare feet, remembering belatedly that he'd shed his boots for better traction. "Oh, my gosh! You have to be freezing!"

He twitched his cheek in a half grin. "My toes are pretty cold, but the rest of me…" he brushed her hair behind her ears and pinned his bright blue gaze on her "…is burning."

As if to prove his point, he tucked her chilled hands inside the collar of his shirt just above his collarbone. His skin was hot, and by inching her fingers up toward his throat, she could feel the steady throb of his pulse in the vein at the side of his neck. The tender spot rescuers used for proof of life.

Not only was Zane alive, he was warm and tantalizing and making her feel more alive than she had in many years. Since her brother had died, a part of her had been dead, as well. Even after she'd helped root out the truth about his murder, his absence in her life was a void she'd not moved past. Never would.

She gave her head a little shake. She didn't want to think about Sean now. She wanted to savor this moment with Zane. Because she knew by dawn's light tomorrow, she'd have come to her senses about a physical entanglement with someone she was, technically, investigating.

Did she really think Zane was involved with the sabotage to his family ranch? No. But losing objectivity would not help her find the real culprit.

She stroked the back of her fingers from his throat along his strong, square jaw, murmuring, "What do you say we give the lights some juice and enjoy our handiwork, then get your feet inside and warmed up?"

"An excellent idea." He swung down from the roof of the cab to the bed and held out a hand to help her down. While he tugged his socks and boots back on, she jumped from the tailgate to the frozen ground.

At the base of the spruce tree, she plugged all of the light strands together, then to an extension cord. Zane took the coiled power cord from her and marched toward the barn, unlooping the cord as he disappeared across the shadowed ranch yard.

"Ready?" he called a moment later from inside the barn.

Seized by the desire to have him by her side when the tree was lit, she bent to unplug the extension cord from the linked light strands. "Yes," she called back.

A moment later, he approached, groaning when he found the tree dark. "Well, damn. That's anticlimactic. There must be a bad wire or blown bulb or—"

"Or—" she held up the two loose ends of the power cords "—I was waiting for you."

A grin ghosted over his lips as he moved up beside her. "Shall I provide a drumroll?"

"I'd rather have a kiss for luck."

Something hot flashed in his eyes, and he bent to capture her lips in a tender, lingering kiss.

Before he could lift his mouth from hers, she connected the cords, and the magical glow of lights from the tree flooded the yard with holiday cheer. Sliding an arm around Zane's waist, she leaned sideways into him as she drank in the wondrous sight.

A bittersweet joy filled her chest as she admired the shimmering lights. As much as she loved the holiday and the twinkling bulbs, their gleam always reminded her of the brother she'd lost. Decorating the family tree had been a tradition she'd shared with Sean from the time they were old enough to walk. Being older and several inches taller than her, Sean handled the top of the tree while she and their sister, Kelly, decked the lower branches with as many baubles and tinsel as their annual fir could hold. Thinking back, she knew her zealous decor must have looked gaudy, but their parents never tried to modify her efforts and would praise the tree as the most beautiful ever. Moisture gathered in her eyes as she admired the towering spruce, and she would swear the wink of lights reflecting from the red glass balls was Sean sending a hello from beyond. *It's the most beautiful tree ever*, she heard him whisper in her mind.

Erin blinked hard and cleared the thickness that her sentimental sidetrack left in her throat.

"Good work. It looks great," Zane said, draping his arm over her shoulders and giving her a little squeeze.

"I only finished what Dave and Brady had started. I believe in giving credit where it is due."

"Well, thank you for finishing it. It may have gone neglected otherwise, and you are right that the ranch could use a bit of cheer." His expression dimmed as if his thoughts had turned to the misfortunes the ranch had suffered in recent months.

She wanted to pick his brain about those events and decided she had the perfect opportunity at hand. "I propose we toast our handiwork with a cup of hot cocoa in the guesthouse. Will you join me?"

He inhaled slowly and deeply, his mouth twisted in a skeptical pucker.

"We can build a fire to warm your feet up," she added before he could refuse. "And…I think I saw some bourbon in the kitchenette if you want your cocoa with an extra touch of holiday cheer."

The reluctance in his face softened, and he lifted a corner of his mouth in a faint acquiescent smile. "All right, then."

He returned to the driver's side of his truck to turn off the satellite radio and retrieve his keys from the ignition.

As they reached the door of the guesthouse, she glanced back at the spruce, glowing in the dark of the cold winter night like a beacon of hope. Hope was what the folks at the Double M needed amid the recent setbacks and sadness. And hope was what she intended to give them.

Zane crouched in front of the stone fireplace in the guesthouse, arranging the logs and kindling just so. Josh was more haphazard when stacking wood for a fire, but

Zane believed any job worth doing was worth doing right. With precision.

"That's funny," Erin muttered in the kitchenette.

He cast her a side glance and found her chewing her bottom lip as she stared into the upper cabinets. His brain flashed back to the kiss they'd shared and the feel of those lips beneath his own. Soft and warm. Inviting. Sweet and tantalizing.

His body hummed with a renewed arousal as his gaze drifted over her feminine curves. As if she felt his perusal, she turned her face toward him.

"I don't see it here anymore." She propped her hand on her hip and closed the cabinet door.

"Don't see what?"

"The bottle of bourbon. I would swear it was up there yesterday." She stooped to check the bottom cabinets. "But it's not here."

"Doesn't matter. Plain cocoa is fine." He faced the fireplace again and struck a match. The tinder caught and blazed, and he bent to gently blow on the flames, feeding them the oxygen. As the fire grew brighter, he sat back on his heels and admired his handiwork before closing the fire screen.

Erin met him at the small couch and handed him a steaming mug of hot chocolate. "Some mischievous elf must have appropriated it while I slept."

"Hmm?" Zane hummed as he sipped his cocoa.

"The bourbon." She tucked her feet under her and angled her body toward his. "Honestly, the promise of booze was not a ruse to coerce you here. I *know* it was there." A dimple pocked her forehead as she frowned, and he longed to rub away with his fingers. Although she did look awfully cute with that little wrinkle over her nose.

He waved a dismissive hand. "Don't worry about it." Then hesitated. "Unless you'd like me to get more to replace it. I can—"

She shook her head vehemently. "No. Not necessary. It's just...puzzling."

Because Erin found it significant, Zane took a moment to consider what could have happened to the liquor. Since Roy's stint in the rehabilitation clinic, the family had made a point of being more discreet about their own alcohol consumption. Had someone removed it in deference to the foreman? Or had—?

"So," Erin said, cutting into his musing. She set her mug aside and grabbed the lower leg of his jeans. "Give me those feet. Let's get them warmed."

"They're good now." He took her hand and tugged it from his jeans.

Erin angled a defiant look at him. "Come on, cowboy. Give me your feet. I promise you'll enjoy it."

Heat slammed into him. And curiosity. What did she have in mind? When she started tugging on his boots, he helped her remove the dusty things as well as his socks. She lifted his feet into her lap, and using both hands, she began massaging his left foot. His feet were, in fact, still a bit numb from the cold, and her warm touch sent shock waves of pleasure through him.

"Do you often go outside in the winter without shoes, Mr. McCall?" She grinned at him as she dug her thumbs into the arch of his foot.

He moaned his approval of the deep massage and, closing his eyes, let his head loll back on the sofa cushion. "Only when I need traction on my truck roof to keep pretty journalists from breaking their neck."

Her hands stilled for a moment, and he cracked one eye open to peer at her. Her gaze was locked on his feet, her expression troubled. In the next moment, she pushed whatever had stopped her aside and continued working her fingers into his frozen foot.

"How is your article coming along?" he asked to fill the awkward silence.

Her Christmas-green eyes flicked to his. "Well enough. Still fact-finding and mulling what angle to take."

"Is there anything I can do to expedite—" When she stroked both thumbs along the length of his foot and gave his toes a firm squeeze, he swallowed the rest of his sentence. A satisfied groan slipped from his throat. Not only did her efforts loosen sore muscles and stimulate his chilled blood circulation, an intoxicating sensation rolled through him that shot desire straight to his groin. Who needed bourbon? He was getting drunk off Erin's sensual caress.

He swallowed hard and curled his fingers into a throw pillow beside him. Dear God, he'd never realized a foot rub could be so damn erotic.

"Anything to expedite…?" she prompted.

Zane sent her a hooded glance. "I have no idea. Who the hell can think while you're doing those incredible things to my feet?"

She flashed an impish grin. "You like?"

He returned a throaty chuckle. "Oh, yeah."

The longer she rubbed his soles, flexed his toes and worked out pressure points in his heels, the more relaxed he became. He was paradoxically sleepy and turned on at the same time. And as much as he wanted to lean his head back on the sofa, close his eyes and simply savor the sensual massage, he was enjoying his view of Erin too much.

She was a feast for the eyes, her quiet beauty made more vibrant in the glow from the fire. The flames cast gold highlights in the waves of her brown hair, and rosy stains still rode her cheeks from the outdoors' cold. A mysterious half smile curved her lips as she worked, and he found himself staring at the pale pink bow of her mouth. Even void of any lipstick, her mouth looked dewy soft and enticing.

The soft light from the fireplace danced across her face, animating the gentle curves and delicate angles of her chin, cheeks and nose, and giving her eyes an elfin twinkle. Watching her now, remembering her pure joy seeing the lights in the spruce tree, nudged at the somber mood that had managed to imprison him in recent months.

The seriousness of the family's finances and looming threat of the saboteur had placed a dark cloud of worry over him he couldn't shake. Josh said he took things too personally, too seriously. His father told him the Double M's problems weren't Zane's to solve and tried to shoulder the responsibility and burden alone, which only worried Zane more because his father's blood pressure was a powder keg waiting to blow. Again.

But when he was with Erin, things were different. Especially tonight, both decorating the tree and now with her magic hands working weeks of hard work and boot fatigue from his feet, Zane felt a comprehensive lift in his mood, a release of the pressure that like a thunderstorm had clouded his mood and filled him with stress for months.

Yet for a woman with such an effect on him, Erin was a blank page to him. She was at his ranch, asking questions about him and his family and their ranching business, but he knew almost nothing about her. He cocked one eyebrow and tipped his head in query. "Who are you, Erin Palmer?"

Her startled gaze darted to his. "What?"

Shrugging one shoulder, he asked, "I know so little about you. Tell me something about you."

"Oh, well…" Her expression softened, and after she'd relaxed, he realized how much his initial question had rattled her.

Curious. Why had his question about who she was bothered her? Was she hiding something?

She paused to take a sip of her hot chocolate, then licked the foam from her lips. A kick of lust swamped Zane, and he almost missed her opening comment.

"I grew up in Colorado Springs, moved to Boulder after I graduated from college and that's where I call home at this point. I love movies, and football, and Christmas—but you knew that one," she said with a twist of her mouth.

She moved her massage from his left foot to his right and fresh waves of arousal flowed through him. With effort he kept his thoughts focused on the topic at hand. "Hobbies?"

"A little photography…although that's less a hobby and more work-related. I read a lot. Mysteries and romances. I like gardening. Flowers, not vegetables."

"Why not vegetables?"

She wrinkled her nose. "Don't know. I'm more in it for pretty landscaping than a meal, I guess."

"Pets?"

"Not at the moment. I'm thinking about getting a cat."

He lifted an eyebrow. "Oh? Have you met Zeke?"

"Zeke?"

"Our family cat. He's a real character."

She grinned. "Would he be the one that jumped on the table at dinner the other night or the shy black cat with the white bib?"

He scoffed and shook his head. "Oh, right. Zeke did act up at dinner the other night, didn't he? The black and white one is Sadie."

"I'd love to meet Zeke and Sadie officially, if that's okay? Maybe tomorrow?"

"Research for the article or are you a cat person?" he asked with a wry grin.

"Both. Cats with character, two dogs that herd cattle, horses... The Double M's animals are part of your life here." She twitched a grin. "And, yes, I love cats, so..."

"Then I will introduce you to the hellion on paws that is Zeke and his new sidekick, Sadie. Now...tell me more about *your* family."

She cupped her cocoa between her hands and stared into the drink silently for a moment. He rued the loss of her massaging fingers, but swung his feet to the floor, so he could reach for his own mug then pull his socks back on.

"My parents are both living in Colorado Springs still, in the same house we grew up in."

"Do you have siblings?"

"Two." She furrowed her brow, set her mug aside,

then cleared her throat. "Well, one now." She took a deep breath. "My older brother, Sean, died." She drew a shaky breath, and tears filled her eyes. "He was murdered."

Chapter 10

Zane jerked taut, his spine straightening from his relaxed slouch. "What!"

He blinked hard, waiting for her to tell him she was kidding, or that there was some explanation that would soften the harsh word she'd used. *Murdered?*

A bitter scowl hardened her mouth, and she nodded. "By his fraternity brothers during rush. A hazing incident gone wrong." Her expression soured further. "That's what they claimed. But I never bought it. It was reckless endangerment, plain and simple, and they deserved to be held responsible. Seeing justice served was the reason I—"

When she cut her words short and dropped her gaze, Zane leaned toward her. "The reason you what? Erin?"

She shook her head, sniffed, dabbed at her eyes. "Nothing."

Her abrupt silence after the passion that had instigated the half comment rankled. Hadn't they just pledged to trust each other? He might have pressed the issue, but the abject misery on her face pummeled him.

He reached for her hand, which he discovered was trembling. How would he feel if he lost Josh or Piper? The possibility was too ugly to consider, and when his gut roiled, he determinedly shoved the notion aside. He refused to go there, even in theory.

"Hey," he said, leaning toward her, his thumb stroking her knuckles. "I'm so sorry for your loss. For bringing up a bad memory. I understand if you don't want to talk about it."

He studied Erin for a moment, who stared at the fire, her face a mask of grief. She wiped her thumb beneath her eye to dry the moisture there, then whispered, "It's okay. Talking about it helps. It keeps him alive just a little bit. And I won't let the pain of what happened because of those jerks steal the last bits I have of Sean."

She shot him a look as heated as the flames crackling in the grate. "They wanted to bury it, to make it go away quietly and cover their guilt. The university, the fraternity's national office and especially the guys' lawyers. They swore up and down under oath that it was a sad and tragic accident." Her grip on his hand tightened. "But I knew in my gut there was more to the story. And I proved that I was right."

Zane blinked, his heart drubbing a beat of dread. He didn't want to dwell on her unpleasant memory, wanted to recapture the lighthearted conversation they'd enjoyed moments earlier. But something—her passionate reaction over the injustice of Sean's death, a desire to better understand what made Erin tick—or maybe just morbid curiosity—led him to ask, "What happened? How did he die?"

"The official report says asphyxiation due to anaphylaxis. Sean had a severe peanut allergy, a fact he *didn't* keep quiet, because even a little nut residue caused him to react. It was in his application to the university, the forms he filled out for the fraternity dietary staff, and he had told his roommate, who had already pledged to the fraternity. In fact, Sean told us some of the brothers had grumbled to him about the fact that they'd eliminated peanut butter and nut products from the house on his account. So when the brothers of the fraternity claimed they didn't know about his allergy—" She scoffed and pressed her mouth into a taut line of frustration. "Bull malarkey. Complete bull malarkey."

"I take it they gave him something with nuts. Willfully?" Zane ventured, his mouth feeling dry and a sense of disquiet swelling in his chest.

"Not only willingly, maliciously. I've talked with people who were there, people who tried to help him and were blocked in their efforts to save Sean."

"What?" A ripple of shock flowed through him, hiking his own tension up another notch.

"The whole thing was couched as a stupid contest for the pledges." Her anger vibrated in her tone, and she shoved to her feet to pace. "They were blindfolded, hands tied behind their backs, and placed at a table where they were supposed to have an eating contest. The first one to finish the plate of brownies in front of them would win a pass on the next challenge. But it was a setup. They wanted to embarrass Sean, wanted to cause an allergic reaction, so they could make fun of his distorted face and blotchy skin. So the brownies were made with peanut oil. On purpose."

Zane muttered a scorching curse under his breath and tracked her agitated movement around the room. Her hands balled and flexed, as if itching to punch something...or someone. He had the same gnawing impulse and rubbed his jittery palms on his jeans.

"He had gobbled quite a bit of them before the first symptoms showed up," she continued. "His roommate said that his face started swelling and a rash popped out on his arms and cheeks within a minute or two. Sean had stopped eating as soon as he realized what was happening, but it was too late. He'd ingested too much to stop the reaction's progress."

"And when they saw how serious his reaction was—?"

"The brothers who'd planned the stunt just laughed at him. Supposedly, they didn't realize how serious his symptoms were. Sean couldn't talk because his throat had swollen shut. He couldn't use his hands to signal his distress, because they were tied behind his back. When his roommate tried to call 9-1-1, another guy snatched his phone away and told him, quote, 'not to be a pussy.'"

Zane scrubbed both hands over his face as a prickling ire heated his cheeks. "Those bastards!"

His fury on her behalf made him edgy. He struggled to find an outlet for the sharp-edged sense of disgust and injustice—a feeling far too close to what he'd been carrying for months regarding the unresolved sabotage at the ranch. "Surely, knowing about his allergy, he had some epinephrine on hand for emergencies."

"He did. But he couldn't talk to tell anyone where it was. And though the brothers claimed they didn't realize how serious the attack was, my witnesses said they were too busy guffawing and imitating his swollen face and choking sounds to think about what was actually happening." She paused by the fireplace and dashed angrily at another tear on her cheek. "They were, of course, drunk as skunks, and when they *did* realize the seriousness, the idiots thought first of saving their own sorry hides. Most of them fled the scene like sniveling cowards. His roommate tried to find Sean's EpiPen, but Sean suffocated before Danny got back with it."

Zane struggled to draw air in his lungs. The story was too horrifying, too maddening, to process. Finally in a strangled-sounding voice, he said, "Please tell me the reprobates were prosecuted and held responsible."

"Not initially. The incident was originally dismissed as a tragic accident. The fraternity's lawyer even tried to put blame on Sean, saying he should have had his EpiPen with him, he should have inquired about what was in the brownies—like they'd have told the truth. It was a setup."

"You're sure it was?"

She nodded. "My witnesses talked, laid out the whole story in exchange for immunity."

"*Your* witnesses?" He cocked his head. "What do you mean by that?"

She gave him an odd look, then rubbing her hands on her jeans, she returned to the couch and sat facing him. "My parents accepted a settlement from the school and fraternity in exchange for an agreement not to pursue litigation. I tried to convince them not to, but they wanted to make it all go away. The stress and grief was killing my mother, and they seemed to think that out of sight would mean out of mind."

Zane grunted his disagreement. But who was he to

condemn her family? Everyone handled grief in their own way. "So the creeps got away with it?"

She held up a hand, asking for patience. "*But...*I learned from a family friend, who was our lawyer, that the agreement only said they wouldn't file *civil* charges. That didn't mean the state couldn't file criminal charges if enough evidence or witnesses who'd testify were found. So I changed my plans for the next fall—I'd been accepted to Duke, but I decided to go the university that Sean had attended—and I did some investigating of my own."

Zane sat taller, his pulse kicking up. "Duke's such a good school, though! Why—?"

"I know! But finding justice for Sean was more important to me. He was my brother! Surely you can understand the need that compelled me? The sense of unfinished business, of imbalance and inequity in my world?"

A strange sense of connection filled him, warm and gratifying. He'd lived with a feeling his life was out of balance, weighted by injustice, for much of the last two years, since the sabotage had begun—and gone unresolved. He reached for her, shifting his body closer and curling his hand around her. "I do understand. Completely."

Her gaze dropped to their joined hands, and when she lifted her eyes to his again, a warmth shimmered from their evergreen depths.

He brushed a coil of her silky hair from her eyes. "And did you find what you wanted at Sean's school?"

She lifted a corner of her mouth, nodding slowly, and the satisfaction that transformed her face nestled in his core like a private victory.

"How?"

She took a breath and exhaled before explaining. "I went to parties at the fraternity, using my middle name—Moira—as a last name, so I wouldn't tip my hand, and when the brothers started drinking, the alcohol loosened tongues. The more information I gathered, playing the part of a gossip-hungry coed, the more I knew where else to dig, who to question, where to obtain documents from the fraternity's internal investigation, where the truth had been reported and then buried. When they thought they were earning points with me, revealing juicy details about the previous year's scandal, the brothers were willing to give up their secrets in exchange for sex." She arched one eyebrow in disgust. "Or rather the suggestion they'd get sex. I wouldn't have slept with them for anything."

He returned a dark scowl, imagining the cretins pawing at her. Jealousy and protective ire surged in him.

"Anyway..." She paused to moisten her lips, and his attention snagged on the soft, pink skin.

A wave of heat flooded him, and for a moment, all he could think about was how much he wanted to kiss her again. Kiss her and—

"...I compiled enough proof of criminal neglect, conspiracy and negligent homicide..." Her voice cut through the hum of desire vibrating from his core, "Along with witnesses who promised to testify in exchange for immunity, that the case was reopened by the police. The frat guys responsible were convicted of second-degree murder and members of the fraternity council and university hierarchy were charged with conspiracy to conceal a crime."

He blinked slowly, staring at her mouth while his

mind played mental catch-up to her words. Charged... murder...convicted...

His heart lifted, and a smiled tugged his cheek. "You got them? You found the evidence needed and got Sean justice?"

Her grin was rife with satisfaction and pride. "I did."

The joy that blossomed in his chest, the relief he felt knowing she'd won her battle with injustice was a balm to his own edginess and dissatisfaction. Something he might call hope squeezed into the ragged edges of his discontent and gave him more peace than he'd known in many months.

He leaned into her, stealing a kiss, and whispered, "You're amazing!"

She blinked in surprise, then smiled. "Thank you." Wrapping an arm around his neck, she held him close for another searing kiss, one he felt to his marrow.

But when she pulled back from the earth-shaking kiss, she was frowning.

"Erin?" Again he brushed her unruly curls away from her face. "What?"

"I had a moral victory, but...nothing can ever bring Sean back." She heaved a cocoa-scented sigh. "And I miss him every day."

Zane slid closer to her, framing her mournful face between his hands. "I'm so sorry. A grief like that... Well, I just—" He wanted to say something comforting and profound, but the truth was he barely knew what to do with his own feelings.

Piper was always quick to point out how out-of-touch he, the left-brained geek, was with his feelings. Emotions were, in fact, something of a foreign language to him and a constant source of frustration. If he were honest, strong emotions scared him. He tried to avoid them, when possible.

And so now, in the face of her deep grief, he redirected the conversation, because the topic of personal loss left him feeling raw and disturbingly off balance. "Did you know before all that happened that you wanted to be a journalist? I mean, you certainly showed your investigative skills in uncovering the truth about what happened to your brother."

She lowered her gaze and drew her bottom lip in between her teeth for a moment then nodded. "Yeah, you could say the work I did to bring my brother's killers to justice shaped my career path." She raised her chin and regarded him with soft eyes. "Now it's your turn. Tell me something about you."

"Me? I'm boring. I thought we established that the other day. I'm a rancher through and through. An open book. Nothing to see, people. Move along."

"Hmm," she hummed, a doubtful lift to her eyebrow. "Everyone has secrets. I told you about my darkest hour. Do really think I'm gonna buy that you have nothing titillating beneath your protective layers?"

He snorted. "Titillating?"

"It's a word. Look it up."

"I know it's a word. It's just not a word anyone ever applied to me."

"Indulge me." She leaned back against the sofa cushions and propped her feet in his lap.

Zane swallowed hard. Somehow, having her socked feet inches from his groin was the sexiest thing to happen to him in months, maybe years. He wrapped his fingers around her toes and dug his thumbs into the arches of her feet. An erotic moan rolled from deep in her chest.

"C'mon, cowboy. Tell me something no one else knows about you."

He concentrated on rubbing her soles and searched his memory. "Well…best I can come up with isn't a secret from the world, just my family. Well, my siblings."

"Oh, do tell!" She tapped the tips of her fingers together like a greedy gangster.

"In high school, I joined the debate team."

She stared at him with a blank face. "And?"

"And nothing. I didn't want my brother and sister to know I'd done anything as geeky as the debate team—"

"Hey! I was on the debate team! It's not geeky!"

He shot her a dubious look. "For a high school quarterback, first baseman and weekend ruffie, the debate team is definitely geeky."

"Ruffie?"

He nodded. "Rodeo term. A risk-taker."

"You? A risk-taker?"

His hands stilled on her feet. "That surprises you? We are opening an adventure ranch. Josh isn't the only one who enjoys the high-adrenaline stuff. Back in high school, I rode some of the meanest bulls in the area."

"Huh." She twirled a wisp of her hair around a finger. "And now? Are you still a bull rider?"

Zane shrugged. "Not in a while. No time for it."

She nodded thoughtfully. "So you hid the debate team from your family…"

"Yep." He moved his fingers to rub her heels. "I was already the butt of enough nerd jokes because of my study habits and grades. I didn't need to fuel that fire."

"Next question…"

He sighed. "Erin."

"What would you say is your biggest fear, Mr. Ruffie?

If mean bulls and high-adrenaline sports don't scare you, then what does?"

He twisted his mouth in thought. "Probing interviews? Relentless, uncomfortable questions?"

"Very funny."

"I'm serious." He arched an eyebrow. "Are we done here?"

She fell silent, not conceding, but not pressing him for further answers, either. Turning her head, she stared into the fire with a thoughtful moue molding her mouth.

And though she didn't push, her question nagged him. What did he fear? Probing questions, sure. No lie there. But, if he were honest with himself, something he supposed he could call fear had been an underlying stress in his life for months. He couldn't escape the cloud of worry that... What? What was it exactly that haunted him?

"Loss," he muttered aloud, surprising himself.

She met his gaze, her green eyes gentle and understanding.

He nodded, more certain of his answer. "Losing."

She tipped her head a bit. "Competitions? Your identity?"

He dragged in a deep breath, analyzing the tension that had plagued him recently, despite the knot in his gut such soul-searching caused him. "That stuff bothers me but... I meant losing things I care about. Things...I love. People." His voice sounded thick, and he cleared his throat. "The ranch."

"Home and family." She nodded. "I get that." She bit her bottom lip. "Me, too. Especially since losing Sean. I know now how much it hurts."

His hands tightened on her foot. He exhaled harshly.

"Yeah." He leveled a hard look at her. "Can we find a happy subject to discuss now?"

"Of course. Please!"

He quirked a half grin of relief at her and pushed her feet to the floor as he scooted to her.

She took his hand, wrapped her fingers around his. Squeezed. "Thank you. For sharing that with me."

A warm, tingling sluiced through him from her touch, but it was completely unlike the erotic pleasure he'd experienced when she'd massaged his feet. This new sensation balled in his chest and stirred a tender ache, a fullness, a warmth in his chest. Sympathy? Compassion? Affection?

He considered it an achievement that he recognized the shift in his mood and the subtle changes in his attitude toward Erin. For him, that was enough, without analyzing the feeling too carefully.

He saw her wince, frown, and he asked, "What?"

She tucked her foot under her as she moved to face him more fully. "I shouldn't have gone off about Sean like that. I spoiled the mood. And we were having a nice evening, too."

"Don't apologize. I asked about your family. Blame me."

"You couldn't have known." She toyed idly with a button on his shirt and gave her head a small shake. Raising her gaze, she infused her expression with forced cheer. "Anyway… I also have a younger sister. Kelly. She's in grad school at Stanford. Bio-technology. She got the lion's share of brains in our family."

He acknowledged the tidbit with a nod. "So… Sean, Erin and Kelly. I'm guessing your family is Irish?"

She laughed, and the sound bubbled inside him like

carbonation, lifting his mood. "Guilty. On my mom's side. We kids were all named for maternal grandparents or great-aunts."

He canted his head to the side. "And your dad's family didn't feel left out?"

"Hey, we're all Palmers because of his side," she said, chuckling. "He was happy with that."

"And when you marry and change your last name?"

She gave him a haughty look. "Who says I'll marry? Or that I'd change my name if I did?"

Zane blinked, more unsettled by her response than he could explain or wanted to admit. "You don't plan to marry?"

She shrugged. "Who knows? I'm not opposed to marriage if the right guy comes along. I was just yanking your chain for assuming I would and that doing so automatically meant I'd change my name."

"So you're a feminist?"

"I didn't say that, either." She gave him a wry grin. "I'm just disputing your assumptions and clichéd generalizations."

Zane sat taller and squared his shoulders. "Ouch." Then twisting his mouth, he added, "And touché…"

He studied the spark that lit her eyes as she debated him, and he acknowledged that their conversation was invigorating. He liked the way she challenged him, not allowing him to get away with stale, lazy reasoning.

As he leaned toward her and brushed his lips against hers, all the reasons he'd had for caution with Erin and keeping his attraction to her in check fled on a wave of heat. Desire pounded through him, blinding him to everything except Erin.

Chapter 11

Zane needed her kiss, this moment. Needed to lay her down on the couch and feel her body pressed fully against his. He acted on the impulse, easing her back onto the cushions and wrapping himself around her as he nuzzled her neck and traced a tendon toward her shoulder.

She hummed her approval and lifted her chin to provide better access. Her legs hooked around his, and she arched her body in a way that made her hips grind against his groin. His body crackled and popped like the fire in the grate. He'd been celibate a long time, uninterested in empty one-night stands or hollow relationships based solely on sex.

At the corner of his brain, the question prodded him concerning what kind of relationship he thought he was starting with Erin. Was he recklessly dismissing his stance on casual sex for her? With firm resolve, he shut that line of thought down. He didn't want to think or to analyze. When he was with Erin, all he wanted to do was to act, savor, steal a few moments of pleasure and escape.

He stroked his hands down the length of her body and reveled in the purr of contentment that rolled from her throat. Returning his lips to hers, he kissed her deeply, slowly, thoroughly. When she tugged at the back of his shirt, he paused from exploring her mouth only long enough to pull the tail of his Henley from his jeans. A jolt like an electric shock shot through him when she insinuated her hands under the fabric to stroke his skin.

Taking her lead, he fumbled with the top buttons of her blouse, exposing more of her creamy skin and a satin bra. The anticipation and fever in his blood built quickly as he explored more and more of her. The hollow of her throat, a bared shoulder, the swell of a breast…

"Zane…" she whispered breathlessly when he exposed a rosy nipple and covered it with his mouth.

He teased the taut bud with his tongue, and she gasped. Released a fluttering sigh. The pulse of her warm breath tickled his scalp, stirred his hair. And then her fingers were there, tunneling through his short-cropped hair, curling against his head and massaging the base of his skull as she writhed beneath him.

He wanted to be patient, to relish and take things slowly, but something wild and hungry inside him compelled him to hurry. A primal need to have her, to be inside her, to stake his claim to her clawed at him, and he became less careful as he tore at her clothes.

She tugged at his in return, and they stripped to panties and briefs in a frenzy of hands and kisses and moans of satisfaction.

He paused briefly to admire the glow of the firelight on her nakedness. "Beautiful…" he murmured. "You're so beautiful, Erin."

Instead of smiling, she furrowed her brow.

"What?" he asked, kissing the wrinkle at the bridge of her nose.

"I just—" She stopped abruptly, covering his hands with hers when he hooked his thumbs in the delicate material of her last piece of clothing. "Stop."

He blinked, certain he'd heard her wrong in the frantic beat of desire that drummed in his ears. "Erin?"

She squeezed her eyes shut and pushed on his chest. "This…is a mistake. I can't…" She huffed her dejection, and he felt the tension that drew her body tight. "We shouldn't. I mean, I want to, but—"

Disappointment and frustration slapped hard as he levered away from her, but he heard her no and honored it. But it was damned difficult. "What's wrong?"

"I'm sorry. I want to. I want *you*, but I—"

"Is there someone else?" The idea soured his gut and filled him with a poisonous jealousy. "You told me earlier you weren't dating anyone."

"No, I'm not." She shook her head as she sat up and pushed her arms in the sleeves of her blouse.

"Then what?"

"It's just…sleeping with you would be…a conflict of interest." She held the blouse closed over her bare breasts with one hand while she raked her curls away from her face with the other. "It'd be professionally out of line."

He arched an eyebrow. He couldn't say what answer he'd thought he might get, but her citing her journalistic standards was not at all what he'd expected. At the same time, he respected her wish to honor her professional ethics, her ability to place responsibility over personal pleasure.

He rolled to a seated position and swiped his shirt off the floor. "I understand."

"Zane…" She wrapped her arms around herself, and she looked so vulnerable and sorrowful, his heart stuttered. "I didn't mean to play the tease," Erin whispered. "I'm sorry if—"

"No apologies needed." He stood and stepped into his jeans, but couldn't zip them up yet. His body was still too primed, too flushed with anticipation and heat. "Bad timing."

She sat taller, her expression brightening slightly. "Yeah. Maybe when I finish, my…*article*…" She seemed to struggle with the word and glanced away, and it gave him pause. Clearing her throat, she continued. "Maybe later we could revisit…" She waved a hand between them.

His pulse gave a kick. He liked the idea of a later with Erin more than he should.

"Yeah," he said, shoving his feet into his boots without his socks. "Maybe later." He bent at the waist and kissed the top of her rumpled curls, trying not to think about how her hair had become so mussed. "Good night, Erin."

"Wait!" She caught his wrist. "You don't have to go just because—"

"Yeah, I do. It's late. Rancher-late anyway." He tugged free of her grip and jammed his hat on his head as he headed for the door. "I've got an early morning tomorrow."

"All right, then." She heaved a sighed and bit her bottom lip as she sent him a wistful look from the couch. "Good night, Zane."

He had to muster all his strength and conviction to turn and walk out. She looked so damn heartbroken and alluring as she lifted a hand to wave goodbye. But he tore himself away from the kiss-swollen pink lips and tumble of dark brown coils framing her face and stalked out into the frigid December night.

He blew into his hands to warm them as he walked across the ranch yard to his house. He knew what would keep him awake tonight. One word. *Later.*

Erin paid a visit to the family's house the next morning to spend some time with Dave as he recouped after his surgery. Melissa met her at the front door, greeting her with warmth, welcome and an apology. "I'm afraid I haven't been a good hostess to you. Between time at the hospital with Dave earlier in the week and a bunch of last-minute items I'm helping Kate with for the wedding…well, I don't know some days if I'm coming or going!"

"Not a problem." Erin hung her coat on the coat tree in the foyer and gave Melissa a dismissive shake of her head and a smile. "Zane and the rest of the family have been very accommodating. And the last thing I want to be, when you're so busy, is in your way."

Erin explained the purpose of her visit, and Melissa pressed a hand to her chest. "Oh, bless you! I know Dave's felt cooped up, even though we've been trying to keep him company. This way." She waved for Erin to follow her. As they started down the hall, Zeke and Sadie raced past them, the felines causing a surprisingly loud thundering of paws and claws on hardwood as they ran down the hall. Melissa pulled up short as the cats charged past, and Erin stumbled to a stop, narrowly avoiding tripping over the felines darting by.

"Holy cow!" Erin said, laughing. "That was... Wow."

"Yes." Melissa rolled her eyes. "The cats are best friends now, and they turn the hall into the Grand Prix daily, finishing with bouts of wrestling."

No sooner had Melissa finished explaining than the cats raced back the other way and into the bedroom at the end of the hall. They heard an "Oof!" and an "Ow!" and Melissa hustled down to the door with a grimace. "Dave, are you all right?"

Erin caught up and found Dave, sitting on the bed, propped by pillows, with the TV across the room turned on but muted. His casted leg was resting on a large wedge pillow. On the floor, the fluffy brown cat and the smaller black cat were tussling and bapping each other.

"I'm fine. The hairballs made the bed their landing strip and didn't mind running into my leg in the process." Dave sat straighter when he spotted Erin. "Oh, hello, yoga breather."

"Yoga breather?" Melissa gave her an odd look.

She chuckled. "Yes. Better than a mouth breather, huh?

I just showed him how to stay calm when he was injured by focusing on his breathing."

"No 'just' about it." Dave repositioned himself to face Erin more fully. "You were very helpful and a pleasant distraction. Thank you."

"Erin would like to talk with you, if you don't mind? For the article she's writing about the ranch," Melissa said, sidestepping when the two cats took off down the hall again at full throttle. The tinkling of glass and tiny bells drifted down the hall, and Melissa groaned. "They're in the Christmas tree again. I'll leave you two to chat and go save my ornaments from feline destruction. Call if you need anything, Dave."

Melissa pulled the door closed as she left, and Erin took a seat at the foot of the bed. "How are you feeling?"

"Not bad if I don't try to move my leg." He rattled the bottle of pills on the nightstand. "But my pain pills run out in a couple days. Ask me again on Sunday."

She pulled an appropriately sympathetic face, then clicked open her pen. "Are you up to a short interview?"

"If it keeps you here for a little while." He winked at her.

She arched one eyebrow. "Does Helen know how much you flirt with other women?"

He looked mildly chastened but not entirely repentant. "She knows it's only flirting. Though it does irritate her sometimes."

"I'd wager it more than irritates her. If you really care about her—"

He bobbed his head. "I plan to propose on New Year's Eve. Or *had* planned to before this happened." He waved a hand to his leg.

"Why can't you still?"

"Aw, it messes up the romantic plans I had to take her to dinner then hike up to the lookout over the valley where we had our first kiss."

"Speaking as a woman, I think she'll still be thrilled with a proposal, even if you can't hike. Give her the ring at dinner. Hide it in a glass of champagne or some cake or…anything."

He frowned. "The real problem is I don't know if I'm gonna be able to work at the ranch anymore. Doc says the break was bad. I can't ride for at least a few months, and then I have to get therapy in order to walk on it again. It could be six months or more before I'm any use to the ranch. They'll replace me for sure. And I don't blame 'em. They can barely pay me a living wage as it is now. They sure won't be payin' for me to sit on my duff."

Erin bit her bottom lip as she thought about his predicament a moment. "The McCalls strike me as a loyal lot. I'd bet when you can work again, they'll re-hire you."

"And dump whoever they hired to replace me? Come spring, the herd will need tending whether I'm there or not." He pitched his volume lower, adding, "I already overhead Michael making calls to place an ad about hiring a new hand." He aimed his thumb to the wall he shared with Michael's office, and his expression soured. "After everything I've done for this place…" He sighed before adding, "I guess I'm learning the hard way that I'm replaceable."

Erin drew a breath, prepared to defend the McCalls, but caught the words on her tongue. She had no right to speak for the family, and certainly was ill-advised to bias the interview with her softening feelings toward the family…and Zane in particular.

A memory of their tangled bodies, Zane's hands stroking her, his smoldering kisses, caused a flash of wanton heat to wash through her. She struggled for a breath of composure and cleared her throat, almost missing Dave's next comment.

"Should have known that after they tossed Karl to the curb last year," he said with a frown, his voice still quiet.

A prickle of unease chased down her back as she tried to remember if Michael had mentioned anyone by that name. "Karl who?"

"Townsen. A guy who used to work here as a hand."

The name didn't ring a bell, but she did recollect Michael had told her about a hand who had left on his own terms and amiably. Could this Karl be the same man Michael mentioned?

"He was accused of stealing from Michael's office," Dave continued, "and Piper fired him on the spot. Family never blinked." He set his mouth in a grim line, clearly unhappy about that fact. "From what I hear, Karl went to work for another ranch in the area and told them about the plans for an adventure ranch." Dave scoffed. "The other ranch threw together a competing adventure ranch and is in business today. A sub-par outfit by all accounts, but it sure ticked off Josh and Zane."

"I imagine so," she said, while wondering just how ticked off Karl had been. And why Michael had mischaracterized the hand's dismissal.

"Was Karl Townsen fired or did he leave on his own?" Erin asked without preface when she found Michael in the stable a few hours later.

Michael hesitated before answering, blinking and scanning the vicinity as if checking to see if anyone was in earshot.

"There's no one else here," she assured him. "I looked as I came in."

He sighed. "Has your investigation led you to him as the culprit?"

She folded her arms over her chest, both in frustration and warding off the cold. "No, because until this morning when I talked to Dave, I was unaware there was a Karl Townsen, aka fired and disgruntled ranch hand.

Did you not think the nature of his firing was worthy of mention?"

Michael's brow furrowed. "You told me you wanted only facts, not personal impressions because of bias."

She shot him a dubious look. "There was more to the circumstances of his firing than you let on."

Michael squared his shoulders, his expression serious and concerned. "Was there? I wasn't aware that he'd been disgruntled when he left. He and I had a frank conversation. He swore he'd not stolen anything. I gave him the benefit of the doubt and offered to rehire him after Piper let him go. He said he'd already gotten a new position, but to be sure there were no hard feelings, I gave him two weeks' severance pay. I honestly thought he left on good terms."

"Not according to Dave. And I hear he fed information to his new employer about the idea for the adventure company and the other ranch copied the idea."

He twisted his mouth in disagreement. "Not exactly. While the base of operation was at the ranch Karl went to, the rival adventure business was started and funded by Gill Carver."

Erin tensed. "The banker? Gill the Ass? The guy that has been a thorn in Zane's side since he was a kid?"

Michael frowned and nodded. "The same. But, again, you said facts only, and not my personal views. You wanted to form your own opinions about people. But since you mentioned it, Gill has always been a nasty little cuss, looking for ways to stick it to my children."

"Does Gill own the ranch Karl went to?"

"No. He went to the Rockin' J. That's Harold Jackson's place. I've no doubt Gill's bank holds the mortgage." He held up a finger. "But...I have no proof of that." He heaved a sigh. "You think Karl is relevant to the sabotage investigation, don't you?"

"Could be."

He set aside the rake he'd been using to muck one of the stalls and shucked off his work gloves. "I had dismissed him in my own mind because the vandalism started a good year or more before Karl left the Double M. The sheriff's department talked to him, like they did all our employees, after each incident, and Karl always had a solid alibi." He lifted one eyebrow. "But that's why you asked me not to give my personal take, huh?"

"Based on what I'm learning, I'd say he is a top contender. Gill, too, for that matter, alibi or not." She rubbed a hand on her leg as she thought. "If Dave is right about Karl's attitude when he left, I should at least talk to him." She paused before adding, "From now on, tell me everything, no matter how trivial it may seem to you. I need full disclosure from you if I'm going to do my job."

Michael gave her a chastened nod and frown. "Understood." He ducked his head, his brow creasing as he added, "Do you have any idea how disturbing it has been for me, not only dealing with the practical and financial fallout of the sabotage, but because of the way it has made me doubt the people I love most? It kills me to even think of the people I trust, my family, friends and long-term employees, as being deceitful or vindictive toward me."

He rubbed his chest and leaned heavily against the nearest wall.

Knowing Zane's father was at high risk for a heart attack because of his high blood pressure and a previous cardiac event, she hated causing him any further stress, but they needed to reach an understanding. "I can understand that. But you have to be completely transparent about all aspects of the ranch history if I'm going to find the truth. And find the person behind the vandalism."

He nodded slowly. "I hear you. I never meant to mislead you. I honestly believed I'd represented Karl fairly." He paused, adding, "I'm also sorry to hear he was unhappy when he left. That's news to me."

"I need to talk to Karl. I need to cover that base. How do I reach him? What ranch did you say he went to?"

"The Jackson's place. The Rockin' J." Michael sighed. "I've known Harold Jackson for forty years. He's good people."

Erin tugged out her notepad and wrote down the name of the ranch. "I'll let you know what I learn."

"Erin?" Zane called as he stepped inside the guesthouse and cast his glance around the empty living room. He closed the front door against the December chill and noises from the ranch yard and listened. "Anybody home?"

The small table in the breakfast nook was littered with food wrappers, a water bottle and scattered notepads and crumpled paper wads. In the middle of the mess, her laptop sat open with a word-processing document glowing on the screen.

Zane lifted a corner of his mouth. The detritus of the writer at work.

She couldn't have gone far if the laptop hadn't gone to power-saving mode yet. Although he couldn't say what her settings were. Maybe she let the screen stay lit for hours.

Shoving aside the thought, he set his Stetson on the back of the couch and moved to the end of the hall that led to the guest rooms. Her bedroom door was closed. "Erin?"

When he moved a few steps further down the hall, he heard the unmistakable sound of a shower running and a soft humming. He grinned and perked his ears. Yep, she was humming "The Christmas Song." He was transported back to the top of his truck, the glow of holiday lights from the spruce, and the floral scent of Erin's hair surrounding him as he'd kissed her and held her close. On the heels of that memory came one of sharing hot chocolate and having his feet rubbed by his own magic elf. And the heated kisses, the tangling of their bodies that followed.

Later...

That tantalizing promise of future pleasure sent a burst of sparks through his blood.

A thunk sounded down the hall, calling his attention back to Erin. The shower. Had she fallen? His heart drummed harder when he considered the possibility. But her humming continued, so...more likely she'd dropped the soap or her shampoo bottle. When he conjured an image of her bending to collect the lost item, his muscles tightened, tingled, and his groin throbbed. He could picture her bare skin, slick with suds, and her naked body, pink from the hot water. The key words being *bare... naked*. His mouth dried, and his throat felt thick.

He had two choices. Strip off his clothes and join her, testing her promise of *later* and ensuring he involved his heart with a woman he wasn't completely sure he trusted. Or walk away now and preserve his sanity.

His hand moved to the buttons of his coat. Hesitated. If Josh could throw caution to the wind and enjoy sex for sex's sake, why couldn't he? Zane twisted his mouth as he mentally amended. Obviously his brother didn't do that now that he was engaged to Kate. Josh was faithful. In love. Honorable.

The shower cut off, and Zane exhaled deeply, giving himself a mental kick in the shin. Erin had taken sex out of the equation until she finished her article, and he had to respect her wishes. Plowing his hand through his hair, he turned back to the front room, deciding he'd wait in the living room for Erin.

Shrugging out of his coat, he draped it over the sofa, next to his hat, as he strolled toward the kitchenette for a bottle of something to bathe his dry mouth. *Bathe...*

He huffed his frustration. *Get your mind off Erin and her shower, pal.*

Zane bent at the waist to peer into the small refrigerator and selected a soda.

He should let Erin know he was there, waiting in the living room, so she didn't come out of the bedroom underdressed.

Or not. A wicked, teasing grin twisted his lips before he resolutely dismissed the notion of lurking in the living room without her knowledge. Popping the tab, he tipped the can up for a swallow as he strolled back past the table where her laptop *still* showed the open document.

He rolled his eyes. He *could* open settings and set the power-saver for her. He hesitated by the laptop and groaned. No, no, no. Too intrusive and controlling. He had to resist being *that* guy.

But he could recommend the change to her when she came out. Even offer to set it up. Right?

He took another sip of his drink and almost choked when he noticed the words on the screen. Wiping his mouth with the back of his hand, he peered down at the document Erin had open. The heading read *Notes on McCall Sabotage Investigation.*

Heart thumping, Zane set his soda aside and lowered himself into the chair in front of the laptop. He shouldn't read it. He needed to avert his eyes, close the laptop... something. A moment of guilt tickled him even as his eyes moved back to the screen.

Interviews with ranch employees and family members. Plenty of opportunity. Any motives?

"What the hell?" he muttered, scanning further down the page on the screen.

Roy Summers—drinking problem. Went to rehab. Relapse?

Dave Giblan—opportunity. Could he have grudge?

Brady Summers—partner in adventure biz. Illogical to sabotage his own interests.

Michael McCall—police suspect insurance fraud. Could Melissa be involved?

Confusion battled with anger, and he tried to keep his cool as his brain scrabbled to make sense of what he was seeing. Maybe this wasn't something Erin wrote, but a document she'd gathered from someone else for her research, he rationalized. But what did these notes have to do with her feature on the adventure tours?

Shifting his attention to the scattered handwritten pages on the table, he picked up a sheet with names of his family members and ranch employees with circles and arrows connecting them with side notes such as "has alibi" and "no witness" in the margins. He couldn't deny what he was seeing. Erin was researching the sabotage, digging deep and looking to pin the blame on someone at the ranch. Fury slammed into him, blurring his vision. Hurt sliced his chest, the betrayal opening a gash through his soul. He gaped at the swimming words on the screen.

His hand fisted on the papers he held, crumpling them. His jaw tightened, his back teeth grinding so hard a bolt of pain streaked through his head. Anger roiled in his gut, causing his whole body to tremble, and he had to take several deep breaths to regain some control. Slowly he began sorting through the pages of notes on the table. He no longer cared that he was invading her privacy. The mounting evidence of her lies and treachery justified his actions, he told himself.

A loud gasp called his attention across the room.

Erin gave him a startled grin. "Zane, I…" Her smile fell and her brow creased as her eyes darkened. "What are you doing here?"

She had a towel around her neck that she used to pat the ends of her wet hair, which curled around her bare shoulders. She wore jeans and her bra but little else.

He rose to his feet, his strength renewed by the adrenaline and fury that pulsed through him. "Who are you and what are you doing at our ranch?"

Her gaze shifted to the papers and computer before returning to his face. Her expression reflected a kaleidoscope of emotions. "You snooped through my files?"

"Answer the question," he repeated, his voice low and deadly.

She blinked and squared her shoulders. "What are

you doing in here? Do you make a habit of breaking into women's living quarters?"

"This guesthouse belongs to my family. I'll enter it whenever I damn well please."

She scoffed, and crossing her arms over her chest, she snapped, "Well, thanks for the heads-up on that!"

"You have one last chance to answer me before I toss you out on your lying ass! Who are you, and why are you here?"

Something that might have been remorse flickered over her countenance before she firmed her jaw and lifted her chin defiantly. "You had no right to snoop in my—"

"Answer me!" he roared, and the venom in his tone even surprised him. He curled his fingers into his palms and drew a shuddering breath, fighting not to let his frustration, pain and anger swamp him.

Erin glared at him silently for several tense seconds. Slowly her rigid stance melted and moisture filled her eyes. "If I tell you, you have to promise to keep it a secret. You can't tell—"

He snorted his disdain for her requirements. "You have some nerve. I'll promise no such thing. You'll be lucky if I don't call the sheriff to investigate you!"

Her arms dropped to her sides, and her spine stiffened. "For what? Doing my job? That's not a crime."

"Your job?" Zane shook his head and curled up his lip. "You're no travel writer." He grabbed a handful of her notes and threw them at her. "And this is no promotional feature article on McCall Adventures."

She drew a slow breath, her gaze holding his as she said calmly, "You're right. I'm not a travel writer. There is no article. I'm sorry I lied to you."

He shook his head, snarling softly, "Leave."

"Zane, wait. Let me explain."

He took a step toward her, his finger jabbed at her in accusation. "Get your things, and get the hell off our ranch."

Although her eyes widened at his threatening gesture, she didn't back down. "Will you give me a minute to explain? I'm here because your father asked me to come. He hired me to investigate the things that have been happening, the vandalism and murky accidents."

Zane froze. His pulse thundered in his ears. "What?"

"I'm a private investigator, and your father hired me to get to the bottom of the sabotage. He didn't know who he could trust, so he asked me to keep the truth about my work to myself for the time being."

"My father told you to *lie* to me and my siblings? You want me to believe that my father didn't trust his own family to know the truth?" He raised a hand and angled his head, his eyes narrowed in suspicion. "Assuming what you're telling me is the truth and not another one of your lies."

"Ask your father. He'll tell you."

"Oh, I plan to ask him. Meantime, pack up," he said tightly. "I want you gone by tonight."

She shook her head and folded her arms over her chest. "Maybe you didn't hear me before when I said *your father* hired me. Only he can fire me. I leave when I finish my investigation or when he tells me to go. Not before."

Zane jammed a hand through his hair and exhaled through his teeth. The ache in his chest grew sharper as all the implications of her confession came into focus. "Has *anything* you told me since we met been the truth?

Or have the last few days been nothing but a giant false-fest for you?"

Her shoulders drooped. "Zane, I said I was sorry."

"So it was *all* lies? Is that what you're saying?" A sick feeling balled in his gut. Something heavier and more ominous than the dishonesty surrounding her reason for being there clawed his heart, choked him. "What about us? The kisses, the private talks? Was any of it real for you?"

Her throat worked as she swallowed. "Zane, please…"

"Was seducing me part of your plan to get information? Am I one of your suspects or just a tool to manipulate for the investigation?"

"It's not like that," she said, her voice thin and shaking.

She took a few tentative steps toward him, and, straightening his back, he held up his hand as if warning her away. Sharp, icy spikes stabbed his lungs as he said, "I trusted you."

She huffed a humorless laugh. "Did you? Really?" She waved her hand toward the scattered papers. "The evidence would say otherwise."

Her assertion twisted inside him. If he were honest with himself, he *had* clung to misgivings about her. But not over her truthfulness. His doubts had been regarding her feelings, his wariness over letting himself follow his heart with her or fight his attraction based on practicality. He'd opened himself to her, shared his pain and his fears, grieved with her over—

His pulse kicked. "What about the sob story you gave me about your brother dying? Was that true or a ploy to get me to open up to you?"

Her body went rigid, and the pain that filled her eyes told him immediately that he'd crossed a line. He had his answer even before she said through gritted teeth, "Although I have *sobbed* over the loss of him, my brother's murder is no story."

She took a step toward him, eyes narrowed. "It did, indeed, happen, and I took it upon myself to find the truth when the university and the fraternity conspired to protect chapter charters, alumni funding and their negligent asses over justice."

Her eyes puddled with unshed tears. She aimed a trembling finger at him as she stalked closer. "I am what I am today because of Sean's murder. I learned quickly that the world wasn't fair, and no one handed you happiness. You have to fight for what is right. You have to *find* happiness in the moment, because tomorrow is never promised. You count your blessings rather than your troubles, and you never take the people you love for granted." She poked him in the chest with her finger. Her face was flushed, and her eyes flashed with turbulent emotion. "That is my truth. My life. Sean's legacy to me."

Oh, yeah... Erin was thoroughly pissed at him and for good reason. He regretted his callous remark, yet the raw honesty of her response was as real as it got.

Real spoke to him. *Real* cut through the clutter. *Real* stirred a bittersweet ache in his chest that stole his breath.

He lost a huge piece of his heart to her in that moment. He was still mad as hell over her lies, still had to sort through this deception with his father, but her candor, her passion, moved him in a part of his soul he'd fiercely protected for most of his life.

And that scared the hell out of him.

Despite his head warning him about falling for someone he barely knew, someone who lived far away, someone with the potential to break his heart, the physical pull between them had won. His intrinsic attraction to her charm and intelligence, her warmth and beauty, her sass and humor had shouted down the voice of reason and caution. He'd already formed feelings for her, even in a few short days.

"Now, if you don't mind," she said tightly, "I'm freezing my ass off. I'm going to dress and dry my hair. You know the way out. Please use it." She spun around and marched toward the hall to the bedrooms.

Jaw rigid, Zane stalked to the door and slammed it behind him as he left. His heart thrashed, and his gut was knotted. He had no idea where to start making sense of his feelings for Erin and her deception. But he definitely had some questions for his father.

Erin stared at the blinking cursor on her laptop screen. She'd intended to work most of the afternoon, reviewing her notes and planning who to interview next. But her mind, her heart, were not with her. She couldn't get Zane's betrayed expression out of her mind. Nor could she shake the feeling she'd lost something valuable this afternoon. An opportunity. A relationship with the potential to change her life. She hadn't felt this despondent and at loose ends since she'd received the news of Sean's death.

A knock on the guesthouse door interrupted her self-pitying musing. She scraped the chair back and hurried to answer it. Her pulse leaped when she found Zane waiting on the other side of the door, his hat literally in his hands. She was too emotionally exhausted to go another round with him and was prepared to send him away, but his hangdog expression stopped her.

"Can I come in?" he asked.

"The place belongs to you. I hear that means you can come in anytime you want." She stood back and swept an arm toward the living room.

He scowled in response to her snark. "Erin…"

Remorse flooded her and she said, "I'm sorry," at the same time he did.

He cracked a small grin. "See? No woo-woo involved. Sometimes you just speak at the same time as the other person."

She shook her head. His lighthearted banter filled her with hope. "This doesn't count. Josh says it happens all the time to you two. That's woo-woo."

He snorted his disagreement and stepped inside.

Erin closed the door against the blowing snow, and the room seemed somehow smaller with him there. She felt a prickly heat crawl through her, and she lingered at the door, uncertain what to do next.

He remained silent for a long moment before murmuring, "I was wrong to snoop. I apologize."

She nodded. "Forgiven." Swallowing hard, she moved further into the room, stopping inches from him. The impulse to touch him was strong, but she curled her fingers into her palm, waiting to get a better read on his mood and where their relationship stood. "For what it's worth, I hated every minute that I was lying to you. I don't condone deceit, but your father was adamant. He didn't know how far his circle of trust extended and decided that keeping his hiring me quiet was the best move in the long run."

"That's what he said, too."

"So you talked to him." She made it a statement more than a question, but he nodded in answer. She released a slow breath, holding his bright blue gaze. "Anyway…

I am sorry that my part in it hurt you. I asked for your trust and was breaking it at the same time. That was... wrong. No matter how I justify it or what the reason."

He gave a small nod, but his expression remained dubious. "Honesty is very important to me."

"Me, too...actually." She gave him a rueful smile. "Despite evidence to the contrary."

He scrubbed a hand over his face as he exhaled harshly. "So...going forward—" he paused and a muscle in his jaw twitched as his penetrating gaze locked on hers "—we're straightforward with each other?"

She did touch him then. She had to or she'd go nuts. Cupping her hand around his cheek, she nodded enthusiastically. "Yes. Please. I'd like nothing more."

With a somber sigh, he curled his fingers around her palm and removed her hand. "While I can understand why you lied to me, can maybe even forgive it, that doesn't mean I've forgotten it." His eyes were as cool as his tone. "Things have...changed for me."

Erin dropped her hand to her side and stepped back. Pain, as if she'd been kicked by a bull, seized her chest. Had her promise to keep the terms Zane's father had laid out for the job cost her Zane's affection?

He cleared his throat and asked, "So, in your investigation, your interviews, have you found anything? Have you discovered anything we've missed?"

His demeanor was all-business. As if he hadn't just pulled the rug out from under her. Hadn't just shattered her newly formed feelings for him like an icicle fallen from the eaves. "Well..." The intensity of his gaze distracted her and, even in the face of his dismissal of her, stirred a pulsing heat in her core. She clenched her hands and glanced at her laptop to regain her train of thought, to loosen the squeeze of emotion in her throat. "Yes and no. You're welcome to read my notes."

"What do you mean yes and no? What have you learned?"

"Well, for starters…" She paused, feeling like a school tattletale. But uncovering ugly truths and reporting them to Michael was what she'd been hired to do. She'd convinced herself Zane was innocent of any wrongdoing, so what could it hurt to alert him to concerning issues around the ranch? Sighing, she blurted, "Roy is drinking again."

Zane frowned. "What? Are you sure?"

"Pretty sure. I've smelled it when I was in the truck with him, when I was talking with him in close quarters. And I'm guessing that the whiskey I saw in those cabinets—" she aimed her thumb at the kitchenette "—and later disappeared, was his. Remember I couldn't find it when we drank hot cocoa together a few nights ago?"

An odd combination of heat and regret passed over his countenance, and she knew exactly what he was remembering about that night, even before he whispered, "Hard to forget."

"Zane, everything that happened that night was real for me. No lies, no deception. Just me and—"

He shot a hand up, stopping her. "I'll look into Roy's drinking. Thanks for the heads-up." He shoved his hand back into his pocket. "What else have you found out?"

Clearly any further discussion of their feelings for each other was off the table. She'd cracked the hard shell Zane had created around his heart, but once wounded, he'd reinforced the layers of self-protection with concrete and steel.

Disappointment pinged her chest. Without meaning to or wanting to, had she burned her bridge with Zane?

She tucked a curl behind her ear, and the chill that seeped through her had as much to do with her lost connection to Zane as the draft in the cool guesthouse. She edged closer to her computer and straightened some of the paper files on the table. "I have a meeting set tonight with your dad to go over some of my notes. Why don't you join us?"

He jerked a nod. "I will."

She forced down the bubble of dejection filling her lungs and added, "The preview is that I've not found much. The most likely candidates by my estimation also have significant drawbacks."

Her comment clearly piqued his interest. "For example?"

She waved a hand. "Gill Carver makes no bones about his dislike of you. He's openly contemptuous but—"

"But he's been too public with his animosity toward us." He twisted his mouth, glumly. "You mentioned as much at the diner the other day."

She shrugged. "I'm just saying it seems illogical. If he's responsible for the sabotage, why would he draw attention to himself and his feud with you in public?"

"Point taken." He rubbed his cheek, and the stubble on his chin made a quiet scratching noise against his palm.

She remembered the feel of that five-o'clock shadow on her fingertips, the gentle abrasion as they'd kissed. She longed to curl against him on the couch again, to kiss his stern mouth until he smiled, to savor the warmth of his body next to hers...

"Who else is a candidate in your book?" He folded

his arms over his chest, his eyebrows dipping low in consternation. "Not anyone in the family."

She shook her head. "Not that I can determine."

He released a breath as if a weight had been lifted from him. "So who?"

"I haven't talked to Karl Townsen yet. Dave seemed to think he was more angry over his firing than your father had led me to believe. He's high on my list."

Zane furrowed his brow and seemed to ruminate on that prospect for a while. "The sheriff's talked to him already. He—"

"I know. I'm going over a lot of the same territory the sheriff's department has covered. But I still want to talk to him. See what vibe I get. See if his story has changed. See what he says when he's not talking to law enforcement."

Zane nodded. "Okay. I'll go with—"

"No." She smiled to soften her argument. "Thank you, but…I have a car, and I really think he'll be more open if you're not there."

He stared at her silently, his expression pained. She knew him well enough, even in their short acquaintance, to realize the shadows in his eyes were not because she'd rejected his accompanying her. The clouded-blue of his eyes bore into her heart. She hated knowing her deception was largely responsible for the hurt and distance between them.

Heaving a sigh, he shoved his hat on his head and turned for the door. "All right, then. Be careful. I'll see you tonight. What time are you meeting with my dad?"

"Seven."

With a nod, he opened the door and stepped out into the blowing snow. "See you at seven, then."

Chapter 12

Erin's interview with the fired hand proved fruitless. While he admitted having had some hard feelings about his firing, he corroborated Michael's story of a severance payment and claimed to have no ill will toward his former employer.

"What can you tell me about the competing adventure tours company you helped with last summer?" she asked.

He snorted a laugh. "That was just sour grapes for Gill Carver. An in-your-face to the McCalls. I doubt it'll run again next year. He lost money on the deal. Only reason I helped was the extra cash he paid me."

She twisted her mouth. "I see. Just how sour are Gill's grapes? Could he be connected to the vandalism out at the Double M the last couple years?"

Karl shrugged, a wad of chewing tobacco making his cheek bulge. "I don't know. Don't wanna guess." He gave her a hard look. "And before you get any ideas, I've told the sheriff everything I know about all that trouble. The vandalism started before I left, and I have solid alibis for everything that's happened since I left."

She raised both hands as if warding off an attack. "Hey, I didn't ask."

"But you were gonna. Weren't you?" He gave her an irritated look.

She sighed. "Well…maybe in some form. You have nothing to add to what you've told the sheriff? Nothing that'll help find the person responsible?"

He shrugged. "Nope. Frankly, I'm glad to be gone from the Double M. Michael's a good man, but I don't want to be on a sinking ship when all the lifeboats are gone."

Erin's heart squeezed. "And you think their lifeboats are gone?"

He shrugged again and spat tobacco on the ground. "Guess the auction later this week will determine that."

Karl's words haunted Erin as she watched the McCalls prepare to transport their heard to auction over the next few days. The tension level had ratcheted up as the date drew nearer and the family kept one eye on the weather forecast. Bad roads on their travel day could mean they missed their contracted sale date and money lost on the rental of the livestock trailer.

Zane stayed busy, helping bring the herd in from the fields, sorting out which cows would go to market, and seeing that all the ranch vehicles were properly prepped for the trip. Motel reservations near the sale barn, made weeks in advance, were double-checked and stock prices from other sales were monitored hourly.

"The whole year boils down to one paycheck from the price we get for our herd," Michael explained when Erin asked about his obsession with current prices. The day before the men were scheduled to leave, she'd found Michael in his office with Sadie on the floor by his chair patting his arm to get his attention.

Michael waved her in and motioned to a chair. Erin sat, cleared her throat and said, "If it's all right, I'd like to go with you when you take the herd to auction." She didn't know what she'd thought she'd learn about the sabotage on the trip, but knowing how important the one day was made her curious to experience this part of ranch life. Of Zane's life.

"Sure. Tag along. We may even find a job for you."

Sadie tapped Michael's elbow again with her white-toed paw and gave a tiny, kittenish meow. The McCall patriarch glanced at the cat and resumed scratching her head with a chuckle for the feline's persistence. But Michael's smile didn't erase the worry that shadowed his gaze.

"So...what happens if you can't make it to the auction because of weather or—" She didn't finish the question. The stricken look on Michael's face made her worry about his blood pressure.

"We can't miss sale day. Can*not*. Period." His tone was so grave, so determined, a shiver rippled through her.

"Is there anything I can do now to help?" she asked.

He nodded. "Pray."

"Zane, wait up!" Erin called across the ranch yard.

Zane's steps faltered, and, his heart in his throat, he glanced back at her. He'd managed to avoid Erin most of the last couple days, burying himself in the work of prepping for the trip to auction, but she'd never been far from his mind. *Get over it*, he told himself whenever he thought of what could have been. *Get over* her. She'd proven herself untrustworthy, breaking his heart just as he'd warned himself she would. The sooner he forgot about her and moved on with his life the better.

He acknowledged her summons with a nod as he headed into the garage to retrieve one of the ATVs. He wanted to make one last trip to check for strays in the far pasture. Call him obsessive, but they needed every single head of cattle sent to auction this year.

"Can we talk?" she called.

"About?"

"Cows. Turnips. Aliens. I don't care," she said as she approached. "I haven't seen much of you in the last day or two and—"

"That was intentional," he intoned flatly.

She hesitated. "Oh, so you're still mad at me?"

He lifted one eyebrow in reply and tugged open the door to the garage, stamping snow off his feet as he entered. He raised a hand toward the light switch…and paused, sniffing the air. Even over the odor of motor oil, mud and hay that normally scented the garage, he detected an odd smell that sent a tingle up his spine. He'd worked with enough injured animals to know blood when he smelled it. And the odors that accompanied death.

Erin caught up with him then, bringing a fresh blast of wintry air in with her as she swept into the garage. "Look, I get that you're mad. But I've apologized for lying to you, and I'd hoped we could at least be friends. Your dad has given me the okay to accompany you all to the auction, and I was hoping we could use the time on the drive to… I don't know. Sort things out between us?"

He shook himself from the strange trance that had seized him and flipped on the light.

Nothing looked out of place, but the foul smell was distinct.

"Do you smell that?" he asked her. "It smells like… blood."

She took a deep whiff. "All I smell is oil and the usual ranch odors."

He moved forward, glancing around for the source of the odor.

"Do you see anything?" She sniffed again as she cast her gaze toward the parked vehicles.

Zane continued deeper into the garage, looking under trucks and behind boxes as he made his way across the floor. When he bent to peer under the F-350, he spotted a coffee can on the ground under the engine. He reached under and dragged the can out, finding it full of pale yellow fluid. Brake fluid most likely. Damn it! A major leak by the looks of it, but not the source of the smell.

"What's that?" Erin stood over him, staring at the coffee can with a frown.

"Trouble. Brake fluid leak." He handed her the can. "Will you hold this while I look under the hood?" He pushed up from the ground, dusting off his hands and making a mental note to tell Roy about the brake line leak. It'd have to be repaired pronto, so they could use the truck to haul the herd tomorrow. He prayed it didn't mean a huge delay.

He propped the hood open and used the flashlight function on his cell phone to find the brake line. The cut was long and obvious.

Slamming his fist on the truck frame, he bit out a curse.

"Zane? What is it?"

He nudged the slit line. "More sabotage. Brakes were cut."

Erin's eyes widened, and she leaned closer for a better look. "Oh, my God. If you hadn't found that... If someone had tried to drive the truck..."

He pressed his mouth in a grim line and tapped the auto-dial number to call Roy.

"Should I go get your father?" she asked. "And the sheriff needs to be called."

He sighed his resignation. Jerked a nod of agreement. *Hell and damnation!* This was the last thing they needed the day before they left for auction. His mind was already ticking through the contingencies if the truck wasn't repaired in time. Rent a truck? Borrow one from another ranch?

Zane paced the floor while Roy's line rang. When the foreman answered, he sounded groggy.

"Roy, we have a problem with the F-350. I need you in the garage ASAP to work on replacing the brake line."

Zane spotted a red smear on the floor and caught his breath, pulled up short.

Roy mumbled something in reply, but Zane couldn't make out the words over the sudden buzzing in his ears. He'd found the source of the odd smell. As he neared the smear, he found more blood staining the floor behind the truck. And what looked like drag marks.

"Erin?" he said numbly.

He heard her receding footsteps stop. "Yeah?"

He visually followed the trail of smeared blood to a pile of boxes in a corner. A large tarpaulin was draped over the discarded boxes. He swallowed hard, seeing a foot peeking out from the tarp. "Call for an ambulance, too."

"What?" Concern sharpened her voice, and she jogged over to join him.

Zane crossed slowly to the tarpaulin, his gut knotted, his breath still in his lungs.

Over the thud of his heartbeat echoing in his skull, he heard Erin approach, gasp.

With a shaking hand, he drew back the heavy cloth, and bile surged in his throat.

Helen lay with her head at an unnatural angle, bruises on her throat.

He reached for her neck, searching for a carotid artery pulse. Praying. *Maybe...*

Erin mewled in fear. "Is she—?"

Grief slashed to his marrow as he withdrew his fingers from her neck, and his body sagged. "She's dead."

Chapter 13

Erin watched in numb disbelief as the coroner's van pulled away from the ranch, carrying Helen to the morgue. Investigating the sabotage at the ranch was one thing; discovering the murdered victim of the saboteur's escalating menace was quite another. She had met and liked Helen, a young woman in love, with so much life ahead of her.

She cast a glance to Dave, who stared, zombie-like, at the departing coroner. His features were drawn, pale, shocked. Her heart ached for the cowboy. While she knew what it was like to lose someone you loved to tragedy, she imagined losing the person you'd wanted to spend the rest of your life with was a special kind of hell.

Her heart gave a painful throb, remembering Zane's anger and distance since he'd learned her true purpose at the ranch. A deep ache filled her chest and sucked all the air from her lungs. Maybe she did have some inkling of the hurt of losing someone she loved. Her relationship with Zane hadn't progressed to the point of promised matrimony, but knowing she'd lost what had promised to be a once-in-a-lifetime love with him stung. Like a jagged gash in her flesh. Drenched in alcohol.

She hugged herself against the stiff cold wind and searched for Zane among the faces gathered in the ranch yard. *There.* Standing beside his sister. He had his arm around Piper's shoulders as she wept into her hands. As if he sensed her attention, Zane angled his head toward Erin. His gaze locked with hers, and his face filled with heartbreaking pain. She took a step toward him, wanting, needing, to offer him the same consolation and support he was lending his sister. But no sooner had she started toward him than his expression hardened. Stiffening, he turned away.

Tears formed in her eyes, and gritting her back teeth, she battled them down. Now was not the time to indulge in self-pity. She needed to stay in control of her emotions and to do the job she was being paid to do. This was a key moment in her investigation. She should be observing the family and employees with dispassion and a professional eye. Had the murderer returned to the scene of the crime?

For example, where was Brady? Why was he not the one comforting Piper?

The blue and red strobes of the light bar atop the sheriff's vehicles cast an eerie pall in the gathering night. She edged toward Michael, who sat on the tailgate of Zane's truck, wearing a stricken countenance.

"I'm so sorry, Michael," she said, sitting down beside him. "I can't imagine how difficult this must be for you."

He nodded without looking at her. "She was...so young."

Erin put a hand on Michael's shoulder and said nothing for several moments. "Have you seen Brady? Zane is across the way with Piper, but I don't see Brady."

Michael didn't react at first, as if shock had gummed the wheels in his mind, slowing his ability to focus and process.

She remembered that feeling well. *Your brother has been killed in a tragic accident on campus.* She'd walked around in a stupor for days after Sean died.

Michael's brow lowered, and he gave her a dark look. "You're not thinking Brady did this? He'd never hurt a woman!"

"I'm not saying he did this." She held her tongue, not bothering to remind him that his bias and affinity for the people on the Double M were the reason he'd hired her to investigate the recent crimes. Nor did she add stones to his weighted view of his son-in-law by telling him that she agreed with his assessment. Everything she knew of Brady, her observations of his patience and skill with the herd, his dedication to his family and her take-away from interviewing him, composed a picture of a humble, loyal, loving man. A tough cowboy, but not a killer.

Michael's tense face relaxed, and he blinked. "Oh. I, uh, think he's in the main house with Melissa. They're trying to keep Connor away from the scene...and comforting him."

Of course.

"Connor was close to Helen," Michael added softly, and she squeezed his shoulder. "She babysat for him a good bit when he first came to live at the ranch."

A deputy approached, and she could feel Michael tense beneath her comforting touch.

"Mr. McCall, may I speak to you?" The deputy gave Erin a hooded glance. "Alone?"

She recognized him as the officer she'd scolded for his approach to the scene when Dave broke his leg, and judging by his scowl, he remembered her, as well. Erin nodded and scooted down from the tailgate.

At loose ends, she surveyed the somber scene and considered where she could be the most use. Staying busy would help her keep her own grief and frustrating sense of helplessness at bay.

Zane was still comforting his sister. Josh and Kate had moved up next to Dave, though they appeared as shell-shocked as the injured hand. As she studied Dave, she saw his crutches wobble, and he swayed. He was about to collapse. She sprinted toward Dave, shouting, "Josh! Catch him!"

Josh's reflexes had been honed in his high-adrenaline sports, and he snagged Dave under the arms before the ranch hand hit the ground. "Whoa, partner!"

"Dave!" Kate hurried over to him. "You should go back inside. Get in bed."

"Helen…" Dave moaned, and his shoulders began shaking as the tears broke.

Josh and Kate exchanged a look, and Josh hoisted Dave onto his crutches. "Come on, man. Let's go inside."

Kate and Josh helped Dave hobble back into the house, flanking him, supporting him, comforting him.

Erin watched them go for a moment then cast another glance over the mourning family members and the sheriff's deputies, who also looked shell-shocked as they worked the scene. And why not? They were law enforcement professionals, but they were also human. Citizens of the small town who'd, no doubt, known Helen.

A clatter from inside the garage drew her attention, and she headed that direction. The back corner of the garage was marked off with yellow tape as a crime scene, and she gave that area a wide berth. She discovered the source of the noise as she approached the F-350.

Roy was leaning over the engine of the truck, busy working on the brake line.

"Roy?"

He glanced over his shoulder. "Miss Palmer."

"What are you doing?" She'd asked the question in almost a rhetorical way. She knew he was repairing the truck, but his timing...

Roy moved to lie on his back and scooted under the truck to continue working. "Michael needs this truck ready in the morning, so I'm fixing the brakes."

She shook her head, startled a bit by his response. "Surely Helen's death means... Will they really still go to the auction considering...?"

"No choice," he said in clipped tones from under the truck. "Gotta get the herd to auction."

She was staggered by the reality that even a death, a murder on the ranch grounds, wouldn't prevent them from making the trip in the morning. Then she thought of Michael's grave expression when talking about the importance of the auction. The whole year boiled down to one paycheck...

"Roy?"

He didn't answer. Erin sighed, wondering if she should offer to help him repair the truck. She knew nothing about engines or brakes but maybe she could hand him tools or—

A sob broke into her thoughts, and Roy said softly, "She was such a s-sweet girl. She didn't...deserve to die. She didn't—"

So he wasn't unmoved by Helen's death. Erin knelt by Roy's legs and put a hand on his ankle. She heard him sniff, clear his throat.

"I'm sorry. I..." He drew a shaky breath.

"Don't apologize. You need to grieve. It's healthy." And everyone dealt with pain and grief differently. Some people, like her mother and, apparently, like Roy, needed to stay busy. Bury themselves in work. Try to keep the horrible awfulness at arm's length.

"Would you like some help, Roy? I can be your gofer or just keep you company or—"

"No." She heard his heavy sigh. "I'd...rather be alone." She heard the clank of tools as he got back to work. "I'm almost finished here."

She hesitated, then pushed to her feet. "All right."

Erin glanced warily toward the bloodstains on the garage floor, and her gut knotted. What had happened? Why was Helen killed? Her instincts told her it was connected to the sabotage, but she was a long way from proving that theory. Did Helen's death mean she was closer to finding the vandal? The *murderer*, she amended with a chill. Or had the case just taken a tragic and obscure turn that meant she had to start from scratch with her investigation?

Erin left the garage just as the sheriff's forensic team pulled up the driveway. She wanted to stay and watch the evidence collection, but the deputy in charge directed the family to leave the scene while the forensic team worked.

"You heard the man," Michael called, squaring his shoulders as if preparing for battle. "Let them work. We all have our own work to do. We load up at sunrise."

Chapter 14

As morning broke over the horizon, Zane joined his family in loading the heard into two trailers, the larger rented livestock trailer hooked to the F-350 held most of the cattle, and a smaller trailer was hitched to Josh's truck and held the calves.

As soon as the herd was prepped for travel, his dad and Brady had left for the auction grounds to handle last-minute details before the stock arrived. Zane, Josh and Roy were following with the herd. The roads were mostly clear, but there had been reports of icy spots on the mountain road they had to travel. They'd need to go slow and take extra care on the curvy highway.

Erin arrived in the ranch yard as he settled in the F-350. She appeared at the passenger window as he was buckling up for the ride.

He cracked open his door to see what she wanted.

"You're riding here?" she said. "I'd hoped we could talk on the drive over."

He frowned at her. "You're going with us?"

She gave him a funny, awkward smile. "I told you that yesterday when—" She stopped and scrubbed a hand on her chin. "Well, right before we found Helen. I guess I can understand why you forgot."

Roy climbed in behind the wheel and put a large steaming cup of coffee in the cup holder. "Ready?"

Zane nodded. "Let's hit it." Turning back to Erin, he said, "Ride with Josh if you insist on going. I'm sure he'd love the company."

"But—"

His heart twisted when he saw the disappointment that shadowed her face. But he wasn't ready to talk to her about anything, much less their dissolved relationship. His emotions were raw after finding Helen murdered, and the auction had his nerves strung taut. He had enough to deal with today, thank you.

Roy cranked the engine.

"See you at the sale barn," Zane said and closed his door.

As they pulled slowly down the driveway, he watched in the truck's side mirror as she stared after them, her expression wounded. Did she really think he could trust her again enough to build a relationship after the way she'd lied and deceived him? And knowing how much her deception had hurt, did he even want to try?

A little voice in his head whispered to him as Roy pulled onto the highway, and the answer that whisper gave him sent an unsettling ripple to his core. *Yes, he did want to try.*

* * *

"Tell me what's wrong with this picture." Josh waved a hand in a vague gesture between him and Erin.

"Uh, not enough coffee?" Erin guessed, then shrugged. "I give up. Tell me."

He gave her a raised-eyebrows, it-should-be-so-obvious look. "You're with the wrong twin. I should be in the lead truck with Roy, and Zane should be here patching things up with you."

Erin's pulse hiccupped. "Zane told you we fought?"

Josh twisted his mouth in a lopsided grin. "He's my twin. He didn't have to tell me. I could see it."

Erin hummed acknowledgment of that statement. "Do you know why?"

Josh sipped from his coffee. "No. You want to fill me in?"

"Would it suffice for me to say all will be known by everyone in a couple weeks?"

He gave her a puzzled glance. "Is that supposed to make sense to me?"

"Let's just say he didn't like the way I was doing my job, for good reason, and though we've reached an understanding—"

"He's not ready to kiss and make up," Josh finished for her.

"Sort of." Erin fingered the seam of her jeans, fidgeting as she replayed the argument she'd had in the guesthouse with Zane. And the kisses they'd shared. Would they ever "kiss and make up"?

"Here's the thing about my brother," Josh said. "He doesn't do anything halfway. He takes forever to commit to something, but once he does, he's all-in. Especially with people."

Erin glanced at him. "That's what I figured, but I'm kind of afraid he'll never trust me again. I may have burned that bridge."

The possibility that she'd lost her chance at a relationship with Zane sliced through her like a hot blade.

"You broke his trust?" Josh asked with a frown. He gave a low whistle. "It's more serious than I thought."

A pang gripped her chest. "I never intended—"

"I'm not blaming you. You certainly don't seem like a manipulative wench or man-eater."

She gave an ironic laugh. "Thanks?"

"I'm just saying that Zane…" He scratched his ear and shot her a sympathetic look. "Well, he takes loyalty real seriously."

"I get that. And I do, too. Truly. But…circumstances…" She fumbled with the button on her coat. "I was in a bad position because…"

He lifted a hand from the steering wheel. "You don't have to explain it to me. Your business with Zane is your business with Zane. I don't want to interfere."

She nodded. "Thank you."

He curled his bottom lip in, biting it as if fighting the urge to say more as he drummed the steering wheel with his thumbs. Finally he blew a large sigh out in exasperation. "Can I make a request though?"

She lifted a corner of her mouth. "Sure."

He glanced at her with eyes filled with the same cerulean intensity she'd come to love in Zane's gaze. "Don't give up on him. If you love him, stick it out. Only a demonstration of your perseverance and dedication to him will push him past his own stubbornness and fears."

A knot of emotion rose in her throat, and Erin swallowed to find her breath. Did she love him? She had deep feelings and respect for him. She was insanely attracted to him. She longed to spend time with him and felt a hollow ache when he was gone. Was that love?

Rather than examine her own feelings, she said, "I'm not so sure he loves me."

Josh sent her a frown before returning his attention to the road. "Come on. I have eyes. I know what I saw. And I see how he's been the last few days."

"We had a certain chemistry, yeah. But love is…bigger… It's more…" Wow. *For a pseudo journalist, you sure have a way with words.* She groaned at her inability to express herself. But how did she explain to Josh what she couldn't untangle for herself?

"Erin, you make him happy. I caught him whistling as he mucked stalls in the stable last week. Whistling, for cripe's sake! He's been different since you've been around. More like himself. His old self. His true self." The gravitas in his voice, almost a pleading, squeezed her heart. "And by contrast, more…mopey, for lack of a better word, since this argument of yours."

She drew a careful breath and murmured, "He makes me happy, too."

Josh nodded, and his jaw tightened. "Then fight for him."

Roy took a sip from his travel cup, and in his memory, Zane heard Erin saying, *Roy's drinking again. I've smelled it when I was in the truck with him.*

He took a deep breath, trying to sniff the air. Gritting his back teeth and fisting his hands at his sides, he debated how, and if, he should confront Roy about Erin's contention.

When Roy drifted toward the center line, then over-corrected, Zane made up his mind. He reached for Roy's cup, pried off the lid and took a swig. The burn of liquor seared his throat as he swallowed.

Roy cut a startled look at him, panic in his eyes. "That's my cup!"

"I know." Zane rolled down his window and dumped the rest of the heavily spiked coffee on the highway. "Roy, we need to talk."

The foreman's jaw tensed, and he scowled darkly at Zane. "You had no right to do that."

"Don't I?" Zane sighed, his gut in knots. How in the world did he address this? He considered waiting until they returned from the auction, letting Brady deal with it, or—but no. He wouldn't cop out. He cared about Roy, and the man's drinking affected his family's business.

"How long have you—?" He cut himself off. That wasn't what mattered. He gathered his thoughts while Roy stared straight ahead out the windshield, his face flinty. "You'll have to go back to rehab."

Roy drew and released a tremulous breath. "I... can't— You don't understand, Zane. It's not that simple."

"I know it will be hard. But you have to get this under control. We all care about you, and—"

"You *don't* know!" Roy replied sharply.

Zane fell silent, studying the man he'd known his whole life. He'd never heard Roy raise his voice that way. What's more, Roy was shaking, and something frightening and turbulent filled his eyes.

"There's a runaway truck pull-off up ahead. I want you to stop and let me drive."

Roy gripped the wheel harder. "I'm fine."

"No, you're not. I'm going to drive." Zane kept his gaze on his foreman, his second father. Sweat had beaded on Roy's upper lip and forehead, despite the cold temperature in the cab. His breathing had grown erratic, and he blinked rapidly as if fighting back tears. The man seemed to be crumbling before him. When Roy reached up to wipe sweat off his face with his sleeve, the truck swerved.

Zane grabbed his armrest, his pulse thumping loudly in his ears. "Roy." He kept his tone calm but firm. He didn't want to push Roy when he was already visibly upset, but he had to make his point clear. "Pull over, and let me drive."

"It's been so hard, son," Roy said in a low, raspy voice. "So hard. I just want it to be over."

Zane shifted on the seat to more fully face the foreman. "What's been hard, Roy? Your battle with addiction?"

Roy snorted and curled his lip. "Drinking isn't the problem. It's the way I forget. It's how I've survived for all these years."

Zane's mouth grew dry, and the taste of alcohol that was still on his tongue became bitter. He wanted to hear what Roy had to say, but the man was clearly too upset, too inebriated to be driving. Especially while pulling a huge livestock trailer on a twisting mountain road in questionable weather conditions.

"Roy, please. Pull over. We'll talk about it. I don't mean to castigate you. I want to help. Just…pull over."

Whether he ignored Zane or wasn't listening to him, Zane couldn't say, but Roy stared straight ahead, his expression bereft. "I never meant anyone harm. I never… meant…"

A chill rippled up Zane's spine. "Roy? Have you hurt someone? What are you talking about?"

"I did his bidding to keep him quiet. He knew…'bout what I'd done."

Apprehension coiled in Zane's gut, the foreboding of disaster careening toward him that he couldn't prevent. His voice sounded strangled as he asked, "What did you do? Roy, what's going on?"

Roy turned bleary, grief-stricken eyes toward him and held his gaze so long, Zane had to snap him from his inattention, shouting, "Roy, watch the road!"

Heart hammering, Zane slid his cell phone out and started a text to Josh. Then changing his mind, because his brother was behind the wheel, as well, he redirected the text to Erin.

We have a situation. I'm trying to get Roy to pull over and change drivers. May need police assistance.

Roy cut a glance to him. "Are you calling the cops? Turning me in?"

Zane shook his head. "Just letting Erin know we'll be changing drivers just ahead. Okay? Roy, you need pull over and let me drive."

Roy heaved another shuddering breath and nodded weakly. "I know." Then his face crumpled, and tears filled his eyes. "Oh, God… I deserve what I get. I've… I've been a coward. I know that. I just… I was scared. I had a boy to raise. Brady needed… And I thought it had gone away, that no one would ever know. But then…"

The confession spilled from Roy like a dam opened to release floodwaters. His tears flowed, and his past transgressions poured out of his soul. "I killed a woman. A long time ago. Hit her car when I was drunk. Then I ran."

Shock punched Zane. He gaped at Roy, left mute and frozen as Roy continued.

"I left her there and fled before anyone could find me. Or so I thought. But I was seen. And he's held my crime over me all these years..."

Zane forced his jaw to move, but no sound came out. What would he say anyway? He needed time to process this bombshell. The phone in his hand beeped with an incoming text, but he barely registered it.

Because Roy wasn't finished.

Wiping his sleeve across his face, Roy rasped, "He threatened to turn me in if I didn't...help him." Roy's throat convulsed as he swallowed. He turned bleak eyes toward Zane for a moment, then away. His face contorted with agony as he mumbled, "He blackmailed me to... to...sabotage the ranch."

Zane's ears buzzed with adrenaline, and numbing disbelief paralyzed him. *No! He must have misunderstood...*

Roy stared straight ahead, his cheeks wet and his complexion pale. He was trembling hard enough for Zane to feel the vibration in the truck's bench seat. Or maybe that was his own body quaking. As shock faded, Zane was consumed with the slow rise of tangled emotions. Too many to sort out. But riding high and center was betrayal.

"Y-you?" he stuttered, his voice barely recognizable.

Roy licked his lips. "I had to. He...he was going to turn me in. I—"

"No!" he grated. "You *didn't* have to! You *chose* to!"

Roy jerked a startled glance to Zane, then back to the road. "You don't understand. I had to protect Brady. I couldn't—"

"The only one you were protecting was your own

sorry ass!" The full weight of Roy's confession settled on Zane like a granite boulder. "You're responsible for destroying our family's business! We could lose the ranch because of *you* and your selfish deceit!"

"I'm sorry." Roy reached for his travel mug, then frowned at the empty cup.

"Sorry! Sorry doesn't begin to make up for—" Fury and heartsickness welled in his chest, choking his breath. His phone pinged again, and he glanced at the screen, more out of habit than anything else.

What situation?

Then, What the hell is happening? Are you all right?

Zane wasn't sure he'd ever be all right again. Roy, who'd been a second father to him his entire life, had killed a woman in a DUI hit-and-run. Sabotaged the Double M to hide his secret and—

"Who is *he*? Who is blackmailing you?" His heart galloped, thrashing against his ribs.

What little color had been in Roy's face leached away. He shook his head. "No. I can't… He can still come after me. He can hurt us! Brady, Connor…"

The truck drifted across the center line, narrowly missing a car in the oncoming lane. The other vehicle blasted its horn, and the sound jerked Zane from the bubble of disbelief and anger that had blotted out the more immediate danger of Roy's physical and mental condition. He had to get the man out from behind the steering wheel.

"Roy…" Zane took a deep breath, trying to rein in the roiling in his gut. "You have to pull over. *Now.*"

Roy was still shaking his head, his gaze distant and cloudy. "Can't go back now. What's done is done."

"Roy!"

"I don't deserve forgiveness. I've ruined everything..."

Zane was in no mood to disagree with him on that point, but he had to snap Roy out of his funk. The man wasn't fit to be behind the wheel, and his emotional meltdown was only escalating the danger. Would he have to take the wheel by force? That seemed equally risky on this twisty road. He grabbed Roy's sleeve and shook him. "Roy, listen to me. Stop the truck! Now!"

Roy cast a blank side gaze to him, causing the truck to swerve. "I didn't mean to kill her."

Zane scrubbed a hand over his face. Damn, damn, damn! "Forget the accident for now. Stop the truck before you cause anoth—"

"Not that one. Helen." Roy groaned. "She found out. I only wanted her to be quiet. I didn't mean to..."

A fresh bolt of shock and horror streaked through Zane. Roy had murdered Helen? He squeezed his hands into fists, trying to tamp down the surge of anger and grief. He had to keep it together until he had Roy off the road.

Roy raised a hand to blot his streaming eyes and nose, and the truck traveled into the oncoming lane again.

"Roy!" He'd run out of time. He had to take control of the truck or someone could die because of Roy's inattention. *Someone else could die.*

Shoving the distracting thought aside for the moment, Zane unbuckled his seat belt and swept the clutter on the bench seat to the floor. "I'm taking the wheel. Don't fight me!"

He slid closer to the driver's side, trying to grip the steering wheel. His actions seemed to wake Roy from his stupor.

"Hey! Stop!" Roy stiffened and raised an arm to block Zane.

"Give me the wheel, Roy, or pull over for yourself." He tried to infuse his tone with calm rationale.

"I can't go to jail! And I won't let that bastard hurt my family!" Roy roared, panic in his eyes. The truck jerked hard to the left then back into their lane, narrowly missing an SUV.

Zane raised a hand, palm out. "Take it easy, Roy. No one is going to jail." *Yet.*

When he tried again to reach for the wheel, he saw that Roy's hands were shaking. Hard. A quick glance at the foreman's face revealed the level of the man's desperation and disconnect. His eyes darted wildly from the road to Zane to the sharp drop-off at the edge of the highway.

"No, no, no, no…" Roy moaned. "I can't… I can't…"

"Roy!" Zane gripped Roy's shirt, shaking him, trying to reach him through his panic. He scooted closer and put one hand on the base of the steering wheel. "Just let go of the wheel and let me—"

"No! I have to—" In that instant the front tires hit a patch of black ice. The truck lost traction, skewing slightly. And Roy reacted in the worse possible way. He slammed on the brakes. The back tires locked, hit the ice patch, skidded. The momentum of the trailer pushed them forward, out of control, and sent the truck in a sharp veer across the oncoming lane. Bumping over the narrow, rocky shoulder. Through the guardrail.

And over the steep embankment.

Chapter 15

Erin screamed, watching helplessly as the lead truck left the road. The truck went nose-first, hitting a boulder that brought the vehicle to an abrupt halt. Zane was thrown through the windshield like a rag doll and slid across the crumpled hood to lie in a heap on the ice and dirt at the top of the hill.

The trailer flipped on its side, skidding over rocks, icy scrub trees and dead grass. The trailer weight dragged the truck backward before friction, a small outcropping and a few aspens managed to catch the trailer's slide on a protruding ridge of earth several dozen yards down the drop-off.

The crash was over before Erin could draw her next shaky breath. Before Josh could bring their truck to a safe stop. He braked hard, guiding his truck to the narrow shoulder of the highway, and they sent each other stunned looks. Erin leaned forward to peer through the windshield. From their vantage point on the lower side of a hairpin turn, looking up at the vehicular carnage, she saw no movement. Her gut churned with fear. Dread.

Josh recovered from the shock first. He cut the engine, whipped out his phone and tried to dial. But the sneer that crossed his face and the bitter curse word he barked told the frightening result.

"No freaking signal!" he shouted, throwing the phone on the seat with a growl. He banged the steering wheel with his fist, muttered a quick, "Please God," under his breath and launched himself from the front seat.

Erin released her seat belt with trembling fingers and a frantic need to reach Zane. With her heart in her throat, she followed Josh as he ran up the highway toward the accident. She said her own prayer as she rushed up the mountain road. She'd already lost one person she loved far too early. She could bear to lose another...

She stumbled as the truth hit her. The thought of Zane being taken from her brought everything into sharp focus. And she knew she did, indeed, *love* Zane.

Zane opened his eyes slowly. He squinted against the winter sun which seemed bright despite the thinly overcast sky. He took a moment to assess. Where was he? Lying on his back. On the ground. He could hear the frightened bellows of cows.

Something had spooked the herd. That thought permeated the fog in his brain, stirred a sense of urgency in him that hiked his pulse.

Get help... Trouble with the herd...

He tried to sit up, and his head swam. Pounded. He raised a hand toward his temple. Then froze. Tiny, bleeding cuts covered his arm. *What the...?* He squinted against the throb of pain in his head and glanced down at his body. Shards of glass sparkled around him, on his clothes, in his skin, on the rocky dirt around him.

Why was the ground moving? Rolling like a wave in the ocean?

Zane blinked, inhaled a cautious breath, and his ribs protested. Damn! Had he been bucked? He hurt all over.

Casting a glance around him, he blinked again at the view of rolling foothills, twisting highway and—

Reality slammed into him with a sobering punch. Adrenaline flooded his veins.

Roy. Murder. Truck crashing.

He jerked his head toward the sound of the distressed herd. The sudden movement caused a paroxysm of pain to roll through him. He gasped, sucking a shallow breath into his sore chest. More carefully, he angled his eyes toward the sound of an engine, the agitated lowing of cattle and restless thump of shifting hooves. The front of the truck teetered at an awkward angle over open air at the top of a sheer drop. The truck's hood was crumpled, the windshield broken out, the back tires askew yet still slowly spinning. Gasoline dripped from the undercarriage.

Roy. Where was Roy?

Rising carefully to his knees, Zane scanned the ledge. No sign of their foreman. Moving unsteadily to his feet, Zane groped for balance, for clarity. Broken glass fell from his clothes, tinkling like tiny Christmas bells as it littered the ground. He took a staggering step toward the truck and craned his neck to peer inside the crumpled cab.

Roy slumped over the steering wheel. Not moving.

Ignoring the pain that throbbed beneath his skull,

Zane edged closer to the pickup, sizing up his options. As the cattle in the trailer moved about in their panic, the trailer jostled, rocking the precariously perched truck. His gut clenched. He had to get Roy out before the truck lost purchase and tumbled down the mountain.

The cattle. Going to auction. The bulk of the ranch's income for the year. Zane hesitated, his pulse beating wildly in his ears.

Roy had betrayed them. Killed innocent women. Brought on the crisis his family now faced.

Resentment boiled in his core.

He glanced toward the trailer. Could the cows be saved? If the cattle were lost, they'd almost certainly lose the ranch within months.

Bile filled his throat. He took a step toward the trailer—then stopped. *What was he doing?* He gritted his teeth, and frustration made his blood surge and his headache swell. As much ill will as he had for Roy, having learned of his betrayal, he had to try to save their foreman before he could think about the herd.

"Roy!" he shouted. No response.

Edging toward the cab, Zane opened the passenger door, which was now facing the sky. He tested the truck's stability with one hand. Then a foot. Half of his weight. Then more…

"Roy?"

Metal creaked, and the truck dipped and swayed. Zane's mouth dried. Any second the truck and trailer could shift and slide over the edge, down the embankment—a free-falling deathtrap. "Roy!" he shouted with more urgency.

The older man moaned. Moved a hand.

Fumbling with the seat belt buckle, Zane hurried to free Roy from the encumbering strap. When the older man groaned again, he pulled Roy back at the shoulder and slapped at his cheek. "Come on, man. Wake up! We gotta get out of here!"

Roy mumbled something Zane couldn't understand. Zane cursed under his breath. He couldn't wait, couldn't count on Roy's help to get him out. Whispering a litany of prayers, he reached around Roy and braced a foot on the steering wheel for leverage. Pain ripped through Zane's rib cage as he hoisted Roy. He dragged the foreman up, toward the open passenger door.

The wrecked F-350 rocked and shimmied as the cattle continued stirring anxiously inside the trailer. Gasping for a breath, Zane took stock of his position, the distance yet to lift Roy. How the hell was he supposed to get the limp man out without sending the truck careening off the tenuous perch? Was he really going to risk his life to save the man who'd ruined his family?

An ache wholly separate from his physical injuries speared Zane's chest. Roy was family. No matter how he'd betrayed the McCall's, Zane refused to let Roy die. He had to find a way to get them both out alive.

"Zane!" Erin called, frantically searching the ledge around the wreckage. She was sure she'd seen Zane ejected from the truck as it crashed. So where was he? The sharp tang of fear filled her mouth. Swallowing hard, she forced down the panic that strangled her.

"Zane!" Josh echoed, his voice sounding equally taut with worry. He scrambled down the embankment at the side of the highway toward the crash site. "Roy!"

"Here!" Zane called back.

The relief that ballooned in her made her knees wobble. She caught her balance, bracing a hand on the crumpled guardrail. *Zane was alive!*

"I need help! Roy's hurt."

She visually tracked Josh's progress down the hill to the large pickup that lay on its side, hanging over the embankment. The precarious position of the vehicle made her breath snag in her lungs. As quickly as she could, she climbed down the ice and rocks at the edge of the road and rushed to the crumpled truck.

Josh's face reflected the same anxiety clambering inside her as he skidded up to the truck. "Are you all right?"

"Good enough," Zane rasped. "Help me get him out!"

Josh put a hand on the F-350 as he positioned himself to grab Roy's arms, and the vehicle creaked and slid a few inches toward the drop-off.

Erin gasped, and Zane shouted, "Careful! It could go over any second."

Biting her bottom lip, Erin turned away, unable to watch as the brothers struggled to drag Roy out of the cab. Knowing that any false move could spell disaster, she held her breath and prayed as hard as she could. She heard grunts and scraping metal, the crunch of gravel and ice. And the clamor and plaintive mooing of frightened cows. Heart thumping, she shifted her attention to the trailer, and with a sinking sensation in her gut, she realized what else was at stake. The cattle. If the trailer went over the edge…

Another car stopped on the highway, and an older woman came to the top of the embankment. "Oh, good gracious! Is there anything I can do to help?"

"Yes!" Erin called back. "Do you have medical training-

"Sorry, no. I'm a hairdresser on my way to fix up a bride for her wedding."

Disappointment pinged Erin's chest. "Do you have a cell signal? We haven't been able to call 9-1-1 yet."

She raised her phone and glanced at the screen. "No. But I'll keep checking as I drive and as soon as I can get a call out, I promise I'll alert the police and ambulance."

"Please do. Thank you!"

The loud scrape of metal on rock drew her attention back to the truck as the trailer and pickup shifted, sliding to a sharper angle. Josh and Zane had Roy out of the pickup, and the older man was rousing, waving the brothers off as they ministered to his injuries. She jogged over to join them, crouching beside Josh. When she glanced at Zane, she gasped.

"You're bleeding!" she cried, seeing the tiny trickles all over Zane's face and hands.

He frowned and swiped a hand along his brow, then blinked at the red stains on his fingers as if surprised by the blood there. "I went through the windshield," he said, as if that were an everyday occurrence and all the explanation she needed. She made a move toward him and he lifted a hand to stop her. "I'm fine. Sore—" he grimaced as he clutched his ribs "—but I'll be okay."

"And Roy?" She leaned to peer around Josh.

Josh cut a glance to her. "His arm looks broken, and he says his hip hurts like hell. He's got cuts from the glass like Zane. But…they were lucky."

Zane grunted, and she faced him again. "What happened?"

His jaw tightened, and he mumbled, "Later."

Later. Despite the dire situation, she couldn't help but

remember the last time Zane had used that word with her. A pang twisted inside her. Their *later* might never come.

She held his gaze and could see deep pain dimming his eyes. Some was physical pain, she was sure, but something more troubled him, and she recalled the text he'd sent just prior to the crash.

We have a situation. May need police assistance.

"Zane, the text you sent earlier said—"

He shook his head, then winced as he raised his palm to a goose egg bulging at his temple. "Not now." He gave Roy a dark look, then rose to his feet and faced the trailer. "We've gotta do something to save the cattle."

She stood and moved beside him, studying the trailer that jostled and rocked as the restless animals moved inside. Erin was no engineer, but even she could tell the only thing keeping the truck from plummeting and dragging the trailer down the mountain was the weight of the cattle. "How, Zane? If you start taking the cows out, the decreased weight in the trailer will throw off the balance with the pickup, and the whole thing will go over."

Josh joined them, staring bleakly at the trailer and the drop-off beyond. "She's right, bro."

Zane glared at them both, saying tightly, "And if we do nothing, the whole thing will still likely fall, and we'll lose the majority of the herd. No herd, no auction, no income. We might as well kiss the ranch goodbye!"

Erin surveyed the small shelf-like outcropping where they stood. "If we can get the cows out of the trailer without it falling—"

Josh snorted. "That's a big *if*."

"There's room for most of the cattle on this part of the hill," she persisted.

"But, Erin, the logistics of getting them out of—" Josh started.

But Zane cut him off with, "We have to try. Are you in or not?"

Roy stumbled over, limping and holding his injured left arm. "I'm in."

Zane shot the foreman another odd look. "You're injured. Sit this one out." He strode to the back end of the sideways trailer and reached for the sliding rod that held the cargo doors shut.

Roy followed Zane, grimacing with each step. The man was clearly in pain and needed medical help.

"Zane, someone…has t' go inside the trailer…steer the cattle out," Roy wheezed, "make sure there's…not a stampede."

Nodding somberly, Zane said, "I know that. I'm willing to take the risk."

Josh stepped forward, frowning, and grabbed his brother's coat sleeve. "Are you kidding me?" he asked, aghast. "No one can go inside the trailer! It's too damn dangerous!"

"The animals 're frightened. Some l'kely injured," Roy started, his tone even, though his words sounded rather slurred. "Someone has to—"

Josh cut a sharp glance from Zane to Roy and back. "No! Are you joking? And you call *me* reckless?"

Erin stepped closer, her heart stuttering a staccato beat. "I agree with Josh. Please, Zane, don't—"

The trailer shifted again with a groan of steel on rock.

"We don't have time to debate this." Zane wrenched open the door now on the bottom as the trailer lay on its side. The door smacked the ground with a thud. Inside, the hooves of the herd could be seen.

Roy elbowed his way in front of Zane with an odd look on his face. "Son, you *know* why…I have to be the one takin' the risk. If fate…takes me today, it's what I deserve."

"Roy?" Josh scrunched his face in dismay. "Roy, no! This is insane! You can't—"

Zane jerked a nod to the foreman and stepped back as he raised the second sideways door, folding it back on the wall of the trailer that was now on top. "Go."

The cattle nearest the open end of the trailer staggered out on their own. Zane watched Roy squeeze past the press of bovine bodies moving en masse toward the opening. The trailer swayed ominously as the cows stomped to the open end.

Zane swatted at the heifer closest to him, directing it away from the drop-off. Already he could see that some of the cows had been injured in the wreck. *Keep your head. Work fast and work smart.* "Erin, help Josh herd 'em away from the drop-off and toward the highway!"

She hustled out of the way as the first of the half-ton cows barreled toward her.

"Wave them away from the edge!" Josh demonstrated as he took his position by the embankment.

Erin edged into place, flailing her arms as the riled Black Angus herd moved toward her.

"Keep this area clear as we move them out," Zane added, seeing that the dazed and frightened cows were bottlenecking the exit.

Trying to refocus the anxiety twisting in his chest into a productive sense of urgency, Zane smacked one hindquarter after another as the cattle disgorged onto the ledge. Some balked at the exit. Others bolted erratically. Still others were clearly injured and hobbled or swayed as Roy shoved and shouted, steering the herd out of the death trap.

More than half of the cows were out when the trailer began sliding, gathering speed as each successive animal was unloaded and the balance of weight anchoring the wreckage changed.

Zane cupped a hand by his mouth, shouting to be heard over the restless herd. "Roy!" He made a giant sweep with his arm, motioning for the foreman to hurry and feeling his ribs throb in protest. "Time to go! We're losing the trailer!"

Roy met his gaze, clearly knew what he was saying…but turned away and continued directing the last of the herd.

Zane grumbled a curse. "Damn it, Roy! Don't play martyr! Get your ass out of there. Now!"

Roy ignored him, and the first wing-beats of panic flapped in Zane's chest. He was furious with Roy and crushed by his betrayal. But he didn't want the man to die.

The truck dipped further over the drop-off, and, with a screech of metal, the back bumper ripped free. The truck fell with a loud crash that reverberated in Zane's chest. In the next instant, the trailer, perched on a boulder-fulcrum like a deadly teeter-totter, rocked back, throwing the front end up as the weight of the exiting cattle re-shifted the balance.

Startled cows charged out, sending Zane stumbling backward. Josh grabbed his brother's arm, narrowly saving him from stepping over the drop-off.

Roy was thrown to the floor of the trailer. He cried out in anguish as he landed on his hip.

Josh turned to the trailer, alarm in his eyes. "Roy, get out of there! It's going over!"

No sooner had Josh spoken than the teetering trailer tilted sharply to the side. Rocks loosened by the crash tumbled down the embankment.

"Roy!" Zane felt his chest tighten, dread fisting around his throat. "We'll work things out! Don't do anything stupid. Just…get out!" His voice sounded strangled even to his own ears.

Josh cut a puzzled look toward him that Zane ignored. His full attention was on Roy. The sliding trailer. The last dozen injured cows.

Roy struggled to his feet, grimacing and grunting in pain. Pushing past cows too wounded to walk, he took a few lurching steps toward the open end of the trailer. In seconds, the trailer rolled past its tipping point. Picked up speed as it slid.

His heart in his throat, Zane reached inside, grasped Roy's outstretched right hand. The trailer careened down the mountain, crumpling and breaking apart as it smashed against rocks and frozen earth. Roy's feet scrabbled for purchase on the loose stones and ice at the edge of the outcropping. He slipped, pulling Zane to his knees as Roy tumbled over the edge.

Erin screamed.

Zane thudded, chest-first, onto the ground, pain slicing through his ribs and streaking up his arm. But he clung stubbornly to Roy's hand.

Josh was beside him in the next instant, grabbing Roy's coat collar, his belt, and hauling the man up.

Roy bellowed in agony as he flopped on the ground, and the foreman's shout shot splinters of pain beneath

Zane's skull. He, too, laid back on the icy rocks, panting and trying not to think about the lost cattle.

"We got most of them," Josh said quietly, echoing his thoughts. "The one's we lost...well, many were injured and...now they're not suffering."

Leave it to Josh to try to put a positive spin on tragedy. His ever-optimistic brother.

"You shoulda let me go with 'em," Roy muttered, clutching his left arm to his chest.

"What?" Josh shook his head, frowning at their foreman.

"Better dead than where I'm going."

Josh turned a confused and dismayed look to Zane. "What the hell's going on?"

Before he could answer, Erin called to them, her tone agitated. "Guys, a little help? They're wandering toward the edge! Some are clearly hurt. Time to cowboy, fellas!"

He crawled slowly to his feet, every muscle in his torso cramping and throbbing. His head felt ready to explode. But there was work to do. The rescued cattle had to be herded to the road, a replacement trailer brought to collect them.

And the sheriff needed to be called to take Roy into custody.

Chapter 16

"Anyone have a cell signal?" Zane asked once the herd had been moved out of immediate harm's way. They'd moved the second truck and smaller trailer to block the road, the emergency flashers on to warn other cars the highway was temporarily impassable because of the cattle. From the other direction, another driver had angled his SUV and was helping keep the herd corralled. The three men and Erin were spaced about ten feet apart, guarding the edge of the road, a human fence. Roy, who couldn't stand without excruciating pain, half sat and half lay on a large bolder near the road.

Zane held his phone up and squinted at the screen. "Even if you can get a text out to Dad, it'd help. We need a replacement trailer, ambulance..." He glared at Roy. "And police."

Erin huffed a sigh. "All right, the worst of the crisis

is past. Mind telling us what precipitated this disaster? Why do you keep looking at Roy like he's the devil's own son?"

"Because I deserve it," Roy mumbled darkly. His face was pinched with pain, but Erin sensed that physical discomfort wasn't the main source of his agony.

Josh, who'd been trying to get better reception on his phone from atop a rock a few yards away snapped his attention toward the foreman. "What?"

A dawning realization settled over her like a cold morning fog, seconds before Zane groused, "Meet our saboteur. Roy has been the one vandalizing the ranch all this time."

Josh scoffed. "Don't be ridiculous! Roy wouldn't—"

"He's right." Roy's voice was barely audible, and yet his confession was like a scream in a sacred place. "I betrayed your family. I deserve whatever happens to me."

The weight of the revelation juttered through Erin's body, leaving her gut swirling. She gaped at Roy in disbelief...but a sad recognition of the truth whispered through her, as well. She liked Roy, had admired his loyalty to the family. If she was this stunned, how must Zane and Josh feel?

She divided a look between the brothers. Zane was still grim-mouthed and tense. A shadow lurked behind his injury-and-pain-induced paleness. He'd had longer to grapple with the news, but Josh looked poleaxed.

She could see the subtle shift in Josh's expression as he sorted through the ramifications. His thoughts likely were reeling through the similar questions and scenarios that hers were.

"The zip line... Did you—?" Josh rasped, his eyes growing hot with fury.

Roy's throat worked as he swallowed. He briefly met Josh's gaze, then looked away. "I'm sorry," he whispered. "I…didn't mean for it to fall. It was only supposed to force you to delay opening. I thought someone would find it before—"

Josh charged at Roy with a feral growl. "You son of a bitch!" He grabbed the front of Roy's coat and snarled in his face, "Kate could have died! She almost did! You prick. I should—"

Erin rushed to Josh's side and grabbed his arms. "Josh, stop! He's injured."

"I'll kill him!" Josh roared, his face flushed and his body shaking.

Roy hung his head, and his shoulders jerked as he sobbed. "Do it. I deserve…"

Beneath her hands, Josh jerked taut. Drew a strangled sounding breath. "Helen…"

A chill rippled through Erin, remembering how the young woman's body had looked in death. She angled her head toward the foreman. "Roy, d-did you kill Helen?"

He refused to meet her eyes as his uninjured arm lifted to wipe tears from his face. "It was an accident," he croaked. "She caught me…draining the brake fluid. She was going to talk. I only wanted to—"

Josh bit out a curse and staggered back, his face distorted with disgust and betrayal. He seemed unable to breathe, and Zane seized his brother's wrist. "Josh?"

His twin turned bleak eyes on Zane, his expression shifting again as some new realization hit him. "Zane, what do we tell Dad? This… This will kill him! And Mom… Oh, geez." He drew a ragged breath. "And Brady…"

Roy's head snapped up then, his eyes wide and blood-shot. "Brady."

Erin tasted a sour dread at the back of her throat. "Does Brady know?"

Roy shook his head vehemently. "No. H-he had nothing to do with…any of it."

Josh panted a few shallow, agitated breaths, then snarled, "For the love of God, Roy! *Why?* Have we not been good to you?" He jerked his hat off and shoved a hand through his hair. His face crumbled in anguish. "Do you hate us that much? We…we considered you family! You—"

The distant wail of a siren filtered through the winter air over the mooing of cattle and rumble of car engines as travelers tried to stay warm while waiting out the blockade of the highway.

Erin saw the shudder that raced through Roy, but he said nothing else to Josh.

Josh sent his brother a devastated look as if begging his twin to tell him it was all a sick joke. Instead, Zane said, "He was being blackmailed. He killed a woman years ago in a drunk driving hit-and-run. Someone saw, and that someone is using Roy to hurt us."

Erin stepped forward, vaguely aware of the ambulance creeping along the shoulder of the highway toward them. "A blackmailer? Who?"

Zane pressed his mouth in a line of frustration and shook his head. "He refuses to say."

Erin glanced over her shoulder to Roy, who hung his head and clutched his arm to his chest, the image of defeat. Roy wouldn't tell Zane who'd blackmailed him, but perhaps she had enough sway, the right arguments or persuasion, to get the name. Before the cops took him away, she knew she had to try.

Erin sat in Zane's exam room at the hospital as he relayed the story of Roy's confession to his mother. Melissa sat beside her, and judging from the woman's pale complexion, bereft eyes and shaking limbs, his mother was equally, if not more, shell-shocked.

"No," Melissa murmured, shaking her head slightly. "That can't be right. Roy would never... I can't... Oh, Zane, no!"

Zane rubbed a hand gingerly over his taped ribs. Two were cracked, others bruised, and he had a concussion along with multiple tiny cuts, scrapes and contusions from the accident. He refused to be admitted for observation, contending he'd have multiple nurses hovering over him at the ranch.

That much was true. Erin could imagine Melissa wouldn't let her firstborn son out of her sight for days. Erin was of the same inclination, though she wasn't sure Zane would be interested in her company.

"I know it's hard to take in, but he admitted all of it. Even before the ambulance arrived, he'd told the first officer on the scene most of what he'd done. I think...he was relieved to have purged his conscience, even though it means..."

"He'll...go to prison," Melissa finished quietly. She lowered her face to her hands and wept. Erin scooted her chair closer to put an arm around the grieving woman.

"You said someone put him up to it, that he was blackmailed. Did he say who that someone was?" Melissa asked, meeting Zane's gaze.

"No," Erin answered. "I tried to cajole a name from him, but no luck. He's still protecting the person's identity."

"He thinks the asshole—sorry, Mom—the *cretin* could come after his family."

Melissa's back stiffened. "Brady and Piper? Connor!" Her breathing grew shallow and quick. "Oh, no!"

"It's okay, Mom," Zane said, his tone low and comforting. "We're not going to let anything happen to them. Forewarned is forearmed."

As if summoned by mention of him, Brady stepped into the exam room, and from under the rim of his black cowboy hat, he sent Zane and Melissa a stunned and apologetic look. "So I, uh, saw Dad."

Zane's mother rose on unsteady legs and embraced Brady. "Oh, darling boy, I'm so sorry."

Brady squeezed his eyes closed as he clutched Melissa. "No. I should be apologizing to you. I should have known. I should have—" His voice broke and, with it, the barbed-wire tension in the room. Erin felt tears rush past her sinuses, and Zane turned away, rubbing his eyes, while Brady openly wept.

Melissa, for all her grief and hurt, gathered herself first. "How is he, your father? What did the doctors say about his x-rays?"

Brady stepped back, swiping his face and clearing his throat before he answered. "Fractured hip. Broken ulna. He's getting his arm in a cast now." Brady scoffed, and his face contorted with misery. "Under police guard."

The room fell silent for a moment. Erin surveyed the grim faces, knowing each of them was grappling with the staggering revelations and complications of the accident.

"No one blames you, Brady," Zane said at last. "So don't blame yourself."

Brady nodded, but he removed his hat and swatted it against his legs. "I just feel like I should have—"

Melissa gripped his arms and shook him gently. "Stop." She pinned an all-business look on Brady that Erin had seen so often on Zane's face, it took her breath away. "Your father made his choices, son."

Brady twitched, and emotion flooded his face when Melissa used the familial moniker.

"You cannot be responsible for decisions he made, or the reasons he made them. Do you hear me?"

Brady bobbed his head, thumbed moisture from his eye. Then, drawing a deep breath, asked, "Have you heard from Michael or Josh?"

Erin lifted a corner of her mouth in a brief smile, recognizing the change of subject as a deflective and protective technique. Too much heavy emotion for one day. She could imagine the alpha cowboys were on overload trying to sort through the mess.

"Josh checked in about twenty minutes ago." Zane shifted on the exam room bed, wincing as he moved. "They got the herd—what was left of it—to the auction house just before they closed for the day."

Brady nodded. "Good."

"They expect to be back around ten tonight," Erin added.

"How much… How much money was lost because of the smaller herd?"

Zane shrugged one shoulder. "We'll sort that out another day."

Brady blew out a weary sigh. "I, um…should get back

to my Dad. He…" Without finishing the thought, he started for the door.

"Brady?" Melissa called. "Have you spoken to Piper? Is she coming to the hospital?"

"I have. And…no. We thought it best she stay home with Connor until…things can be explained to him."

Melissa's throat worked as she swallowed, and she blinked rapidly as tears leaked from her eyes. "That's probably for the best." When Brady turned back toward the door she added, "Brady?"

He held his cowboy hat between his hands, his chin lowered to his chest.

"Brady, we love you. All of us do. That hasn't changed," Melissa said with a mix of tenderness and steel. "You— and Roy—are family. We'll get through this. Together. We'll figure it out, honey."

Without looking back, he rasped, "Thank you," and strode quickly down the hall.

"I'm going to get some coffee at the cafeteria," Erin said, rising stiffly from the chair where she'd been sitting the last two hours. The emergency room was apparently hopping, and they were still waiting for the results of Zane's CT scan, checking for internal injuries, before the doctor would sign discharge papers. "Can I get anyone anything?"

"No," Zane grunted.

"Yes. Please. Black coffee," Melissa said, trying to hand her money. "Thank you, sweetheart."

Erin waved away the cash and paused by Zane's bedside long enough to lay her hand on his. "Are you sure I can't bring you something? Water? A snack?"

His gaze shifted to their hands, and his mouth firming, he pulled his hand away. "I'm sure."

Erin's heart sank. If she'd thought the accident had changed anything about where she stood with Zane, his withdrawal now cured her of those delusions. She swallowed hard, choking back the tears that knotted her throat.

She spotted the police officer parked on a chair outside Roy's exam room, and her heart lurched. Maybe she was expecting too much from Zane to sort through his feelings for her while he dealt with his family's crisis.

She wished he'd let her in though. If only he'd allow her to help him navigate this dark time in his life.

You lost that privilege when you hurt him.

She hurried to the cafeteria and returned with the two coffees to find the doctor in Zane's exam room, signing papers.

"So go slow in the next couple weeks," the doctor was saying, "Use those prescriptions only as needed, and be sure to get plenty of rest."

With that, they were free to go, and she and Melissa escorted Zane to Melissa's car and back to the ranch.

The next couple of days were beyond miserable for the McCalls as they dealt with the shortfall of income, attended Helen's funeral and answered endless questions from the sheriff's department with regard to Roy's crimes. Kate even offered to delay her and Josh's wedding, scheduled for the next weekend, but the family voted unanimously to go ahead with the nuptials, needing the happy occasion to dispel some of the gloom.

For her part, Erin drove in to Zoe's diner on the third evening after the accident, knowing no one would be in the mood to prepare dinner. She decided buying the family take-out was the least she could do for them under the circumstances.

She hadn't been inside the diner two minutes before Walt Anderson, the former rancher she'd interview at the Feed and Seed, approached her. She greeted him and could immediately tell something was on his mind. "Is there something I can do for you, Mr. Anderson?"

"Well, I hate to be nosy, but...word's spread in town about the accident with the McCalls' trailer on the way to auction. Folks are sayin' Roy Summers has been arrested, too."

"Oh." She drew a deep breath, remiss to delve into the gory details. "The grapevine in Boyd Valley is certainly healthy and quick."

Walt's eyes widened. "Then it's true?"

She hesitated, but finally bobbed a nod. "Who told you?"

"Well, a couple ladies were discussing it at the store earlier. Millie Taylor heard it at Helen's funeral. And Sarah Hinchcliff heard from her husband about the road being closed because of the accident. The rest was just tidbits that came in the Feed and Seed over the last couple days."

Zoe stepped up to the register, ready to take Erin's order, and shamelessly eavesdropping. "What can I get for you, sugar?"

Erin placed her order, deflected a few of the more probing questions from patrons, and hurried back to the car with a large box of hot food ten minutes later.

Zane opened the back door when she knocked and eyed the bags of food as she arranged them on the countertop in the kitchen. Zeke and Sadie, smelling the food, appeared at her feet, meowing loudly.

"The small-town rumor mill is in high gear," she told Zane as she shucked her gloves and unpacked the food. "They already know about Roy and the accident."

Zane let a groan rumble from his throat and pushed Zeke back onto the floor when the cat jumped on the counter to go after the fried chicken. "Swell."

She pulled out her phone and texted Josh and Michael, letting them know dinner had arrived. Returning her gaze to Zane, who winced as he reached in the cabinet to get plates down, she mused over implications of the rumor mill's activity. "Do you think Roy's blackmailer will have heard about his arrest?"

Zane cut a sharp look at her. "I hadn't considered that. But…could be."

She gnawed her bottom lip. "What do you think he'll do?"

He stilled, gave her a strange look, then grumbled, "Why ask me? You're the PI."

His sour tone cut her, but she excused it, given the rough time he'd had the last couple of days. Despite his surly mood, she pursued the line of thought. "Do you think he's left town? Gone to ground? He has to be worried about what Roy is telling the police."

Pausing with a furrow denting his brow, Zane grunted softly and nodded. "Yeah."

Erin took a plate and selected a piece of chicken. "I'm worried that he'll do something intended to warn Roy to keep quiet."

Zane grunted. "I've considered that, too."

"I mean, suppose Roy gets released on bond and this

blackmailer comes after him? Or after Brady or Connor or—"

When his expression darkened, she snapped her mouth closed. She didn't need ESP to know what he was thinking. His concern for the Double M and his family was clearly etched in the lines that bracketed his mouth and eyes.

"The thing is…" She licked fried chicken grease from her fingers, and Zane's gaze zeroed in on her mouth. Her heartbeat stumbled, and she cleared a sudden tightness from her throat before finishing, "I'm not a cop. I have a certain amount of self-defense training and what I feel are pretty good observation skills, but…maybe you all should hire a security guard or—"

Zane's derisive snort interrupted her. "And pay him with what? Magic beans?"

She opened her mouth and closed it again. She had no answer.

"Speaking of…how much do we owe you for dinner?" He withdrew his wallet and opened it.

She waved him off. "Nothing. Please. My treat."

Her answer clearly didn't sit well with him—male pride?—but he jammed his wallet back in his pocket. "Do you really think that with my dad, Josh, Brady and myself—" he said, his tone skeptical "—and Dave for that matter, all on the premises, all skilled with rifles and handguns, all with a vested interest in protecting our family and property, that we need to pay someone to come guard us?"

She lifted a hand in surrender. "Just trying to consider all the angles and possibilities."

Zeke jumped on the counter again, sniffing the chicken. She twitched a small smile for the feline's bold persistence as she nudged him away from the family's dinner and scratched his head as she lifted him to the floor. "Silly kitty."

Bold persistence. The words reminded her of Josh's advice regarding Zane. *Fight for him.*

As she straightened from putting Zeke on the floor, Zane said, "I guess you'll be leaving soon?"

She blinked at him. His words were so in the face of her line of thought, she had to wonder if he could read her mind. "Leaving?"

His level gaze was haunted, shadowed with pain, fatigue and abundant worry. And something else she'd never seen in his eyes before. Was it regret?

"With the vandalism solved, I assumed you'd be moving on. The police can take over now, rooting out the blackmailer."

The notion of leaving the ranch hurt more than it should, and it took her a moment to form her reply.

"On the contrary, I intend to stay and lend my assistance in finding the blackmailer. Although…I guess that it's really your dad's decision when my job is done."

Her phone pinged with an incoming text. Josh.

On our way! Starving!

"However," she added, willing her voice not to crack, "I will probably go home for Christmas, get out of your family's way for the wedding." She heard voices from the back of the house. The rest of the family making their way in for dinner.

As much as she'd grown to admire and care for the McCalls over the past weeks, as much as she wished she might have a future as a member of the ranching family, she was an outsider. Her chest squeezed. Suddenly she had no appetite. Pushing her plate aside, she gathered her gloves and headed for the back door. "Well, enjoy your dinner. I think I'm going to head to bed early and read."

As she left through the back door, she glanced back at Zane. He met her eyes for a few seconds, and she'd swear there was a question in his gaze. Hope filled her like a balloon. He seemed about to speak but...instead inhaled deeply, firmed his mouth and jerked a dismissive nod. Deflated and shivering in the icy December air, she trudged toward the guesthouse.

Once she'd had a hot shower, she plugged her phone into her laptop at the breakfast table to charge and headed to bed, weary to the bone. But for all her bodily fatigue, her mind wouldn't rest.

She replayed Roy's confession, the guilt in his expression and tears of shame. She saw the shock, pain and anger that crossed each of the McCall's faces as they learned the news. Brady's torment over his divided loyalties. Knowing how easily Zane could have been killed in the truck accident. And most off all, his reticence around her. The melancholy, conflicted shadows in his eyes when he'd looked at her over the past few days.

Even after everything they'd been through together, he remained distant, quiet, guarded around her. Knowing her deception was at the heart of why she'd lost Zane's trust was an open wound she didn't think would heal anytime soon. Zane was not like the men she knew in Boulder. Not like any man she'd met before. He was scrupulous to a fault, and when she'd chipped past his protective wall, she'd known a man whose heart was as good, as loving, as true as any she'd ever known. More so. He was fiercely loyal, protective and smart as a whip. And oh, Lordy, could the man kiss! He had a raw sex appeal and chemistry with her that—

She determinedly shoved aside thoughts of her physical attraction to him, the intimate moments they'd shared. She'd never get to sleep if she roused the tingling, heated flush of desire that memories of his hands on her evoked.

Punching her pillow, she rolled over and blanked her mind...for all of a minute. And then the circle of thoughts began again. Finally, about two hours later, she managed a light sleep.

But a creaking noise, as if someone was walking across the hardwood floor in the living room, woke Erin soon after she'd drifted off. She sat up in her bed and listened, straining her ears for another sound while her heart beat an anxious rhythm. Was it Zane coming to talk? She remembered his angry declaration that as the owner of the guesthouse he would come and go from it as he pleased.

A scraping sound, as if the chair at the kitchen table had been moved, was followed by thumps and bumps, cracking noises. Paper tearing. Was Zane snooping through her research again? But why, since Roy had confessed to the vandalism...?

Heart racing, she rolled toward the bedside stand in search of her phone. Remembering belatedly she'd left the phone plugged into her laptop to charge, she bit her bottom lip, debating her options.

She tossed back the covers and started down the hall to confront Zane. About the time the hardwood floor squeaked under her feet, her sleep-and-fatigue-fogged mind considered another option.

What if the late-night visitor wasn't Zane? She'd

locked all the doors to the guesthouse, but was it possible that—

A strong arm seized her around the throat, and a gun was jabbed under her chin.

And Erin loosed a scream.

Chapter 17

Zane scuffed his boot against the frozen ground in frustration. He hadn't been able to sleep, despite the painkillers. But his sore ribs and head weren't what had kept him awake. He'd been groping through the dense forest of his emotions, trying to understand the hows and whys of the tumult inside him. The hurt in Erin's face as she'd left the kitchen that evening, like that of a scolded puppy, twisted in his gut. He knew deep down she was sorry for her lies and deceit. He wanted to truly forgive her, to give her a second chance—give *them* a second chance—but something held him back. What? And why?

He mentally recounted the special moments they'd shared, the way she lifted his spirits, challenged him, inspired him. And she'd changed him—for the better. So if she was good for him, made him happy, had all the qualities he wanted in a lover and friend, why did the thought of her rattle him so deeply?

When he sighed, his breath formed a frosty white cloud that wafted like a ghost in the moonlight. He always came out to the corral to think, even at night, even in the dead of winter. The quiet appealed to him. The vast open sky lulled him. The proximity to the horses gave him a sense of rootedness. The night, the sky, the animals were soothing in their predictability, their steadfastness. They didn't change, and Zane had never liked change. Change brought with it an uncertainty that unsettled him.

He gritted his teeth as the familiar roil in his gut started when he thought of the recent upheaval in his life. He was losing any control he ever had over—

He paused, his thoughts snagging on the word *control*. Josh always countered Zane's criticism of his recklessness with accusations that Zane was a control freak. He'd shrugged off the term. Sure, he liked order and predictability. So what? But what if his need for control was more deeply rooted? A tickle started at the base of his neck. What if—?

A muffled woman's scream pierced the night, jerking him from his thoughts.

Zane's pulse spiked as he whirled around. Where had it come from? His gaze flew first to the guesthouse. Erin was alone, unprotected if she—

A shadow moved past the dimly lit front window of the guesthouse, and Zane ran across the ranch yard, heedless of the jostling to his ribs. He skidded to a stop near the front step, reining in his impulse to burst through the door. He had no idea what or who he'd find. He needed to use caution.

He'd left his phone in the house on his nightstand. He debated for the briefest instant taking the time to retrieve his cell phone and call the sheriff. But a crash inside the guesthouse, another muffled cry, resolved the issue. Erin needed him—*now*.

He tested the front door, and though the knob didn't twist, indicating it was locked, the door swung open. A chill slithered through him. By the glow of Erin's laptop, he spotted a man near the table where Erin had worked. He had his arms around Erin, and she was struggling to get free.

With a slap of his hand, he flipped on the light. "Let her go!"

Erin gasped, and the man holding her jerked taut as the overhead light flooded the room.

Zane filled the front door, his face dark with the vehemence of an avenging angel. Her relief at seeing him shattered in the next moment as her captor swung his weapon toward Zane.

"Gun!" she shouted.

Zane dove behind the couch.

"Stop!" Erin pleaded with the man. "Don't hurt him! I'll give you what you want. Just…don't shoot anyone. Please!"

The weapon shifted back to her.

"Now we're getting somewhere," the man growled.

From behind the couch, she heard Zane moving. Groaning. Her gut knotted. "Zane?"

"Put the gun down, Hugh!" Zane shouted. "We can resolve this without anyone getting hurt."

Hugh?

"You know him?" Erin asked, and the gun jabbed harder into her neck.

"Shut up! Both of you!"

"Yeah, I know him," Zane said, rising from behind the sofa with his hands in the air. "His name is Hugh Carver. He's Gill's father."

Erin scrambled back through her memory for what she'd learned about Gill Carver's father. "You—" she turned her head and angled her eyes to see her captor's face "—were a rancher. Before…"

Hugh curled his lip in disdain, and he waved the gun in Zane's direction. "Before this punk and his family took advantage of my bad luck and profited from my family's misery? Yeah."

Zane shook his head. "That's not how it happened. You were bankrupt before my father ever bought anything at the auctions. We had nothing to do with your losses."

Erin searched for something close at hand she could use as a weapon to defend herself, to help Zane if the situation spiraled further out of control. Papers, her dirty coffee mug, a pen.

"Didn't stop your father from licking his chops and tearing into my carcass before my body was even cold," Hugh said.

Erin's gut turned at her captor's morbid analogy, but she used the man's distraction to inch her fingers toward the pen on the table.

Zane took a step forward, hands still up. "Look, Hugh, put the gun down and we'll talk."

"Talk?" the man scoffed. "It is way too late for talking."

"Then what do you want? Why are you here?"

"I had to come. Had to get rid of the evidence." Hugh

heaved a sigh, and his chest vibrated as he growled, "Summers blew it."

"Roy?" Zane asked.

"Of course, Roy. I had no way to know how much the drunk idiot told the cops." Gill's father shifted his weight, and his grip around her waist tightened. "I knew this one—" he jabbed the muzzle harder against her throat "—had been snooping around, asking questions. I told Roy to get rid of her, destroy her notes, but he refused. So I had no choice. I had to come myself. Get rid of anything, *and anyone*, who could implicate me."

Erin's breath froze in her chest. If she'd any question about the man's intentions before, he'd erased those doubts. He wanted to silence her. Permanently.

She watched the color leach from Zane's face as he drew the same conclusion. "Hugh, don't be rash."

"I have no choice. I will *not* go to prison because Roy Summers screwed up!"

"Roy didn't sell you out." Erin said, her voice breaking. "He confessed to what he did, but didn't tell anyone who put him up to it!"

Hugh grew quiet, still. "You're lying."

Zane shook his head slowly. "He was worried that you'd hurt his family. He wanted to protect them. He never said a word about who was blackmailing him."

Which meant Hugh had blown his own cover by panicking. Erin knew the moment the older man realized that truth, because his grip on her sagged briefly. And she took advantage of that instant of distraction.

With her hand fisted around the pen, she jabbed it into the old man's leg as hard as she could. When he screamed and grabbed for his injured thigh, she allowed her body to go limp, crumple to the floor. While he roared curses at her, she rolled away and scrambled to her feet, ready to feint or dodge as needed.

Zane was at her side in an instant, shoving his body in front of hers as a shield.

"Damn you, bitch!" Hugh raised a ferocious glare as he aimed the gun at them and fired.

Zane jerked her to the floor, and she heard the thud as the bullet lodged itself in the hardwood, inches from her ear. They scuttled behind the couch for protection, and Zane rose to a crouch to peer over the back at Gill's father.

"Hugh, stop! Think about what you're doing! By now my family has heard the gunshot, her screams, and they've called the police."

Erin closed her eyes and said a quick prayer that Zane's claim was true.

"If you shoot us, you'll only add to your troubles. Think of *your* family. Don't—"

"My family?" he shouted. "Now you care about my family? What about ten years ago when you and your father were driving me out of business and buying up my land and equipment like vultures?"

Erin estimated the distance to the door. Could she crawl to it and escape, get help without getting shot? Did she dare leave Zane here with Hugh, a man clearly not thinking rationally and full of rage toward the McCalls? Her heart drummed a frantic tattoo.

Maybe if Zane distracted Hugh, she could ease quietly from the other end of the sofa, work her way behind the gunman and reach her phone. Text the other McCalls. Call 9-1-1.

"Think about what you are doing, Hugh," Zane said, his voice remarkably calm and reasonable.

"I'm done thinking and waiting," Hugh grumbled. He shoved her laptop on the floor and fired at it. "It's time for justice. Time for my revenge."

She touched Zane on the arm, drawing his attention. *Keep him talking*, she mouthed. *Distracted.*

He frowned in query, then seemed to understand her intention, because he shook his head, mouthing, *No!*

She nodded and made hand signals of her plan to retrieve her phone.

His mouth firmed, and his eyes flashed with vehemence. *No!* he mouthed again and pointed to the floor. *Stay here!*

I can do this, she mouthed back.

More bumps and crashes drew their attention back to Hugh, who had knocked over a chair and was throwing files into the fireplace, reigniting her banked coals.

She didn't wait for any other reply. Easing to the opposite end of the sofa, she rose in a squat. She peeked toward the spot on the floor where her mangled laptop lay with her phone still tethered by a short cable. And crept toward it.

Zane grabbed for Erin as she moved from behind the couch. Missed. Panic flared in his chest as she slipped away, out from the protection of the sofa. What the hell was she doing? Why wouldn't she listen to him? If she'd just do as he'd told her and—

A jolt of reality chilled him to the bone. He had no control over Erin. No control over this standoff. Things could go very wrong, very quickly, and he'd be at the mercy of other people's choices, of fate, of luck—whether good or bad. But he still controlled his own actions, and he'd do whatever it took to rein in this situation and direct the outcome.

He drew a ragged breath as he hurried back to the other end of the couch to find something to distract Hugh.

"Hugh," he said, allowing himself to be seen as he peered around the couch, not only snagging the old rancher's attention but stealing a glimpse of Erin's progress. In a squat, she was silently duck-waddling in her bare feet toward the laptop.

Hugh glanced toward him, firing a wild shot over his head.

Zane ducked back down, his pulse thundering. Damn it, he'd get himself shot, die if he had to, if only he could be sure Erin would be all right.

"I had Roy under my thumb until that nosy bitch from out of town came poking around. She ruined everything! But I won't let her and Roy destroy me!"

"No," Zane answered, rising slightly to survey the situation again. "You're doing that by yourself. Your bad decisions are what brought you here and caught you in this snare. You are the only one to blame, Hugh."

Music filled the air suddenly, cheerful and incongruous to the tension of the standoff. Erin's ring tone.

Hugh swung around, startled by the sound. And spotted Erin, who'd frozen about a yard short of her phone.

Zane's heart stuck in his throat. No!

When Erin lunged for her phone, Hugh raised the handgun.

And Zane surged from his crouch, took two running steps and tackled Hugh.

The gun fired as Hugh and Zane grappled for control of the weapon.

Erin gasped and flattened herself on the floor, hoping to make herself a smaller target for stray bullets. She angled her head to monitor the struggle between Zane and her intruder. Zane had a grip on the man's gun hand and was slamming it on the ground, trying to force Hugh to lose his grip on the weapon.

Another shot fired, and Erin rolled back toward the sofa, weighing her options as fast as her stunned brain could process the rapidly changing situation. *Get the gun. Help Zane.* That much was obvious but...

And then Hugh's hold on the gun faltered, and the revolver skittered across the hardwood floor. Erin pounced, snatching up the weapon and aiming it at the two men who were still grappling, throwing punches, battling for the upper hand. She stood there for a second or two, shaking and trying to steady her aim. But she couldn't shoot Hugh without risking hitting Zane.

Her phone was still ringing, and with the gun now in her control, she hazarded a glance at the caller ID. Piper.

She thumbed the answer icon and immediately heard Piper's voice. "Erin? Erin, are you there? We heard gunfire! Are you all right?"

"Call the cops! We need help!" With that, she tossed the phone aside without even disconnecting the call.

In the next instant, the door burst open, and after a quick glance around the door frame, sizing up the situation, Josh and Michael charged into the room.

Michael held a rifle and aimed it at the wrestling men.

"Are you all right?" Josh shouted to Erin, his gaze darting briefly to her.

She gave him a jerky nod and slowly lowered the gun.

"It's Hugh Carver," Erin cried over the buzz of adrenaline in her ears and crash of furniture as Hugh and Zane knocked over chairs as they fought. "He came to kill me and destroy any evidence I had of his blackmailing Roy."

Josh shot her a frown of dismay, then set his jaw as he dove into the fray with his twin.

With Josh's assistance, Zane soon had Hugh subdued, and Michael stepped over to press the muzzle of the rifle between Hugh's eyes.

Teeth clenched, Michael grated, "Give me an excuse, you bastard."

"Dad." Josh put a hand on the rifle and pinned Michael with a hard glare. When Josh tugged on the rifle, Michael released it, and Zane dragged Hugh to his feet.

Hugh divided a glare among the three McCall men before him, then spat at Michael.

Zane's father balled his hand and smashed his fist into Hugh's nose. Stepping back, he heaved a sigh and divided a look between his sons. "Now, let that be the end of it."

Chapter 18

"Aren't you going to see Erin off? Say goodbye?"

Zane glanced up from the desk in his office when his father stuck his head in the door, aiming his thumb toward the front of the house. "She's leaving? Now?"

Michael turned up a palm as if the answer should be obvious. "The case I gave her to work on has been resolved. Her job is done, so she's going to surprise her family a day early for Christmas." He jerked his head toward the front hall. "C'mon. Josh says she's loading up."

Zane sat in his chair, feeling a bit shell-shocked. Erin was leaving.

Of course, she's leaving, idiot! You've given her no reason to stay.

Last night, after the sheriff arrived to take Hugh into custody and the deputies had taken all the statements they needed, he'd simply told Erin good-night. Everyone had retired to bed, given the late hour and the exhaustion that had quickly settled over each them in the wake of the sabotage mystery being solved, the blackmailer captured. As if the tension of the crimes against his family had been all that held them upright, once removed, they'd all collapsed.

All, that is, but Zane. Zane had believed that with the threat to his family removed, he'd have a clearer mind about his relationship with Erin. And that he'd have time today to sort through his emotions and have a frank conversation with her. He'd been deluding himself on both accounts.

He'd spent the hours until daybreak reliving the terror of seeing Erin on the business end of Hugh's gun. The ice that had settled in his marrow brought his love for her into stark relief. The possibility of losing her, of her being killed in front of him, had been a nasty wake-up call. His life without her would be bleak and painful. Full of regret.

Zane drew a shuddering breath and gripped the edge of his desk. Death was only one way to lose her. Even now she was packing her car, about to walk out of his life. He was about to lose her because of his own mulish pride and blindness.

Did you really expect otherwise when you've been so distant the last few days? Zane's heart sank. Clearly she had taken her cues from him and drawn the only conclusion she could.

He shoved to his feet, his heart galloping. He saw the truth now. He'd used her deception about her reason for being at the ranch as an excuse to justify pushing her away. But he'd been lying, as well. To himself. He'd held her at arm's length, built walls around his heart, because his feelings for her confused him. Frightened him. He'd fallen for her so hard and so fast, his logical mind hadn't had time to catch up. Loving her so deeply meant greater pain if he lost her. Stupid, stupid! In trying to avoid that pain, he'd brought it about.

"And you're supposed to be the smart one," he mumbled to himself as he grabbed his coat and hurried outside.

Josh was closing the trunk of Erin's car as Zane strode out into the ranch yard. He watched her give Josh then Kate and Piper each a hug, and panic beat its wings inside him.

Don't blow it, he thought as he stepped forward. "Erin."

She turned to him with a melancholy expression. "Goodbye, Zane. Thank you for your help last night. I owe you my life."

Her soft curls tickled his chin as she rose on tiptoe to brush a kiss on his cheek. As she stepped back, turning toward her car, he caught her sleeve. "Erin, wait."

She glanced up, her eyes full of expectation and... trepidation?

"I, um..." He drew and exhaled a cleansing breath. "I forgive you."

She blinked. Scoffed a gentle laugh and pulled her arm free of his grip. "Good to know."

Piper's groan matched his internal one.

I forgive you. What was that?

Erin climbed into her car quickly and started the engine. With a last wave to the family, she headed down the driveway.

And Zane's heart crashed to his toes.

From behind, Piper gave him the head slap he wanted

to give himself. "Why didn't you let her know how you feel, Dork?"

Kate added a look of disappointment and shook her head. "You missed your chance, Zane. While Josh's showing up at my door days after I left the ranch was romantic and all, he could have spared me days of agony thinking I'd lost him."

Josh strolled closer, one eyebrow raised in disappointment. "Dude…"

Piper gripped his arm. "Get her back here! Tell her you love her!"

"You need a gesture," Kate said. "Something special to let her know how serious you are, how much she means to you."

"Oh, yes! A big, romantic gesture!" Piper said, nodding.

"Agreed." Josh shoved his hands into his pockets and gave him a nod. "She'll love it."

Zane frowned. "A gesture? What does that even mean? Like flowers?"

"Come on, Zane," Piper said, her nose wrinkled. "Flowers are nice and all, but you're fighting for her heart! Time to think outside the box. Break the mold. Be less…Zane-ish."

"Less Zane-ish? What the hell does Zane-ish mean?" he asked.

"If it is practical or well-planned or safe…throw that idea out." Piper gave him the stink-eye. "Your normal is the opposite of the spontaneity that will sweep her off her feet."

"Great. That's a big help," he groused.

"Well," Kate said and tapped a fingernail on her teeth as she thought. "Is she coming back for mine and Josh's wedding? You could do something sweet for her there."

"That's a good idea!" His sister gushed. "And it counts as spontaneous, considering the wedding is in a week. Anything that gives you less than a month to plan counts as impromptu."

His sister's teasing typically rolled off his back. But something about her gibe stuck with him. Not unpleasantly, just...

"Uh, except..." Josh said, twisting his mouth and motioning toward where he'd been helping Erin load her car, "she just told me she wasn't coming to the wedding. I invited her, of course, but she declined." The look his brother gave him told Zane he was the reason Erin was avoiding the wedding.

But the seed Piper had planted was taking root, and he ignored his brother's accusing frown. Slipping his phone from his pocket, he sent Erin a text he hoped was enough to convince her to turn around.

Erin heard her phone ping with an incoming text. She'd been sitting at the end of the long driveway to the Double M, trying to battle back the sting of tears before she pulled out onto the highway that would take her out of town, away from the ranch, away from the man she'd grown to love.

When she saw who the text was from, she almost deleted it, unread. Even knowing she was about to leave the ranch, the best Zane could do was tell her he forgave her for her false cover story?

She'd had to leave in a rush or risk breaking down in front of him. Josh had urged her to fight for Zane, and she'd tried to reach out to him. Only to be rebuffed time and again. Her heart could only take so much.

But through the blur of tears, she saw the simple message he'd sent her.

You forgot something.

She frowned. Had she driven off so fast that she'd neglected one of her bags? She supposed it was possible. But returning to the house meant facing Zane again. Her heart was already in tatters. She banged her fist on the steering wheel. Damn it, she didn't want to drag her crushed soul through the mud again just because she'd forgotten her toothbrush or a pair of gloves.

She eyed the highway, her escape route. Then sucked in a deep breath for strength and executed a Y-turn.

Her gut churned harder with every inch she traveled back up the long, gravel driveway. She could see Zane waiting for her. His tall frame topped by his gray Stetson, his wide shoulders and confident stance sent a bittersweet yearning through her. He was so incredibly handsome, and her heart betrayed her with a painful squeeze. She loved him, but she would move on. She'd have to.

His family was still gathered in the yard, as well, which both surprised her and pleased her. Piper, Michael, Kate and Josh would serve as buffers.

Get in, get the forgotten item, get out.

That had been her plan but Zane was at her driver's-side door before she'd even stopped the car.

"Thanks for coming back." He opened her door and reached for her elbow to help her step out.

"What did I leave?"

Rather than answer, he tugged on her arm, encouraging her to get out of the car. "You'll see."

"Zane—"

"Please?"

She glanced to the others, searching for a clue to what was going on, but their faces reflected the same confusion that churned inside her.

He nudged her again, his expression pleading, hopeful. "Erin, please?"

Reluctantly she climbed out and met his piercing blue eyes. "Zane, please, don't make this harder than it has to be."

Placing his hands on her shoulders, he urged her to face him. "What if I made it easier?"

Her pulse thumped warily. "What do you mean?"

He dropped to one knee and blurted, "Marry me."

She blinked. "What?"

Piper and Kate gasped joyfully.

"Next week," he added.

Josh made a choking sound. "What!"

Zane glanced over his shoulder and sent Josh an apologetic look. "Oh, I guess I should ask if you'd mind a double wedding. I don't want to steal your thunder, but I thought—"

His sister's giddy shriek and Kate's squeals of delight interrupted him.

Erin was numb. Stunned. Her jaw dropped.

"We don't mind!" Kate called. "It's perfect! Twins should get married on the same day!"

Josh's mouth opened and shut without a sound before he stuttered, "Wh-what's happening?"

Piper trotted up and hugged Zane, nearly knocking

him over in her zeal. "Our brother is being un-Zane-ish! Oh, my gosh! This is a wonderful idea!"

He untangled himself from his sister's embrace and cleared his throat. "Uh, Pipe… Erin hasn't answered yet."

All eyes turned to Erin. She was, she realized, staring, owl-like, at the assembly surrounding her. Still blinking. Still gaping. Still reeling.

"Erin," Zane said, taking her hand, drawing her full attention back to him, "I love you. The last two-plus weeks with you have changed my life. You've brought me a happiness and sense of completion like nothing I've ever known before. I feel more alive around you, more joyful, more eager to see what tomorrow will bring. What better way to celebrate that than to do something completely out of character for me and get married without overthinking it."

Erin's breath left her in a wheeze. "A-are you sure?"

"Never more sure of anything in my life. It feels good. It feels right. Please, sweetheart. I know I haven't given you a lot of reason to be sure of my feelings. Mainly because I haven't known how to. Emotions are something that I've avoided for years."

"Your whole life," Josh muttered.

"Do you mind?" Zane asked, shooting his brother a quelling look. "This isn't an audience-participation proposal."

Josh waved a hand toward Erin and took a step back.

When Zane turned back to her, tears filled her eyes. Was this really happening?

Zane studied her face, and his expression grew concerned. "I, um…" Zane drew a fortifying breath and plunged on, as if he needed to say everything in his heart or he knew he'd lose the opportunity.

"Giving in to my emotions felt like…giving up control. Giving power to something I couldn't manage or steer. And losing control scared me." He huffed a humorless laugh. "Hell, it still scares me. Figuring out how I felt about you, knowing what to do with those feelings while so much else was going on with the family, wasn't easy for me. Until you said you were leaving."

The breath she'd been holding shuddered out of her, and he paused as if to analyze what it meant. She raised her eyebrows, silently asking him to continue. Zane pressed Erin's hands between his. "And like a light being turned off, I knew immediately the darkness I'd be living in if you left. I knew how much I needed you in my life. You…help me make sense of everything in here." He tapped his chest. "I've been a brooding, business-obsessed killjoy for the last few years because…"

He paused, glanced back at his family. "I was terrified of losing the people that I loved. My father's high blood pressure scared me. Piper's stalker scared me. Kate and Josh's accident on the zip line scared me." He cast another brief glance behind him where Josh stood. His brother, his best friend, looked gob-smacked, but gave a nod of encouragement. *Keep going*, he could hear Josh saying in his head.

"But the thing that scares me most now is the thought of living the rest of my life without you. Before today, I didn't know how to tell you what I was feeling, because…I couldn't really understand it myself. But after seeing Hugh hold a gun on you, I finally realized—"

"Yes," Erin said, a whisper in the frosty ranch yard.

Zane lost his line of thought. Stared at her dubiously. "What?"

"As I recall you started this speech by asking me to marry you."

He blinked, his pulse racing, and two heartbeats later his brain caught up. "Right! I—"

"Ask her again," Josh muttered through a fake cough.

Excitement, joy and a heavy dose of incredulity swamped him. He patted his chest as if searching for a ring box. "I... Oh, I don't have a ring." He grimaced then rushed on. "But I'll get one! Today! I'll go into Denver and—"

"Just say the words!" Piper said, crowding closer.

Nervous energy pumped through him, and when he raised his eyes to Erin's this time, the sparkle of tears in her eyes was accompanied by the familiar light of love and happiness that had filled him with warmth from the first day they'd met. He squeezed both her hands between his, cleared his throat and asked, "Erin Palmer, will you make this the merriest Christmas of my life and stay here to celebrate this holiday and every other one together for the rest of our lives?"

Her eyebrows furrowed. "Uh, well...no. I can't do that."

His heart plummeted and behind him he heard the women groan softly. "But... I—"

Erin shook her head. "It's just the way you worded it. I've promised my parents I'll be home for Christmas. Since Sean died, having the family together at Christmas has been all the more important. Kelly is flying in and, well...I can't stay *today*."

"Geez, Zane," Josh said, laughing, "just spit it out, for cripe's sake!"

When Zane sent his twin a glare, he saw that his mother had joined the entourage. Piper and Kate had inched closer and were huddled just behind him, their faces expectant. Rather than being irritated with his family invading his space during this momentous event, he grinned. Aiming a thumb over his shoulder, he said, "You see what you'll be getting yourself into, right?"

"Zane!" his family said en masse.

But it was the antsy look on Erin's face that spurred him to blurt, "I love you deeply, Erin. Will you please marry me?"

"Finally!" Josh said.

"I will," Erin said, nodding and dropping to her knees to hug him.

And suddenly more bodies were wrapped around them, squeezing, congratulating and welcoming Erin into the fold. And Zane had never been happier.

Epilogue

Melissa put her arm around Michael's waist and leaned in to kiss his cheek. She surveyed the small wedding reception, spreading from their dining room into the living room and den. The addition of Erin's family and a few of her closest friends crowded things a bit, but she was pleased to accommodate them.

"Well, we did it," Michael said. "Got all three of our children married off to devoted spouses."

She snorted a laugh and elbowed him. "Married off? This isn't *Pride and Prejudice*, and you're not Mr. Bennet."

He rolled his eyes. "You know what I mean." Nodding toward the living room, where the furniture had been pushed back to create a dance floor, he motioned to the newly wedded couples. "Our children are in love, and all is right with the world."

Almost all, she thought, but wouldn't for the world dim Michael's happiness. Especially not today, her boys' wedding day. She cut a glance toward Brady, her heart aching for him, knowing how Roy's imprisonment weighed on him. As hurt and angry as she was over Roy's betrayal, she ached for the man who had been part of their family for so long. Thankfully, his cooperation with the authorities in building their case against Hugh Carver had helped his lawyer negotiate a plea deal that included a lower-security prison and the possibility of parole down the road. Brady had been named his father's successor as foreman, and his first duty would be hiring a new hand.

The thought of the new hand brought a pang of grief. Melissa searched the room for Dave, and she found him sitting in the corner of the room talking with Erin's father. Dave was strong, resilient. His leg would heal, and he'd have a job waiting when he was ready to work again. Losing Helen would be hard to get past, but she'd make sure he didn't travel that path alone.

"Did I tell you?" Michael said, cutting into her thoughts, "I had a call this morning from the Carver family lawyer."

Melissa tensed. "Oh?"

He nodded. "Gill, in a classic 'cover your ass' move, has asked their attorney to negotiate a settlement with us in return for us not suing his father for the damages he caused our business."

She turned to face Michael fully, her grip tightening on his arm. "And?"

"And who am I to turn down money when we're gonna need income from somewhere to get us back on our feet?"

Frowning, she started, "But it's—"

"I know." He met her eyes. "Hugh will still face the criminal charges, but signing will prevent us from taking them to civil court." He sighed. "And, honestly, I just want to put this chapter of our lives behind us. I want to accept the settlement and move forward." He nodded toward the dance floor where Zane was smiling at his bride, Josh and Kate were sharing a private laugh, and Connor was sharing a three-person dance with Piper and Brady. "I want this day to be the new beginning we all need."

Melissa let her arguments go and smiled warmly at Michael. "Okay."

He raised one eyebrow. "Then I have your consent to sign the settlement?"

She place a kiss on his lips and nodded. "Of course."

"Good." He turned to snag two glasses of champagne from the bar behind them and handed one to her. Lifting his glass he said, "To new fresh starts."

She clinked her glass against his. "And to happy endings."

* * * * *

*Don't miss the rest of the McCall
Adventure Ranch miniseries:*

Rancher's Deadly Reunion
(Piper and Brady's story)

and

Rancher's High-Stakes Rescue
(Josh and Kate's story)

*Available now wherever Harlequin Romantic Suspense
books and ebooks are sold!*

Read on for an exclusive sneak peek at Fatal Invasion, *the next sizzling book in the Fatal series from* New York Times *bestselling author Marie Force...*

ONE

"THIS IS A classic case of be careful what you wish for." Nick placed a stack of folded dress shirts in a suitcase that already held socks, underwear, workout clothes and several pairs of jeans. Only Nick would start packing seven days before his scheduled departure for Europe next Sunday, the day after Freddie and Elin's wedding. "That's the lesson learned here."

"Only anal-retentive freakazoids pack a week before a trip." Sam sat at the foot of the bed and watched him pack with a growing sense of dread. "*Three freaking weeks.* The last time you were gone that long, I nearly lost my mind, and I don't have much of a mind left to lose."

"Come with me," he said for the hundredth time since the president asked him to make the diplomatic trip, representing the administration on a visit with some of the country's closest allies. Since President Nelson was still recovering—in more ways than one—from his son's criminal activities, several of the allies had requested he send his popular vice president in his stead.

Sam flopped on the bed. "I *can't.* I have work and Scotty, and Freddie is going on his honeymoon for *two* weeks and… I can't." No Nick at home to entertain her. No Freddie at work to entertain her. The next few weeks were going to totally suck monkey balls.

"Actually, you *can.*" Nick hovered above her, propped on arms ripped with muscles, his splendid chest on full display. "You have more vacation time saved up than you can use in a lifetime, *and* you have the right to actually use it. Scotty will be fine with Shelby, your dad and Celia, your sisters, and the Secret Service here to entertain him. We could even ask Mrs. Littlefield to come up for the weekends."

Their son's former guardian would love the chance to spend time with him, but Sam didn't feel right about leaving him for so long. However, the thought of being without Nick for three endless weeks made her sick. His trip to Iran earlier in the year had been pure torture, especially since it kept getting extended.

"Why'd you have to tell Nelson you wanted to be more than a figurehead vice president?" She play-punched his chest. "Everything was fine when he was ignoring you."

He kissed her lips and then her neck. "You're so, *so* cute when you pout."

"Badass cops do *not* pout."

"Mine does when she doesn't get her own way, and it's truly adorable."

She scowled at him. "Badass cops are not adorable."

"Mine is." Leaving a trail of hot kisses on her neck, he said, "Come with me, Samantha. London, Paris, Rome, the Vatican, Amsterdam, Brussels, The Hague. Come see the world with me."

Sam had never been to Europe and had always wanted to go, so she was sorely tempted to say to hell with her responsibilities.

"Come on." He rolled her earlobe between his teeth and pressed against her suggestively. "Three whole *weeks* together away from the madness of DC. You know you want to go. Gonzo could cover for you at work, and things have been slow anyway."

There hadn't been a homicide in more than a week, which meant they were due, and that was another reason to stay home. "Don't say that and put a jinx on us."

"Come away with me. Scotty will be fine. We'll Face-Time with him every day and bring him presents. He'll be well cared for by everyone else who loves him." He kissed her neck as he unbuttoned her shirt and pushed it aside. "You'd get to meet the Queen of England."

Sam moaned. She *loved* the queen—speaking of a badass female.

"And the Pope. Plus, you'll need some clothes—and shoes. *Lots* of shoes."

"Stop it." She turned her face to avoid his kiss. "You're fighting dirty."

"Because I want my wife to come with me on the trip of a lifetime? I *need* you, Samantha."

As he well knew, she could deny him nothing when he said he needed her. "Fine, I'll go! But only if it's okay with Scotty and if I can swing it at work."

"Yes," her husband said on a long exhale. "We'll have so much fun."

"Will we actually get to see anything?"

He pushed himself up to continue packing. "I'll make sure of it."

"Um, excuse me."

"What's up?"

"My temperature after your attempts at persuasion."

A slow, lazy smile spread across his face, making him the sexiest man in this universe—and the next. "Is my baby feeling a little needy?"

She pulled her shirt off and released the front clasp on her bra. "More than a little."

"We can't have that." Stepping to the foot of the bed, he grasped the legs of her yoga pants and yanked them off.

"Lock the door."

"Scotty's asleep."

"*Lock the door*, or this isn't happening." With Secret Service agents all over their house, Sam couldn't relax if the door wasn't locked.

"This is definitely happening, but if it'll make you happy, I'll lock the door."

"It'll make me happy, which will, in turn, make *you* happy." She splayed her legs wide open to give him a show as he returned from locking the door, and was rewarded with gorgeous hazel eyes that heated with desire when he saw her waiting for him.

"You little vixen," he muttered.

"I don't know *what* you're talking about."

"Sure, you don't," he said, laughing as he came down on top of her and set out to give her a preview of what three weeks away together might be like.

THEY BROKE THE news to Scotty the next morning at breakfast. "So," Nick said tentatively, "what would you think if Mom came with me to Europe?"

Thirteen-year-old Scotty, never at his best first thing in the morning, shrugged. "It's fine."

"Really?" Sam said. "You wouldn't mind? Shelby, Tracy and Angela would be around to hang with you, and Gramps and Celia, too. We thought maybe Mrs. Littlefield could come up for a weekend or two if she's free."

"Sure, that sounds good."

Sam glanced at Nick, who seemed equally perplexed by his lack of reaction. They'd expected him to ask to come with them, at the very least.

"Is everything okay?" Sam asked her son.

"Uh-huh." He finished his cereal and got up to put the bowl in the sink. "I'm going to finish getting ready for school."

"Okay, bud," Nick said.

"Something's up," Sam said as soon as Scotty left the room.

"I agree. He didn't even ask if he could miss school to come with us."

"I thought the same thing."

"We'll have to see if we can get him to talk to us before we go—and not in the morning," Nick said.

"I'll ask Shelby to make spaghetti for dinner. That always puts him in a good mood." Sam's phone rang, and when she saw the number for Dispatch, she groaned. "Damn it. You jinxed me!" So much for getting out of Dodge without having to worry about work. She took the call. "Holland."

"Lieutenant, there was a fire overnight in Chevy Chase." The dispatcher referred to the exclusive northwest neighborhood that was home to a former US president, ambassadors and other wealthy residents. "We have two DOA at the scene," the dispatcher said, reciting the address. "The fire marshal has requested homicide detectives."

"Did he say why?"

"No, ma'am."

"Okay, I'm on my way." Thankfully, she'd showered and gotten dressed before she woke Scotty. "Please call Sergeant Gonzales and Detective Cruz and ask them to meet me there."

"Yes, ma'am."

Sam flipped her phone closed with a satisfying smack.

That smacking sound was one of many reasons she'd never upgrade to a smartphone.

"You'll still be able to come with me, right?" Nick asked, looking adorably uncertain.

Sam went over to where he sat at the table and kissed him. "I'll talk to Malone today and see if I can make it happen."

"Keep me posted."

A RINGING PHONE woke Christina Billings from a sound sleep. Two-year-old Alex had been up during the night with a fever and cold that was making him miserable and her sleep deprived. Her fiancé, Tommy, had slept through that and apparently couldn't hear his phone ringing, either. He was due at work in an hour and was usually up by now.

"Tommy." She nudged him, but he didn't stir. "*Tommy.* Your phone."

He came to slowly, blinking rapidly.

"The phone, Tommy. Answer it before it wakes Alex." He needed more sleep and so did she, or this was going to be a very long day.

Tommy grabbed the phone from the bedside table.

Christina saw the word *Dispatch* on the screen.

"Gonzales."

She couldn't hear the dispatcher's side of the conversation, but she heard Tommy's grunt of acknowledgment before he ended the call, closing his eyes even as he continued to clutch the phone.

Christina wondered if he was going back to sleep after being called into work. She was about to say something when he got out of bed and headed for the shower.

Nine months ago today, his partner, A. J. Arnold, had

been gunned down right in front of Tommy as they approached a suspect. After a long downward spiral following Arnold's murder, Tommy had seemed to rebound somewhat during the summer. But the rebound hadn't lasted into the fall.

In the last month, since his new partner, Cameron Green, had joined the squad, Christina had watched him regress into his grief. He'd said and done all the right things when it came to welcoming Cameron, but he was obviously spiraling again, and she had no idea what to do to help him or how to reach him. Even when lying next to her in bed, he seemed so far away from her.

Sometimes, when she had a rare moment alone, she allowed her thoughts to wander to life without Tommy and Alex at the center of it. She loved them both—desperately—but she wasn't sure how much more she could take of the distant, closed-off version of the man she loved. They were supposed to have been married by now. Like everything else, that plan had been shoved aside to make room for Tommy's overwhelming grief. It'd been months since they'd discussed getting married. In the meantime, she took care of Alex and everything else, while Tommy worked and came home to sleep before starting the cycle all over again.

They didn't talk about anything other than Alex. They never went anywhere together or as a family. They hadn't had sex in so long she'd forgotten when it had last happened. She was as unhappy as she'd ever been. Something had to give—and soon, or she would be forced to decide whether their relationship was still healthy for her. She did *not* want to have to make that decision.

Only the thought of leaving Tommy at his lowest moment, not to mention leaving Alex, had kept her from making a move before now. She loved that little boy with her whole heart and soul. She'd stepped away from her own career as Nick's chief of staff to stay home with him and had hoped to add to their family by now. When she thought about the early days of her relationship with Tommy, when they'd been so madly in love, she couldn't have imagined feeling as insignificant to him as a piece of furniture that was always there when he finally decided to come home.

Christina hadn't told anyone about the trouble brewing between them. In her heart of hearts, she hoped they could still work it out somehow, and the last thing she needed was her friends and family holding a grudge against him forever—and they would if they had any idea just how bad things had gotten. Her parents had questioned the wisdom of her giving up a high-profile job to stay home to care for her boyfriend's child, especially when she'd made more money than him. But she'd been ready for a break from the political rat race when Alex came along, and she had no regrets about her decision. Or she hadn't until Tommy checked out of their relationship.

This weekend they'd be expected to celebrate at Freddie and Elin's wedding, and she'd have to pretend that everything was fine in her relationship when it was anything but. She wasn't sure how she would pull off another convincing performance for their friends. Tommy was one of Freddie's groomsmen, so she'd get to spend most of that day on her own while he attended to his friend.

Dangling at the end of her rope in this situation, more than once she'd thought about taking Alex and leaving, even though she had no legal right to take him. Another thing they'd never gotten around to—her adoption of him after his mother was killed. What would Tommy do if she left with his son? Call the police on her? That made her laugh bitterly. She'd be surprised if he noticed they were gone.

Tommy came out of the bathroom and went to the closet where he had clean clothes to choose from thanks to her. Did he ever wonder how that happened? He put on jeans and a black T-shirt and then went to unlock the bedside drawer where he kept his badge, weapon and cuffs.

She watched him slide the weapon into the holster he wore on his hip and jam the cuffs and badge into the back pockets of his jeans, the same way he did every day. Holding her breath, she waited to see if he would say anything to her or come around the bed to kiss her goodbye the way he used to before disaster struck, but like he did so often these days, he simply turned and left the room.

A minute later, she heard the front door close behind him.

For a long time after he left, she lay in bed staring up at the ceiling with tears running down her cheeks. She couldn't take much more of this.

TWO

SAM WAS THE first of her team to arrive on the scene of the smoldering fire that had demolished half a mansion in one of the District's most exclusive neighborhoods.

"What've we got?" Sam asked the fire marshal when he met her at the tape line.

"Two bodies found on the first floor of the house, both bound with zip ties at the hands and feet."

And that, right there, made their deaths her problem. "Do we know who they are?"

He consulted his notes. "The ME will need to make positive IDs, but the house is owned by Jameson and Cleo Beauclair. I haven't had time to dig any deeper on who they are."

"Are we certain they were the only people in the house?" Sam asked.

"Not yet. When we arrived just after four a.m., the west side of the house, where the bodies were found, was fully engulfed. That was our immediate focus. We've got firefighters searching the rest of what was once a ten-thousand-square-foot home."

"Any sign of accelerants?"

"Nothing so far, but we're an hour into the investigation stage. Early days."

"Has the ME been here?"

"Not yet."

"Could I take a look inside?"

"It's still hot in there, but I can show you the high-lights—or the lowlights, such as they are."

Sam followed him up the sidewalk to what had once been the front door. Inside the smoldering ruins of the house, she could make out the basic structure from the burned-out husk that remained. The putrid scents of smoke and death hung heavily in the air.

"That's them there," the fire marshal said, pointing to a space on the floor by a blackened stone fireplace where two charred bodies lay next to one another.

Sam swallowed the bile that surged to her throat. Nothing was worse, at least not in her line of work, than fire victims. Though it was the last thing she wanted to do, she moved in for a closer look, took photos of the bodies and the scene around them, then turned to face the fire marshal. "Anything else you think I ought to see?"

"Not yet."

"Keep me posted."

"Will do."

He walked away to continue his investigation while Sam went outside, carrying the horrifying images with her as she took greedy breaths of fresh air. As she reached the curb, the medical examiner's truck arrived. She waited for a word with Dr. Lindsey McNamara.

The tall, pretty medical examiner gathered her long red hair into a ponytail as she walked over to Sam.

"Fire victims," Sam said, shuddering.

"Good morning to you, too."

"Hands and feet bound with zip ties."

"Here we go again," Lindsey said with a sigh. "Looks like it was quite a house."

"Ten thousand square feet, according to the fire marshal."

"I'll get you an ID and report as soon as I can."

"Appreciate it." Sam opened her phone and placed a call to Malone. "I'm at the scene of the fire in Chevy Chase."

"What've you got?"

"Two DOA, bound at the hands and feet, leading me to believe this was a home invasion gone bad. I need Crime Scene here ASAP."

"I'll call Haggerty and get them over there."

"I want them to comb through anything and everything that wasn't touched by the fire, and they need to do it soon before the scene is further compromised. We've got firefighters all over the place."

"Got it. What's your plan?"

"I'm going to talk to the neighbors and find out what I can about the people who lived here while I wait for Lindsey to confirm their identities."

"Keep me posted."

Sam slapped the phone closed and headed for her car to begin the task of figuring out who Jameson and Cleo Beauclair had been and who might've bound them before setting their house on fire. If the bodies were even those of the Beauclairs. Cases like this were often confounding from the start, but they would operate on the info they had available and go from there.

Her partner, Detective Freddie Cruz, arrived as Sam reached her car, which she had parked a block from the scene.

"I guess it was too much to hope our homicide-free streak would last until after the wedding," he said.

"Too much indeed. We've got two deceased on the first floor of the west side of the home, hands and feet bound."

"Do we know who they are?"

"We know who owns the house, but we're not a hundred percent sure the owners are our victims," she said, passing along the names the fire marshal had given her. "Let's knock on some doors and then go back to HQ to see what Lindsey can tell us."

"I'm with you, LT."

"Any word from Gonzo?"

"Not that I've heard yet."

"He can catch up."

Don't miss Fatal Invasion *by Marie Force,*
available now from HQN Books.

COMING NEXT MONTH FROM

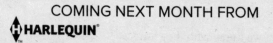

ROMANTIC suspense

Available December 31, 2018

#2023 COLTON COWBOY STANDOFF
The Coltons of Roaring Springs
by Marie Ferrarella
After walking out on Wyatt Colton six years ago, Bailey Norton is back—and asking him to father her child. But a crime spree puts Bailey, their child and Wyatt's ranch in danger. They suddenly have bigger problems than mending their past relationship.

#2024 SNOWBOUND WITH THE SECRET AGENT
Silver Valley P.D. • by Geri Krotow
Instant chemistry between undercover agent Kyle King and local librarian Portia DiNapoli spells instant trouble. Kyle is now torn between completing his mission and getting out of Silver Valley, and protecting the woman with whom he shares the most intense attraction of his life.

#2025 A SOLDIER'S HONOR
The Riley Code • by Regan Black
A security breach has exposed Major Matt Riley and the secrets he's kept for fourteen years, putting the woman he's never stopped loving and their son in grave danger.

#2026 PROTECTING THE BOSS
Wingman Security • by Beverly Long
Designer Megan North has four new boutiques to open over the course of a twelve-day road trip. But someone is targeting her and her business. When the dangers turn deadly, can security specialist Seth Pike save her?

YOU CAN FIND MORE INFORMATION ON UPCOMING HARLEQUIN® TITLES, FREE EXCERPTS AND MORE AT WWW.HARLEQUIN.COM.

HRSCNM1218

SPECIAL EXCERPT FROM

H HARLEQUIN®

ROMANTIC suspense

A security breach has exposed Major Matt Riley and the secrets he's kept for fourteen years, putting the woman he's never stopped loving and their son in grave danger.

Read on for a sneak preview of the first book in USA TODAY *bestselling author Regan Black's brand-new Riley Code miniseries,*
A Soldier's Honor.

She wasn't accustomed to sharing a bed with anyone.

"And what about us?"

"Us as in you and me?" His gaze locked on her, hot and interested. "Is that an invitation?"

She backpedaled. "I meant us as in what are Caleb and I supposed to do while you're fixing the problem?"

He watched her steadily as he took a long pull from the beer bottle. Setting the bottle aside, he took a step toward her. "Which part concerns you most? Sticking with me for safety, or maybe just the idea of sticking with me?"

The last one, a small voice in her head cried out. But she wasn't that overwhelmed nineteen-year-old anymore. She was a grown woman, a mother with a son and an established career. No matter the circumstance, Caleb's safety was her top priority.

She planted her hand in the center of his hard chest. His heart kicked, his chest swelled as he sucked in a breath. He leaned into her touch, as though his heart was drowning and she was the lifeline. Good grief, her imagination needed a dose of reality.

"Bethany," he murmured.

The blood rushing through her ears was so loud, she saw him speak her name more than she heard it. The blatant need in his brown eyes triggered an answering need in her. Any reply she might have given went up in flames when he lowered his firm lips to her mouth. He kissed her lightly at first, but she recognized the spark and heat just under the surface, waiting for an opening to break free and singe them both. Her hands curled into his shirt, pulled him closer. Oh, how she'd missed this. She'd thought time had exaggerated her memories and found the opposite was true when his tongue swept over hers, as he alternately sipped and plundered and called up all her long-ignored needs to the surface.

Our second first kiss, she thought. As full of promise as the first first kiss had been when they were kids.

"Oh. Ah. Sorry. Never mind." Caleb's voice, choked with embarrassment, doused the moment as effectively as a bucket of ice water.

She muttered an oath.

Don't miss
A Soldier's Honor *by Regan Black,*
available January 2019 wherever
Harlequin® Romantic Suspense books
and ebooks are sold.

www.Harlequin.com